A *NEW YORK TIMES* B

A *BUZZFEED* BOOK OF THE YEAR

A BUSTLE.COM BOOK OF THE YEAR

A GOODREADS CHOICE AWARDS FINALIST

"Chokshi's prose is captivating, and the pages come alive. . . . A fantasy about sacrifice, self-discovery, and making your own destiny."
—*PUBLISHERS WEEKLY* (STARRED REVIEW)★

"A stunning debut filled with lush writing, smart characters, and a mysterious plot that provides as many twists as it does swoons."
—*SCHOOL LIBRARY JOURNAL* (STARRED REVIEW)★

"Richly imagined, deeply mythic, filled with lovely language . . . this is an author to watch."
— *KIRKUS REVIEWS*

"A unique fantasy that is epic myth and beautiful fairy tale combined."
—*BOOKLIST*

A BARNES AND NOBLE BOOK OF THE YEAR

AN AMAZON BOOK OF THE MONTH

A KID'S INDIE NEXT LIST PICK

A *PASTE* MAGAZINE BOOK OF THE MONTH

A GOODREADS BOOK OF THE MONTH

THE STAR-TOUCHED QUEEN

THE STAR-TOUCHED QUEEN

ROSHANI CHOKSHI

St. Martin's Griffin
New York

TO MY FAMILY:

FOR BEING THE FIRST TO LISTEN

AND THE LAST TO DISSUADE

www.stmartins.com

The Library of Congress has cataloged the hardcover edition as follows:

Names: Chokshi, Roshani.
Title: The star-touched queen / Roshani Chokshi.
Other titles: Star touched queen
Description: First edition. | New York : St. Martin's Griffin, 2016. |
Identifiers: LCCN 2016001958 | ISBN 9781250085474 (hardcover) |
ISBN 9781250085481 (e-book)
Subjects: | CYAC: Fantasy. | BISAC: JUVENILE FICTION / Fantasy & Magic. | JUVENILE FICTION / Legends, Myths, Fables / General.
Classification: LCC PZ7.1.C54 St 2016 | DDC [Fic]—dc23
LC record available at https://lccn.loc.gov/2016001958

ISBN 978-1-250-10020-7 (trade paperback)

Our books may be purchased in bulk for promotional, educational, or business use. Please contact your local bookseller or the Macmillan Corporate and Premium Sales Department at 1-800-221-7945, extension 5442, or by e-mail at MacmillanSpecialMarkets@macmillan.com.

First St. Martin's Griffin Trade Paperback Edition: March 2017

10 9 8 7 6

ACKNOWLEDGMENTS

This book would not exist without the help of so many. I don't have the room to thank everyone who made an impact, but I'd like to give my sincerest thanks to the following.

To my parents (May and Hitesh), siblings (Monica and Jayesh) and cousins: Thank you for cross-country trips, Father Cat constructions, Amish excursions, bad Filipino accents, quests for the mythical "jetty," boundless love and patience, sneaky-raptor attacks and wells of inspiration. I love you.

To Ba and Dadda (Vijya and Ramesh), Lalani (Apollonia), Kaki and Kaka (Alpa and Alpesh), Foi and Foua (Anita and Kamlesh): Thank you for your storytelling and patience, for picture books and piano-playing—you planted these stories in my head before I knew they were there. To Shiv and Pujan, Sohum, Kiran and Alisa: Thank you for your infinite sass, nose-tugs, affectionate interrogation, curiosity, and first reads. To Kavitha Nallathambhi: Thank you for taking on the mantle of talented older sister and inspiring me from a young age to write.

To Victoria Gilrane: Thank you for the phenomenon of our childhood, for 5 A.M. breakfasts, crinkled codfish, and eon-long phone calls. Niv Sekar: Thank you for tea and digestive cookies, meandering musings on fairy tales and art that always ended in laughter. Bismah Rahmat: Thank you for the smattering of French, lavish meals of scrambled eggs and chai on the reg., and forays into hip-hop slang.

To Ms. Diana Koscik, Mrs. Sandra Slider, Dr. Jim Morey, Dr. Harry Rusche, and Dr. Bonna Wescoat—I am deeply grateful for your wisdom, guidance, and instruction.

To my agent, Thao Le: Thank you for believing in this story, for countless reads, critiques, and bunny pictures to restore my sanity. To my editor, Eileen Rothschild: From our first phone call, I knew I couldn't trust this book in anyone else's hands. To the SMP team: I am so lucky to have had the opportunity to work with all of you.

To Terra LeMay: I am honored to call you my friend. Your countless reads, sharp insights, and fearless belief in me have shaped both this story and my writing. To Ella Dyson and Nicole Slaunwhite: Thank you for reading through my awful first drafts! Your comments helped me unearth what this story wanted to be. To Kat Howard: Thank you for the invaluable mentoring, amazing critiques, and thoughtful advice on everything from law school to writing.

To the fabulous bloggers who gave me a community and

shared their excitement for this book. So many hugs and heartfelt thanks to: Rachel at A Perfection Called Books, Nicola W. at Queen of The BookShelves, Liran at Empress of Books, Kris at My Friends Are Fiction, Mishma at Chasing FaeryTales, Adriyanna Zimmerman at LifeWritings, Pili at InLoveWith-Handmade, and Kit Cat at Let The Pages Reign.

And finally, to Aman Sharma Jaan. Thank you for the promise of midnight tea parties, fox ears in a nimbus of rain, improbable snow drifts, and lost cities. With you, magic is no fantasy.

PART ONE

THE LOST PRINCESS

•» 1 «•

NOT A GHOST

Staring at the sky in Bharata was like exchanging a secret. It felt private, like I had peered through the veil of a hundred worlds. When I looked up, I could imagine—for a moment—what the sky hid from everyone else. I could see where the winds yawned with silver lips and curled themselves to sleep. I could glimpse the moon folding herself into crescents and half-smiles. When I looked up, I could imagine an existence as vast as the sky. Just as infinite. Just as unknown.

But today, there was no time to let my head wander. Duty kept my gaze fixed on the funeral pyre slowly winding its way toward the harem. I choked back a cough. Charred incense filled my lungs, thick and over-sweet with the smell of burning marigolds. Beside the pyre, mourners screeched and wept, tearing their hair and smearing ash across their faces. It was an impressive show, but their bored eyes betrayed them. Hired help, no doubt. Real grief had no place in my father's court.

An ivory screen separated the harem from the funerary procession, but I caught snatches of him through the lattice. He wore a white *sherwani* jacket, and around his throat coiled a necklace strung together with the birthstones of his children. There, by the crook of his neck, my birthstones—a handful of muted sapphires—caught the watery morning light. My father's head was bent to the ear of a pale-faced courtier, his voice low. He wasn't talking about the dead wife on the pyre. He probably didn't even know her name. It was Padmavathi. She had a round face and used to sing in the morning, crooning to her swelling stomach with a secret smile. I never once heard her say a cruel thing about anyone. Not even me.

No, my father was discussing war. The shadow of it looms over us constantly, sometimes hidden. Always present. I only know of the war in glimpses, but I see its pall everywhere. I see war in my father's face, pinching his cheeks sallow. I see war in the courtier's brows, always bent in grief. I see war in the empty coffers, in the tents where once-spirited soldiers await the crematory grounds.

I leaned closer to catch his words, only to be yanked back.

"Get away from there," Mother Dhina hissed. "It's not right for you to stand at the front."

My jaw tightened, but I stepped back without a word. I couldn't risk giving the wives more venom. They may have covered their lips with silk, but their words were unsheathed daggers. According to the royal physician, childbirth had killed Padmavathi, but no one believed him. In the eyes of the court, there was only one killer—

Me.

In Bharata, no one believed in ghosts because the dead never lingered. Lives were remade instantly, souls unzipped and tipped into the streaked brilliance of a tiger, a *gopi* with lacquered eyes or a raja with a lap full of jewels. I couldn't decide whether I thought reincarnation was a scare tactic or a hopeful message. *Do this, so you won't come back as a cockroach. Give alms to the poor, and in your next life you'll be rich.* It made all good deeds seem suspect.

Even then, it was a comfort to know that there were no ghosts in my country. It meant that I was alive. To everyone else, I was a dead girl walking. But I was no ghost. I was no spectral imprint of something that had lived and died and couldn't leave this place behind. It meant I still had a chance at life.

By the time the funerary procession ended, the sun had barely begun to edge its way across the sky. The mourners had dispersed as soon as the royal announcement ended and only the flames presided over Padmavathi's burial. When the noonday bell rang throughout the palace, even the smells—smoke and petals, salt and jasmine—had disappeared, scraped up by the wind and carried far into the shadowless realm of the dead.

Before me, the halls of the harem glittered, sharp as a predator's eyes. Light clung to the curved torsos of statuettes and skimmed the reflections from still pools of water. In the distance, the great double doors of the harem yawned open and the mellow midday heat crept in from the outside. I could never trust the stillness of the harem.

Behind me, the living quarters and personal rooms of the

harem wives and my half-sisters had melted into shadow. The caretakers had set the children of the royal nursery to sleep. The tutors had begun droning to the betrothed princesses about the lands and ancestries of their soon-to-be husbands.

I had my own appointment. My "tutor of the week." Poor things. They never lasted long; whether that was their decision or mine just depended on the person. It wasn't that I disliked learning. It was simply that they couldn't teach me what I wanted to know. My real place of study hovered above their heads. Literally.

Outside, the thunder of clashing gongs drifted through the harem walls. Parrots scattered from their naps, launching into the air with a huff and a screech. The familiar shuffle of pointed shoes, golden tassels and nervous voices melted into a low murmur. All of my father's councilors were making their way to the throne room for his announcement.

Within moments, my father would reveal his solution for dealing with the rebel kingdoms. My heart jostled. Father, while never on time, was nonetheless efficient. He wouldn't waste time on the frivolities of the court, which meant that I had a limited amount of time to get to the throne room and I still had to deal with the most recent tutor. I prayed he was a simpleton. Better yet—superstitious.

Father once said the real language of diplomacy was in the space between words. He said silence was key to politics.

Silence, I had learned, was also key to spying.

I slipped off anything noisy—gold bracelets, dangling earrings—and stashed them behind a stone carving of a mynah bird. Navigating through the harem was like stepping into a riddle. Niches filled with statues of gods and goddesses with plangent eyes and backs arced in a forgotten reel of a half-dance leaned out into the halls. Light refracted off crystal platters piled with blooms the bright color of new blood, and flickering *diyas* cast smoke against the mirrors, leaving the halls a snarl of mist and petals. I touched the sharp corners. I liked the feeling of stone beneath my fingers, of something that pushed back to remind me of my own solidity.

As I rounded the last corner, the harem wives' sharp laughter leapt into the halls, sending prickles across my arm. The harem wives' habits never changed. It was the one thing I liked about them. My whole life was crafted around their boredom. I could probably set my heartbeat to the hours they whittled away exchanging gossip.

Before I could run past them, a name rooted me to the spot . . . my own. At least, I thought I heard it. I couldn't be sure. No matter how much I wanted to plant one foot in front of the other and leave them behind, I couldn't.

I held my breath and stepped backward, pressing my ear as close to the curtains as I could.

"It's a pity," said a voice sultry from years spent smoking the rose-scented water pipes.

Mother Dhina. She ruled the harem with an iron fist. She may not have given the Raja any sons, but she had one enduring quality: life. She had survived seven pregnancies, two stillbirths and a sweating sickness that claimed eight wives in the past three years. Her word was law.

"What is?"

A simpering voice. Mother Shastri. Second in command. She was one of the younger wives, but had recently given birth to twin sons. She was far more conniving than Mother Dhina, but lacked all the ambition of real malice.

"It's just a pity Advithi didn't go the same way as Padmavathi."

My hands curled into fists, nails sinking into the flesh of my palms. Advithi. I didn't know her long enough to call her mother. I knew nothing of her except her name and a vague rumor that she had not gotten along with the other wives. In particular, Mother Dhina. Once, they had been rivals. Even after she died, Mother Dhina never forgave her. Other than that, she was a nondescript dream in my head. Sometimes when I couldn't sleep at night, I'd try to conjure her, but nothing ever revealed itself to me—not the length of her hair or the scent of her skin. She was a mystery and the only thing she left me was a necklace and a name. Instinctively, my fingers found her last gift: a round-cut sapphire strung with seed pearls.

Mother Dhina wheezed, and when she spoke, I could almost smell the smoke puffing out between her teeth. "Usually when a woman dies in childbirth, the child goes too."

Mother Shastri chided her with a hollow *tsk*. "It's not good to say such things, sister."

"And why is that?" came a silvery voice. I couldn't place that one. She must have been new. "It should be a good thing for a child to survive the mother. It is a shame Padmavathi's son died with her. Who is Advithi—?"

"*Was*," corrected Mother Dhina with a tone like thunder. The other wife stuttered into silence. "She was nothing more than a courtesan who caught the Raja's eye. Mayavati is her daughter."

"*Her?* The one with the horoscope?"

Another wife's voice leapt to join the others': "Is it true that she killed Padmavathi?"

Bharata may not believe in ghosts, but horoscopes were entirely different. The kingdom choreographed whole lives on whatever astral axis was assigned to you. Father didn't seem to believe in horoscopes. He spoke of destiny as a malleable thing, something that could be bent, interpreted or loosened to any perspective. But that didn't change the mind of the court. Whatever magic had unearthed meaning in stars, my celestial forecast was shadowed and torn, and the wives never let me forget. It made me hate the stars and curse the night sky.

"She might as well have," said Mother Dhina dismissively. "That kind of bad fortune only attracts ill luck."

"Is it true, then?"

How many times had I asked myself that question? I tried to convince myself that it was just the idle talk of the harem wives and a series of bad coincidences, but sometimes . . . I wasn't so sure.

"The Raja needs to get rid of her," said Mother Shastri. "Before her plague spreads to someone else."

"How can he?" scoffed another. "Who would marry her with that horoscope? She brings death wherever she goes."

The new wife, with the silvery voice, piped up eagerly, "I heard her shadow doesn't stay in one place."

Another voice chimed in, "A servant told me that snakes bow to her."

I pushed myself off the wall. I knew all the rumors, and I didn't care to hear them again. Their words crawled over my skin. I wanted to shake off the insults, the laughter, the shadows. But all of it clung to me, thick as smoke, pushing out the blood from my veins until I pulsed with hate.

The second gong rang in the distance. I walked faster, feet pounding on the marble. As I ran through the gardens, sunlight slanted off my skin and a feeling of *wrongness* struck me. It didn't dawn on me until afterward, until light knifed through the fig trees and striped me like a tiger, until I caught the shadow-seamed imprint of a leaf against the paved walkway to the archival buildings.

My shadow.

I couldn't see it.

•» 2 «•

LESSONS IN SILENCE

The archives were cut like honeycombs and golden light clung to them, dousing every tome, painting, treatise and poem the soft gold of ghee freshly skimmed from boiling butter. I was only allowed to visit once a week—to meet with my weekly tutor before I inevitably scared him away. Every time I left the archival room, my arms brimmed with parchment paper. I loved the feeling of discovery, of not knowing how much I wanted something until I had discovered its absence.

The week before, I had lost myself in the folktales of Bharata. Stories of elephants who spun clouds, shaking tremors loose from ancient trunks gnarled with the rime of lost cyclones, whirlwinds and thunderstorms. Myths of frank-eyed *naga* women twisting serpentine, flashing smiles full of uncut gemstones. Legends of a world beneath, above, beside the one I knew—where trees bore edible gems and no one would think twice about a girl with dark skin and a darker horoscope. I wanted it to be real so badly that sometimes I thought I could *see* the Otherworld. Sometimes, if I closed my eyes and pressed my toes into the ground, I could almost sense them sinking into the loam of some other land, a dream demesne where the sky cleaved in two and the earth was sutured with a magic that could heal hearts, mend bones, change lives.

It was a dream I didn't want to part with, but I had to settle for what magic I could create on my own. I could read more. Learn more. Make new dreams. But the best part wasn't hoarding those wishes to myself. It was sharing everything I learned with Gauri, my half-sister. She was the only one I couldn't scare away . . . the only one I didn't want to.

Thinking of Gauri always made me smile. But as soon as I caught sight of my tutor of the week, the smile disappeared. He stood between two pillars of the archive section marking the kingdom's history. Beyond the sheer number of things to read in the archive room, what I loved most was its ceiling. It was empty, wide enough to crawl through and conveniently linked to my father's inner sanctum.

The tutor, as luck would have it, stood directly below my hiding spot.

At least Father's announcement hadn't started. The courtiers still murmured and the footfall of tardiness fell on my ears like music. But if I was ever going to get to hear that meeting, I had to get rid of the tutor first.

"Punctuality is a prize among women," said the tutor.

I bit back a cringe. His voice was sticky. The words drawn out like they would morph into a noose and slip around you in the dark. I stepped back, only to see his eyes sharpen into a glare.

He was heavyset and tall. Soft-rounded jowls faded into a non-chin and thick neck. Greasy black eyes dragged across my body. In the past, my tutors had all been the same—a little doughy, a little nervous. Always superstitious. This new tutor held my gaze evenly. That was unexpected. None of my other tutors had ever met my eye. Sometimes the tutors sidled against the dark of the archival chambers, hands trembling as they pushed a set of notes toward me. History lessons, they said. Why did they always start with history? Show me a dream unrealized. Don't show me unchangeable paths.

The tutor cleared his throat. "I have no intention to teach you history or letters or speech. I intend to teach you silence. Stillness."

This time I didn't even try to hide my scowl. I did not like this replacement. Tutors generally left me alone. I never had to raise my voice. I never had to scowl. I didn't even need words. What scared them most was much simpler and sweeter than that—a smile. The moment I smiled—not a real one, of course, but a slow, crocodile reveal of teeth and a practiced manic gleam—the tutor would make an excuse, edge along the wall and flee out of the archive rooms.

Who wanted to be smiled at by the girl that trailed shadows like pets, conjured snakes and waited for Death, her bridegroom, to steal her from these walls? Never mind that none of it was true. Never mind that the closest I had come to real magic was making off with an entire tray of desserts without anyone noticing. The shadow of me always loomed larger than the person who cast it. And sometimes that had its benefits.

This tutor, however, was not as easily cowed. I strained my ears, listening for the footfall of more courtiers, but it was silent. The meeting would start any minute now and here I was, stuck with some fool who wanted to teach me the virtue of silence.

I grinned at him . . .

. . . and he grinned back.

"It is unseemly to smile at strangers, Princess."

He took a step closer to me. Shadows glommed around him, choking off the honey light of the room. He smelled *wrong*. Like he had borrowed the scent of another person. Sweat slicked his skin and when he walked closer, red shimmered in his eyes—like coal smoldering in each socket.

"Let me teach you, lovely thing," he said, taking another step closer. "Humans always get it wrong, don't they? They think a bowl of rice at the front door is strong enough to keep a demon away. Wrong. What you know is a false promise of strength. Let me show you weakness."

The room had never felt this empty, like I was trapped between the space of an echo and a scream. I couldn't hear anything. Not the parrots scuttling on their branches or the court notary droning his list of the afternoon's agenda. Silence was a silhouette, something I could trace.

The tutor's voice transcended sound, muddying my thoughts. "Let me teach you the ways of demons and men."

My knees buckled. His voice echoed with all the desperation of someone who had not slaked his thirst in eons and had just spied a goblet of water sweating beads of condensation, thick as planets. His voice lulled me, coated me. I wanted to move, but found myself rooted to the spot. I glanced up, fighting the drowsiness, and saw his shadow smeared on the wall—horned, furred belly skating over the floor, shifting into man and beast and back. Devil. *Raksha*.

Somewhere in my mind, I knew he wasn't real. He couldn't be. This was the court of Bharata, a city like a bone spur—tacked on like an afterthought. Its demons were different: harem wives with jewels in their hair and hate in their heart, courtiers with mouths full of lies, a father who knew me only as a colored stone around his neck. Those were the monsters I knew. My world didn't have room for more.

The drowsiness slipped off me. When I shook myself free of it, my smile was bitter smoke, my hackles raised until I thought my skin had given way to glass. Now, he seemed smaller. Or maybe I had grown bigger. My surroundings slid away, and all that was left was fire licking at the earth, the edge of a winter eclipse, stars whirling in a forest pool and the pulsing beat of something ancient running through my veins.

"I don't care for the ways of men and demons," I hissed. "Your lessons are lost on me."

Whatever darkness my mind had imagined melted. Parrots singing. Fountains gurgling. The distant voice of a courtier droning about wars. Sound pushed up between those lost seconds, blossoming into fierce murmurs, hushed tones. What had I imagined? I searched for the tutor's shadow splayed against the wall. I waited to see something slinking along the ground, darkness stretched long and thin over tomes and cracked tiles, but there was nothing.

"You," he hissed in an exhale that ended in a whimper. He backed into a corner. "It's you. I thought . . ." He gulped down the rest of his words. He looked lost.

I blinked at him, shaking off the final remnants of that drowsiness. I felt groggy, but not with sleep. A moment ago, I thought I had seen horns limned in shadow. I thought something had coursed through me in defense—a low note of music, the bass of a thunderclap, a pleat of light glinting through a bruised storm cloud. But that couldn't be right. The person before me was just . . . a person. And if I had heard him say something else, saw him morph into something else, it was all distant and the fingers of my memory could do nothing but rummage through images, hold them to the light and wonder if I hadn't slipped into a waking nightmare.

The tutor trembled. Gone was the blocky figure choking out the light and lecturing me on silence. Or had he said something else in those lost moments? Something about weakness and demons. I couldn't remember. I clutched a table, my knuckles white.

"I must go," he said, his face pale, like blood had drained from him. "I didn't know. Truly. I didn't. I thought you were someone else."

I stared at him. What did he mean? How could he not know who I was? Someone must have told him that I was the princess he would be tutoring this afternoon. But I was wasting time. He was just another tutor scared by a reputation pronounced by faraway lights in the sky. Curse the stars.

"Leave," I said. "Inform the court that we completed a full

session, but that other commitments prevent you from teaching me again. Do you understand?"

He nodded, his hands still raised to his face like he thought I would hit him at any moment. Then, he bowed, stumbling backward. He stood in the arch of the doorway, body cast in shadow, face an inscrutable inkblot. He bowed once more before I blinked and realized he was gone. Nothing. Not even that telltale seep of cold that invaded a room when another body had just left.

I kneaded my hands against my forehead, rubbing out the shadows of horned silhouettes and flashing eyes. I couldn't shake the sense that the world had split for a moment, separating like oil and water.

A moment passed before I shook myself of that strange grogginess with a horrifying jolt.

The announcement.

My heart lurched. How much had I missed? I spared one last glance at the arch of light where the tutor had disappeared. Perhaps he was just more superstitious than normal. There had been a funeral, after all. *That was all. That was all.* I repeated the words in my head, bright as talismans, until I had all but forgotten the feeling of two worlds converging across my eyes—dazzling and prismatic.

I pulled myself up the ladder propped against the shelves that led directly to the hollowed roof and rafters of my father's inner sanctum.

The wood beneath my palms was rough and scratchy. I gripped the rungs tighter, smiling when splinters slid into my hands. *I am here. I am no ghost. Ghosts don't get splinters.* Heart calm, hands still,

I slid through the loose space in the rafters, kicked my feet behind me and disappeared into the ceiling.

The first time I had snuck up the rafters, my heart raced so fast, I almost didn't hear all the debates between the courtiers, the advisers and my father. Women weren't allowed in the inner court sanctum and getting caught would mean severe punishment.

Over time, sneaking above the sanctum became easy. Now, I could wriggle my way through the empty space like a blind lizard. Safely perched in the rafters, I curled my knees beneath me and snuggled into my hiding spot. I didn't know how many hours I had spent perched in this corner, listening to them. Up here, I could pretend that I ruled over them all, silent and mythic. From here, I could learn what no tutor could teach—the way power settles over people in a room, the way language curls around ankles like a sated cat or flicks a forked tongue in caution, the way to enthrall an audience. And I could understand, almost, the lives and histories scrawled into the lines and lines of the records stowed away in the archival building. The inner sanctum was where my father met foreign dignitaries, it was where the war meetings were held, where crops were discussed and decisions were made. It was the heart of the kingdom and at its throne, my father. According to the archives, he had ruled since the age of ten. If he had siblings, the records never mentioned them.

I flattened myself against the wall and settled in to listen. Whatever I had missed from the beginning had taken its toll on the courtiers. Even from my hiding spot, some faces gleamed white and the air was thick and sour with anxiety.

The inner sanctum held every reminder of the war that had

raged on for at least six years. Dented helmets lined the walls like iron skulls. It unnerved the courtiers. Some of them refused to sit beside the armor of the dead, but father had insisted. "We must never forget those who served us."

Each time I clambered into the rafters, the helmets seemed to grow in size and number. Now, they covered the walls from floor to ceiling. Even though they had been cleaned and scraped of blood, their presence haunted the sanctum. Sunlight glinted off the metal, haloing the helmets so that it looked like my father held court before ghosts.

"Sire, we cannot abide by this decision. There must be a different way to end the war," said Ajeet, a baby-faced councilor with a receding hairline he hid beneath a massive *pagri*. He trembled where he stood, small hands knotted at the base of his ribs like he'd sunk a dagger to its hilt far into his belly. Given the flash of anger on the Raja's face, he might as well have.

"We still have enough soldiers," he cried. "The medics have become more skilled. We might even win this war and sacrifice only a few hundred more."

I frowned. Couldn't Ajeet see the helmets on the walls? *People* had filled that armor. Heads, once brimming with their own hopes and joys and miseries, had worn those helmets. What was only a "few hundred more" to the kingdom could be someone else's lover, brother or son. It wasn't right to honor the dead with inaction.

"You can and you will abide by my decision," said the Raja, his voice hard. He looked careworn, dark eyes sunken so that for a moment they looked like the depthless hollows of a skull.

"But the rebel kingdoms—"

"The rebel kingdoms want the same thing that we do," said my father harshly. "They want food in their bellies. Warmth in their hearths. They want their children to live long enough to possess a name. They fight us out of desperation. Who else will hear their pleas? A decade-long drought? Failing crops? Sweating sicknesses?"

"But, Your Majesty, they turned on the capital."

"Exactly. Their desperation means they have nothing to lose. We are the only losers in this war," he said. "We cannot fight from the fringes. We need to bring them here. Now, do as I say and arrange the *swayamvara*."

A wedding? His tone sent a frisson of ice down my spine. *But all of my half-sisters of marriageable age are already betrothed. The only one who isn't is—*

"—the moment the rebel kingdoms hear about Princess Mayavati's horoscope, they will not go through with the wedding," said another of my father's advisers. Jayesh.

On any other day, I liked him. His voice was soft-spoken, his perspective far more liberal than the rest of the court. But in that moment I hated him, hated him for the words that leapt out of his mouth and chained me to the spot.

Everyone, including me, had thought my horoscope was enough to ward off any proposals. In seventeen years, it hadn't failed me. But now the possibility of a life lived in unwed freedom disappeared, pulled out from under my feet in a matter of seconds.

"Your Majesty, I mean no disrespect, but the princess's horoscope is reputed to have foretold a rather disturbing marriage. One that would partner her with death and destruction. We could offend the—"

The Raja raised his hand. "Hearsay has no place in diplomacy. Our duty is to our people and I will not see them harmed because of superstition. We need to bring the enemy to our court. We need to end this war."

End the war. I knew he was right. Even from the sidelines of the court, death pressed all around us. Jayesh bowed and sat down. I knew they were saying other things. Exchanging details and days, parsing out my life between them like it was ribbon fit for tearing. It was a miracle I didn't stumble through the gap in the rafters. I knew my father better than most did. I had watched him for years. Beneath one plan was always ten. Usually I could find the cracks in his words, pry them open and see what lay beneath the layers of diplomacy, sweet talk and vengeance. But not now. His voice was monotone. Pained, almost. He spoke with the finality of stone and my heart broke beneath it.

"The *swayamvara* will be in a few days' time," continued the Raja. "The rebel leaders will be welcomed as guests and suitors for my daughter's hand. Draw up a new horoscope and hide any evidence of the original. Make it convincing."

A tremor snaked from my head to my toes. Distantly, the clang of the court notary's bell echoed through the walls. Feet shuffled. Voices, sonorous and hard, yielded and blended into one another until only silence remained in the sanctum. I pulled my knees to my chin, back pressed against the wall. Marriage. All I knew of marriage was what I saw in the harem wives—pettiness and boredom with only the comfort of silk and gossip.

There were times when I saw my betrothed half-sisters lost in thought, their faces aglow with hope and wonder. Maybe they thought they would be leaving Bharata behind for a new city that would welcome them with sweet-smelling arms and a husband waiting with a smile fashioned just for them. But I had listened to the stories of the wives and I saw what lay ahead. Another harem. Another husband. Another woman scurried away behind a lattice of elephant bone, staring out to a scene forever marred by the patterns of a gilded cage.

I glanced below me at the empty sanctum. In every tomorrow I had imagined, *this* was never one of them. There were never any prospects beyond the life of a scholarly old maid, but that was a fate I had looked forward to—to live among parchments and sink into the compressed universes stitched into lines and lines of writing. To answer to no one.

There was another sorrow, tucked beneath my surprise. Although I had never envisioned marriage, I had thought of love. Not the furtive love I heard muffled in the corners or rooms of some of the harem wives. What I wanted was a connection, a shared heartbeat that kept rhythm across oceans and worlds. Not some alliance cobbled out of war. I didn't want the prince from the folktales or some milk-skinned, honey-eyed youth who said his greetings and proclaimed his love in the same breath. I wanted a love thick with time, as inscrutable as if a lathe had carved it from night and as familiar as the marrow in my bones. I wanted the impossible, which made it that much easier to push out of my mind.

•» 3 «•

FAVORED DAUGHTERS

Somehow I left behind the rafters and climbed down the rungs and left the honeycombs of Bharata's archives. I didn't care if anyone saw me or asked questions. Bharata had already discarded me. I was no more than a guest in my father's home, whittling away the time until a palanquin bore me away to a different cage.

I was halfway to the harem when I heard feet pounding the walkway behind me.

"Princess Mayavati, the Raja Ramchandra of Bharata requests your immediate presence in the gardens."

I drew my veil over my head before turning. Why did every guard always say the "Raja Ramchandra"? As if I didn't know my father's name. *Oh,* that *Raja. I thought you meant one of the other rulers.* Fools.

"Now?"

The guard blinked. He was young and handsome in a vague, unmemorable way. I had half a mind to ask if he was going to throw in his name with the pack of wolves that would come to Bharata and claim my hand in the *swayamvara*. I must have unknowingly grinned because the young guard masked a flinch. He probably thought I had unleashed some curse on him.

"Yes, Princess. He's waiting for you in the gardens."

That was new. My father never waited for anyone.

"And if I say no?"

The guard stepped back. "I—"

"Don't worry, it was only a question."

"Does that mean—"

"—which is to say," I said slowly, "that I will come with you. Lead the way."

He turned on his heel and, after a moment's hesitation, began marching back down the path. Guilt twinged inside me. He was only doing his duty. He hadn't even done anything openly insulting, like some of the harem wives who would spit on my shadow.

I toyed with the idea of apologizing, but thought better of it. My words were out and that was that. Around us, my father's court shimmered in the early evening. Even though the sun had gone, the sky remained a rich turmeric yellow. A bright vermillion peeled at the edges of the clouds, fading somewhere into the tangle of trees. Around me, the silver reflection pools lapped up the last light and in its waters burned flat flames.

The entrance to the gardens of Bharata was cleverly constructed so that the gates marking it looked like a snarl of roses at first glance. On closer inspection, wrought iron bloomed beneath the petals before snaking upward to bolster the trees—fig and *neem*, sweet almond and tart lime—into living pergolas. My father's guards circled the gardens. In their scarlet robes, they looked like vicious trees poised to spear the sun should it fall.

"One moment, Princess," said the guard quickly. "I believe His Highness is concluding a discussion on matters of state with the crown prince."

Beneath my veil, I arched an eyebrow. If my father was discussing anything with the crown prince, it would be his extravagant ledger. Without waiting for an answer, the guard bowed awkwardly and left. The moment I knew I was alone, I left the path, following the harsh voice of the Raja to a secluded copse of trees. In the middle of the clearing, my half-brother cowered in the Raja's shadow, his head bent as he toyed with the sleeves of his jacket.

"How dare you embarrass us?" the Raja thundered.

"It wasn't my fault, Father, that peasant disrespected me—"

"He sneezed."

"Yes, but on my jacket."

Skanda, my half-brother, was a fool. Where the Raja favored wisdom, Skanda favored wealth. Where the Raja listened, Skanda leered.

"Would you like to know the difference between us and everyone else?" demanded the Raja.

"Yes?"

"Nothing whatsoever."

"But—"

"The worms do not take heed of caste and rank when they feast on our ashes," the Raja said. "Your subjects will not remember you. They will not remember the shade of your eyes, the colors you favored or the beauty of your wives. They will only remember your impression upon their hearts and whether you filled them with glee or grief. That is your immortality."

With that, he strode out of the grove. I ran back to the garden's path, out of breath and hoping he hadn't noticed my presence. By now, the sun had slipped behind the palace, transforming everything that surrounded it to a rosy gold.

As the Raja approached, I saw him as I always did—illuminated and beyond reproach. But as he came closer, new details leapt forward. There were weary creases at the corners of his eyes and a new slope to his shoulders. It didn't look right. I felt like I was truly seeing him for the first time and what I saw was a man stooped in age, wearing a thinning pelt of greatness. The moment our eyes met, I averted my gaze. Seeing him like this made me feel as if I had stumbled into something private, something I wasn't supposed to know. Or, perhaps, just didn't want to.

I knelt before him, the tips of my fingers brushing against his feet in the customary symbol of respect and deference.

"It is good to see you, daughter," he said.

I knew my father in his voice, in his words. The moment he spoke, all of the previous strangeness was forgotten. My father was not known for a pleasing, diplomatic tone. His voice had the gravelly lurch of a thunderclap and all the solemnity of sleep, but the sound clung to me in well-worn familiarity. It lulled me into safety and for a moment, I thought he would say that his meeting with the courtiers had been a sham, that he had no intention of marrying me off to strangers, that I would stay here forever. This was no heaven, but it was the hell that I knew, and I preferred it far more than whatever beast of a country awaited me.

All of that half-hope slipped away with his next words.

"In the manner of the old kings, we are holding a *swayamvara* for you," he said. "You will get the chance to choose your own husband, Mayavati."

His voice filled the courtyard. Cold sweat turned my palms clammy and my practiced calm fell away. My mind scrambled for an escape, but everything felt too close, too slippery and, worst of all, hopelessly out of reach.

He stared at me expectantly.

"Yes, Father," I forced out.

I grimaced, sure he must have heard the curt edge to my speech. I thought he would scold me, but instead he lifted my chin.

"You're the only one I trust to make the correct judgment."

I wanted to yank away from his hold and hide the sudden glistening in my eyes, but his grip was firm, his eyes knowing. He released my chin and sat on a marble bench beneath the tart lime tree. He moved to one side, beckoning for me to join him, but I remained standing. Sitting was agreement to a forced marriage. And I didn't agree.

"The moment you could climb, you were always in the sanctum's rafters," he said in one breath. My head snapped up. There was no accusation in his voice, only something wistful . . . and warm. I glanced into his face, but nothing but pain and age marked his features.

"How—"

"It is difficult not to notice tutors fleeing the archival room every week," he said with the ghost of a smile. "But I never stopped you because I wanted you to know. I wanted you to see how fraught ruling is." He stopped and his chest heaved, shoulders dropping a fraction. "Perhaps I hoped that by letting you see, you might forgive what I must take from you."

I stared at him. This was the longest time we had spent in each other's company. Until now, I only officially saw my father once a year on my annual Age Day. There were times when he had even left me gifts. Not that I was alone in this regard. My half-sisters also received small presents—clusters of gems or fashionable silks. But my presents had always been different. Fragrant sheaves of poetry or treaties of Vedic law. Valuable. I had entertained the hope that he wished to spare me from the stifling fate of my wedded half-sisters, but in the end I was no different.

He rose to his feet and placed a hand on my shoulder. It felt leaden against my skin.

"Even a favored daughter is still just a daughter."

I suppressed a flinch. The warmth of his voice had disappeared, replaced with the cool monotone I knew far better.

"You have always possessed the intellect of a boy, Mayavati," he said. "Should you have the good fortune of a different sex in your next life, you might prove to be a fine ruler."

A semicircle of the scarlet palace guards fanned out around the Raja and, without another word, he left. Despite the evening's warmth, I shivered. His words clung to me. Each sentence was its own barb from which there was no escape.

For the second time today, I found myself in a place without realizing how I got there. I stepped into the harem and a flurry of sounds swelled around me.

"What did the Raja want with you?"

I masked a groan. All my guilt for the young guardsman vanished. Loose tongue. Maybe I should have scared him more.

My half-sister Parvati stepped forward, and her jade green eyes flashed with all the latent menace of someone too beautiful and too bored.

"Are you going to be a royal *devadasi?*" she asked. "No one thought you'd marry, anyway."

I choked back a laugh. I would have far preferred to become a *devadasi* and live my life dedicated to the temple rather than fade into obscurity.

"Is it true that the Raja has denounced you?" asked one of the wives.

I turned to face the wife who had spoken. She was new, or at least I had not seen her before. A pair of buckteeth peeked out beneath thin lips. I doubted my father had wed her for her beauty or out of romantic interest. I wondered if the wife was like me, a bride of political convenience. She stared back at me, first curious and then embarrassed.

"I am to marry," I said to the room.

Shrieks erupted throughout the harem.

"Who?" asked Jaya. "A monster to match your horoscope?"

"Are you sure the Raja was not lying to spare your feelings?" pressed another.

I raised my chin, determined to shove past them all until a small voice caught my attention. Gauri ran to me, brown curls flying as she threw her arms around my legs. I curved around her, burying my face in her sweet-smelling hair and gripping her shoulders tightly, as though they were the only things anchoring me to the spot.

"Are you leaving me?" she asked.

I knelt beside her, searching her face, memorizing the rosiness of her cheeks and her dimpled smile. There was no way I could lie to her. I wanted to tell her that I had no choice and that she would have to find another person to tell her stories and spin her nightmares back into dreams. But before I could wrangle out an explanation, one of the wives rushed past me, pushing me backward.

I looked up to see Mother Dhina and instinctively clutched Gauri closer.

"Don't poison this girl with your bad fortune," she hissed, pulling Gauri away.

Gauri protested but Mother Dhina's grip was relentless. I rose from the floor slowly. I wanted stillness, poise. I wouldn't show Gauri hysteria or rage. Mother Dhina's gaze met mine.

Around me, the line of women converged like a warped mirror. Here was my future—a cage fit for breeding bitterness and spite. I stumbled backward, edging along the walls as if I could avoid that fate through sheer force of will. The voices of the wives and my half-sisters billowed around me, but I couldn't separate their words. They seemed to speak as one.

"Wherever you go, you'll only bring death with you. Take your pestilence elsewhere," spat Mother Dhina.

The marble beneath me was cold and dry, but my feet slipped as if I stood in water. A ringing sound filled my ears and I sprinted out of the halls. Rage vibrated from my heels to my head as I swung open my bedroom door and sank to the floor.

Where my room once glowed rosy in the sunset, now the glint of the walls shone scarlet and flame-like, poised to swallow me. Bharata wanted to be rid of me, just as much as I wanted to be rid of it. But not like this. Not like some parcel of land bartered between countries. That wasn't freedom.

I thought of Gauri's face when I had knelt beside her. I thought about the words that I would have said—I had no choice but to leave. Maybe only half of that was true. I did have to leave, but the manner in which I left could be a choice that was entirely my own. I stared out the window, watching the infinite sky stretch before me. If they didn't give me a choice, then I would make my own.

I would escape.

•» 4 «•

THE INTRUDER

Night coaxed out the stars, my jailers. Above me, the moon burned dull silver. In the dark sky, it looked flat enough to pry and use as a mirror. I had spent the last hour staring out the window, watching the sentinels patrol the vast walls that enclosed everything I had ever seen, touched and known for the past seventeen years. After hours of staring, I had found a spot left unguarded, a hole in the palace's security. All I had to do was reach it and then . . . freedom.

But until I could escape, other tasks clamored for my attention. I faced my room. It was the smallest of the chambers in the harem, shunted to the end of a hall that had no other occupants. They moved me here when I was ten. Mother Shastri told me that it was punishment after a swarm of bees chased my half-brother Yudhistira into a pool of water. He had teased me that day and had kicked over a drawing that I had labored over. I had glared at him, wishing that he would go away. That's when I learned that sometimes my wishes had a strange way of coming true. Over the years I told myself that it was all mere coincidence, but now I hoped that whatever saved me back then from Yudhistira's bullying would save me from the *swayamvara. Stop that,* I scolded myself. Hope and wishing wouldn't save me.

A veil of cold purpose fell over me. Enough meetings in the sanctum had taught me the layout of the city, the demographics of its inhabitants. I could do this. I just had to move fast. I opened up my chest of clothes and began separating the gaudy fabrics from the practical, the nonessential from the necessary. I was halfway through when I heard a voice at the door. Shoving the two heaps of clothes behind a screen, I jumped to my feet.

"Maya *didi?*" called the voice. Immediately, my heart sank. Gauri. I would never see Gauri again. "It's time for my story!"

In spite of myself, I smiled and opened the door for her. She glowed against the dark of the hallways, and it took every last wisp of strength not to hold her to me and weep into her hair. Tomorrow loomed in my mind. I could feel the heft of it like a solid weight against my fingers.

"Story!" she said, shaking my arm in a mock-pleading voice.

"What story do you want?"

It was a tradition between us. The moment evening slipped into night, Gauri would sneak into my room and I would recite fairytales to her—embellishing the beautiful, glossing over the grotesque. Gauri clambered onto my bed, tugging the blankets around her. I sat by her side.

"Tell me about the other realms," said Gauri wistfully. "I'm going to live there when I grow up."

"Which one?"

Gauri frowned. "How many are there?"

As far as I knew, there was only one and it had nothing in it but scheming courtiers, lying wives and gilded menageries. But I wasn't going to tell Gauri that. In all the tomes and folklores I had read from the archives, there was no limit to the worlds around us. Somewhere unseen were demonic realms filled with laughing *asuras* and blackened suns. There were austere kingdoms on the peaks of mountains where phoenixes serenaded the moon and the halls of the gods glinted with lightning. And there was our own, human world, mortal, with only the comfort of stories to keep away the chill of death.

"There's thousands, but mainly three. Think of it like cities within kingdoms," I said when I saw her brows scrunch up. "There's our world, which has you, and is therefore the best one." Gauri grinned. "Then there's the Otherworld, with its Night Bazaar and strange but beautiful beings. And then," I dropped my voice to a whisper, "there's the Netherworld, which holds Naraka, the realm of the dead."

Gauri shivered. "What's there?"

"Demons," I said, raising my arms like a giant bat.

Her eyes widened and she curled closer to me. "Tell me about the Night Bazaar."

I worried the edges of my dress . . . this was the part I made different from the stories. But Gauri didn't need to know that.

"It's a market for the Otherworld people, the beings in our

stories, like *apsaras,* who dance in the heavens, or *gandharvas,* who play celestial music. Or even *naginis,* who want to buy new scales for their serpent tails. All of them."

Gauri wrinkled a nose, unimpressed. "They buy dresses there?"

"Much, *much* more," I said. "It's a place for purchasing nightmares and dreams sweet as *rasmalai.* You can buy sleepless nights or trade your full name for a wish. It's where demon mercenaries lend out their magic like colorful ribbons. There's memories of beautiful women for sale and a thousand potions for things from a broken heart to a sore tooth."

"Really?" asked Gauri, her voice barely above a whisper.

I shrugged. "Maybe. But I've told you and now it's time to sleep. No more tales."

I rolled to the side, feigning sleep, when Gauri poked me.

"How will I find it when I'm done growing up?"

"If I knew, don't you think I would have tried to get there already?" I laughed. "It's hard to find, Gauri."

"I can find it!" she piped up. "Last week, I found slippers beneath a statue. But I don't know why they were there."

I tried to stifle my laugh with a cough. I may have hidden those last week. They belonged to Mother Dhina and had the most irritating tassels. And to add insult to injury, they had bells.

"Did you tell anyone?"

"No. I thought an *apsara* had left them there. Maybe she wanted them back and she'd get mad if I took them."

"So you think finding hidden slippers qualifies you to enter the Otherworld?"

Gauri blinked at me as though this were the most obvious conclusion.

"I'll tell you where to find it, then," I said, laughing. Truthfully, the folktales never said how to get there, but Gauri looked at me so expectantly I couldn't imagine any harm in playing up her imagination. "You have to go when the creatures are at their weakest, on the night of a new moon. The Otherworld is on the other side of a moonbeam and inside a hundred lotus petals. It's in that space of time right before you fall asleep . . ."

Gauri muffled a yawn and looked sleepily at the door.

"I'm going to go someday."

"Are you?" I asked, wrapping my arm around her. "You should take me with you."

"I'll take you, *didi*."

Her voice was heavy with sleepiness, but her body was curled tight and tense. I knew she was trying to keep herself awake, drawing out the minutes where we could lie side by side. But we both knew she had to leave.

"Will we see each other again?" she asked softly.

"Yes."

Gauri fell silent. "In this life?"

I turned to face her. "What do you mean?"

"Mother Urvashi says that if I'm bad in this life then I'll come back as a goat in my next life. Which means that there is another life." Gauri didn't look at me, focusing instead on tightly twisting the hem of her gown. "So will you see me again before I'm a goat?"

"You're too good to be a goat."

"*Didi*, you're not answering me."

"I know," I said into her hair. "I just don't know."

"But if we were sisters this time, we would be sisters again, right?"

"Of course."

"And we were sisters in our last life too, right?"

"Naturally."

"What do you think we were?" asked Gauri, looking up at me. "Princesses?"

"Nothing as boring as that," I said. "We could have been stars, you and me. And not the mean ones that blindly spell out the rest of your life, but beautiful constellations hovering far above fate." I pointed to the open window. "We could have been something magical. Talking bears that built a palace in a mango tree. Or twin *makaras* with tails so long they could have encircled the ocean twice."

"*Makaras* are scary."

"No, they're not."

"They're *huge*," she said, spreading her arms, "and they have lots of teeth." Gauri hooked her fingers into her cheeks and pulled, revealing a number of loose baby teeth and gaps.

"*Er tharp tooth*," she said, still pulling on her cheeks.

"What?"

She let go of her lips. "They're sharp too."

I laughed. "Well, you're very small with lots of teeth and are just as vicious and scary as a sea dragon."

"It's bad to be a dragon."

"Says who? Nothing wrong with a little bit of viciousness. Would you rather be a dove or a dragon?"

"Mother Dhina says—"

"I'm not asking about what Mother Dhina thinks, I'm asking you."

Gauri peeked at me from beneath the blankets. "I think it would be nice to blow fire. I'd never get hungry."

I laughed. "Sound reasoning, as ever."

Slowly, Gauri slipped off the bed. I clenched my hands together so that I wouldn't be tempted to comfort her. I couldn't coddle her. I couldn't lull her with false promises. All I could ask was that she would remember what I said, remember the stories I told and hope that some of that knowledge would, in time, be its own comfort.

"No matter where we are, we'll always share the same sky. We can always find each other in the same constellation."

Gauri sniffed. "Which?"

"The loveliest of them all," I said, pointing at a slight angle in the stars. I may have hated the rest of them, but not this one. This constellation was far from the rest, a lonely cluster of lights. "The Solitary Star. That will be our constellation. Legend says it was built by the celestial architect who made the golden city of Lanka."

"Real gold?" repeated Gauri. "Maybe I'll go there too."

I laughed and pulled her into one last hug. It was better this way, better to go without saying goodbye. After shutting the door behind me, I pulled out the heaps of clothes and set to work scuffing the hems of the saris and cutting holes into silks. I would need to blend in once I was in the city.

Doubt crept up on me. Sneaking out of the harem wasn't the problem. It was what would come next. All those hours spent above my father's inner sanctum, listening and watching. Whatever small hopes I had amassed over the years—to be significant in the eyes of this court, to *rule,* to possess a voice that others would listen to rather than shrink from—now lay bruised and trampled in my mind. If I left, I would live forever as a fugitive. Or perhaps no one would come looking for me. Either fate struck a blow.

Suddenly the small *diyas* that had lit my room extinguished all at once. Even the light from the moon seemed to have swiftly stuttered off into a pitch-black veil, plunging the room into impenetrable black. I crawled blindly along the floor, when a scratching sound stopped me.

Someone else was in the room.

"Gauri?" I called.

Heart racing, I edged closer along the wall. A sharp sound dragged across the floor—a blade. Panic leeched cold into my bones. I held my breath, trying to peer through the blot of darkness that swelled the room. I ran my fingers along the counters, hoping for something sharp, but finding nothing but polished wood.

"Who's there? Show yourself!" I called, trying to keep the tremor from my voice. "Don't stalk me in the shadows like a coward."

A cold laugh rumbled from the middle of the room. High-pitched. Female. I frowned. *A harem wife? No. There's no way they would be able to find a weapon. And even if they did, how would they know what to do with it?*

"Is that any way to greet me after all this time?" said a voice.

Something tugged at my core. The voice had a life of its own and it conjured some wordless secret deep in my mind. Something in me hummed with recognition. I leaned toward the sound of her voice.

"What do you want? Reveal yourself or I will call the guards."

The woman laughed and my arms prickled. "Go ahead and try."

And so I did. But my voice never rose. No matter how much I strained, silence clogged the air. The dark absorbed my screams until the only sound I heard was the frantic beat of my own heart.

"I had no idea where you went, until today. Strange how men can be so unwittingly helpful," snarled the voice. A shiver ran down my spine. The voice came at me from a thousand different directions. I could hear her beside my ear, at the nape of my neck, at the corner of the room. The sound ensnared me. Distantly, I heard her voice, muddled as if it had crossed lifetimes to echo in my head. For a moment, I thought I knew her and the truth of it stirred something bone-deep. But the feeling passed, replaced with panic as a blade growled, dragging across the floor.

A gust of air brushed against my legs. She was near.

"I don't know who you are, but don't come any closer."

"Or what?" laughed the voice. "What can you do in that feeble mortal body of yours?"

Icicle skin brushed against mine and without thinking, I kicked.

Thud.

My foot connected with her chest. I had a half-second to grin before I was forced to the ground.

"Not yet," crooned the voice. "Now I know. I see you. I've seen this . . . home . . . of yours. I need you to lead me."

"I'm not leading you anywhere," I spat. I tried to grasp hold of her, but failed. I tried to scream, but the sound bounded back and all sense of direction spiraled and fell.

A hand closed on my wrist and the touch was iron and ice, so cold I could feel it clattering in my teeth. Cold set in, frosting over my thoughts. I couldn't scream. Panic tore at me. *No. I will not die within these walls. Not this way.*

I pushed through the numbing sensation, willing my body not to snap. It was nothing more than a shift, but I felt it, keyed into it like a groove in a tile. I held on to that small feeling, the faintest specter of warmth. I forced myself to step past the cold, and the pain of it ripped a hundred screams from my throat.

The darkness that glommed around the woman parted. The strength of my screams bounded around me, forcing me backward.

I heard a gasp, the barest muffle of surprise and then—

Nothing.

The silence enveloping the room had lifted. The woman was gone and she had taken all her cold with her. I rubbed my hands together, but my palms were warm and ruddy, as if the cold had been nothing more than a blanket now yanked away.

I couldn't shake out the sound of her voice. I wanted to follow it as much as I wanted to smother it. The familiarity of her voice recalled an old hurt I couldn't place.

Faint light leaked into the room and I cursed. It was dawn already where moments ago my room was plunged in the thick of night. My breathing was still ragged, but I heaved myself to my feet, marching across the room. Just as I reached for the door, a faint clicking sound echoed. It was the sound of a lock falling into place. I thudded my palms against the wood as panic, sharp and acrid, burned in my chest.

"Open this door! Who has locked this entrance?"

A voice no less chilling than the unknown assailant's greeted me.

"Calm yourself, Mayavati," came Mother Dhina's crocodile croon.

I blanched and stepped back. "Someone just tried to invade my room. I need to speak to the guards."

Mother Dhina laughed. "What lies you tell, child. I have half a mind to compliment your imagination. No one can get past the Raja's sentinels—"

"But someone was *here*!" I protested. "Let me out! I demand to speak—"

"Demand?" repeated Mother Dhina. "You are not in a position to make demands. It's a lesson you should learn now before your wedding. The Raja sent me to tell you that the *swayamvara* will be held in two days. Given your past conduct, the realm thought it best to ensure that you stay in one place and not hurt yourself."

"You mean escape?"

"It is also best that you stay away from Gauri," continued Mother Dhina as if I hadn't uttered a single word. "No more meetings until the *swayamvara*. It is best not to infect her with your bad fortune and deplorable manners. Stop spreading ridiculous ideas in her head."

"I'd rather spread ideas than legs," I hissed back. "But I doubt you would agree—"

"*Silence*, you mongrel," said Mother Dhina. "All your life, all I have done is try to be merciful to you and bring you stability. To give you a home."

"You hid me away and shunned me from anyone who might get to know me. You call this mercy?"

"I do. I spared anyone the shame of being in your presence," she said. "The least you could have done was die. But you kept selfishly clinging to life."

"Do you expect me to apologize?"

Mother Dhina laughed and it was a cold, cruel thing.

"When the sickness claimed eight of the wives, I prayed you were next."

She fell quiet and her next words were soft, but no less fierce. "Do you know how many children I have buried because of you? Strong, healthy babies. Ten fingers, ten toes. A full head of hair. They just wouldn't breathe. Because of *you*."

"That's impossible."

"Your shadow touched mine. You poisoned me. You *killed* them. Your horoscope has only attracted darkness to our court. It's your fault."

"You're—"

"Enough," cut in Mother Dhina. "You have no place here. Your mother didn't either. At least she had the good sense to die young."

Mother Dhina cleared her throat and this time when she spoke, it was in the cool and practiced monotone of someone who could watch you burn alive and not blink. "In keeping with Bharata's bridal traditions, you will be isolated to maintain the utmost purity."

"You can't do that!" I screamed, slamming my fists against the door. "I am telling you someone was in here. If you're truly merciful, let me out, let me speak to the Raja."

Footsteps resounded in the distance. I screamed after her, but my sounds chased nothing but echoes. Mother Dhina had left. The panels of wood chaffed, scuffed and scratched beneath my fists, but they never budged. Again and again, I threw myself against the door. I screamed until voice was an echo of something I once knew. I yelled until I felt unspooled and even whispering made me wince. I slid against the door, cradling my bloodied knuckles to my chest.

Perhaps this was a dream, some horrible illusion that would soon collapse into shards of nightmare. I had heard of something like this once. When my father swore to the envoys of the rebel kingdoms that not a single hand would be laid upon the prisoners of war, he had found other means to torture them. Sleep deprivation. But he kept his word. No one touched them. No one needed to. I had listened in the rafters to their horrible testimony, to the nightmare of ears forever ringing, eyes hollow with sleeplessness. The mind was its own escape artist, and who knew what it would concoct in the absence of rest.

That had to be what I was seeing. I was tired, I whispered to myself. That was all. It wasn't real. It wasn't real. I rocked myself back and forth, muttering the words into the cupped hollow of my palms like they were sacred. I closed my eyes and let my body curl around my hurt until eventually, sleep claimed me.

•» 5 «•

A GIFT TO FREE

The next morning, I woke to the other wives assembling in the halls. I stared at my hands, saw the scabs and scrapes, felt the crust of tears along my jaw and knew this had been no dream. Even then, my reality was a muddled thing. In the space of a day my room had become alien and unfamiliar. The voice of my intruder roped around me, tight as a noose. Had she even been there? I didn't know. Or was it like the tutor from yesterday whose stretched form had been nothing more than shadow play?

I pulled my hands through my hair, shivering in my empty room. The air was watery and thin with pale morning light. No matter where I looked, everything bore the telltale signs of a trap. If the sky had ever hinted its secrets in the past, it yielded none now. Twice, I had tried to lift the bars from my windows. I had sawed at them with a rock and dug at their foundations until my fingers were bloody. But there was no escape.

Outside, the wives lined up in front of my door, preparing to recite the wedded tales of their mothers and sisters and selves. The tradition was meant to be joyful, but they would give me no such false hopes. I wasn't sure whether I should be grateful or horrified. I couldn't separate one voice from the other, each one melded into the other, until it swelled into a chorus of pain. The wives told me of sisters murdered by vengeful husbands to safeguard their honor, of wives sewn up to guard their virtue when their husbands left for battle, of the torrent of blood on the first night of marriage. They told me of bruises covered beneath golden bangles, veils meant to hide dislocated jaws, the fear of raised voices. I tried to shut them out. I tried to convince myself that their stories were only meant to scare me. But each time I closed my eyes, all I saw was a menacing man with unforgiving eyes and a cruel mouth.

Night tugged a starless blanket over the palace. I had hardly moved all day. Even when the harem wives' stories burned, even when Gauri slipped drawings under the door, nothing moved me. I tried to imagine the whole of the universe leaning forward to test me. Was this what it wanted? I could conjure fearlessness like a veil. Maybe if I just kept at the illusion, I would fool myself too.

When the kingdom fell silent, I finally moved to light the *diyas* in my room. Near the corner of my room, a pillar carved in the shape of the lion-headed Narasimha grinned wickedly. It was a gruesome tale, of blood and angry gods, but for some reason it gave me hope. The flames flickered bright in the lion-headed statue's eyes, but they yielded no warmth. Everything was a spell of cold. To make matters worse, I had no way of knowing whether my assailant would return. I had gone over her words, but none of it made sense. *I need you to lead me.* Lead *where?* For all I knew, she was nothing more than a nightmare conjured from stress.

But if she wasn't, I would be ready. From the drawer beside my bed, I pulled out a blunt shard of flint. I set my puny weapon beside me and stared at the balcony, willing her to make herself known. Something about her voice had filled me with regret.

A scratching sound startled me out of my thoughts. I lunged for the rock when a voice cut across the room—

"Mayavati, come to the door."

I tensed, my arm still raised. A heavy feeling settled in my gut. I had heard that voice a hundred times, listened for it from my spying place and imagined it saying kinder words. Father.

The door gave way with a sigh and my father's silhouette loomed into the room, a blot against the darkness. He stood alone, no familiar retinue of guards flanking his side. At once, I bolted upright. He wasn't one to flout tradition and yet he'd gone to the trouble of visiting me in secret. For a half-moment, I wondered whether some unknowable power had answered my wishes and freed me. But experience told me otherwise. Father was far too cunning for sentiment.

"I have come with a gift," he said, extending a hand toward me. "One to free you from this marriage."

From the folds of his robe, he withdrew a small violet flask. I took the flask and removed the stopper, careful not to spill its contents before taking a whiff. All the blood slipped from my face. I knew that scent. My breath came in a rasp and a dead chill swam under my skin. It was mandrake soaked in milk—poison.

"No matter who you marry, they will wage war against us. My spies have heard it, my councilors suspect it and my instincts know it," said the Raja, his voice calm and even. "The best chances for the realm are to bring the war to us, instead of letting it play out on the outskirts of our borders. Their attendance at your *swayamvara* is critical in bringing them here. Your death will nullify the bonds of guest hospitality and we may dispatch the rebels on the spot. Your sacrifice would ensure the safety of all our people."

I shook my head, my mouth bone dry. I was no bride. I was bait. The walls stretched above me. An invisible thread running from my head to my feet yanked me, threatening to topple me onto the ground. I inhaled a shuddering breath, but it felt clammy in my lungs.

I hoped that by letting you see, you might forgive what I must take from you.

He wasn't just taking away my independence. Or home.

When I spoke, my voice was hollow, scraped—

"You want me dead."

•» 6 «•

THE WEDDING

Seconds collided into hours, decades, centuries. Eternity itself moved through me, stretching the moments after I'd spoken. In a whirl, I saw my life compressed, folded and distilled into the vial of mandrake poison in my hands.

Clearing his throat, my father clasped his hands behind his back.

"It is not a question of want," he said. "It is a matter of need. If this is what it will take to keep the realm safe for our people, then I have no choice."

Our people. My stomach knotted. Only the thump of my heart told me I was alive. Not yet a corpse. I glanced at the frail vial. If I wanted, I could throw it in his face, pour it on the ground or smash the vial altogether. But of course I couldn't. The vial was Bharata's hope distorted, and I held it in my hand.

"You must understand that your contribution to the realm will exceed that of any of your siblings and any of my councilors. What I am asking of you—"

"What you're asking requires no great sacrifice on my part," I said, my voice shaking. "I am expendable."

"We must show strength," said the Raja. "If any of your rejected suitors believed that your choice was politically motivated, we would be destroyed. Our kingdom would be gone. They know your sisters are betrothed and that you remain a maiden. They also know that we cannot lay siege to their kingdoms if they married a princess of Bharata. The only way to protect ourselves is to have no marriage at all."

His shoulders fell. I looked sharply at him, wild hope pulling at my heart. *Maybe he is changing his mind.*

A half-breath passed before his arm tensed and then his hands fell limply to his sides. A death warrant. Panic rasped in my lungs. My whole body gathered like one frenzied breath. Before he could step back, I lunged forward, grabbing his wrist—

"Please," I said. "Give me a different draught, something that will make it seem like I have died. But not this. There must be another way."

He pulled back his hand. This time when he spoke, there was no hint of doubt, no sign of succor or mercy, or remorse.

"Do you think I have not thoroughly reviewed every option?" his voice thundered. "They would verify your death with their own physicians. The moment they see through our deception, Bharata would be doomed. Would you rather die by your own hand or by the enemy? Trust me, daughter. One is worse than the other."

I set my jaw, my eyes narrowing to slits. "I will not die for you."

He smiled and in that moment I knew I had lost.

"I am no fool. I would not expect you to die for me. But for your sister?" He paused and my heart turned cold. Gauri. "Would you condemn her life so quickly? Or those of your people?"

His words hung in the air, coiling around me like a noose. This time when the Raja stepped back, I made no move toward him. And when he turned to face me—his eyes shadowed and face drawn—no hope glimmered in my heart.

"If you wanted me to know your plan all along, why bother with sending a tutor for me? Why not get rid of all the distractions?"

"Your mind is playing tricks on you, Mayavati," said my father curtly. "There was no tutor assigned to you yesterday. I know because I made sure of it. Take the potion during the ceremony. I have faith in your judgment, daughter."

With that, he left. A heavy thudding sound rang in my ears. Of course there had been no tutor. I had truly lost my mind. I circled the room, my eyes darting over walls and corners. Escape was impossible. My doors were bolted. My windows barred with iron. Light entered the room slowly, like a predator stalking me, cornering me with the truth that there was no escape left but one—death.

The sound of water sloshing up beaten copper basins and the muffled chime of heavy jewels woke me. Fragrant myrrh, rose oil and the starch of brocade silks drifted through the gap in my door. One by one the attendants filled the room, their heads bowed and arms laden.

The moment I saw them, fury shot through me. Fury that I had thought better of my father . . . that escape was out of reach. But most of all fury at myself, for thinking that I was meant for more than this. Fury at my dreams for promising a life *lived*.

Quickly and quietly, the attendants scrubbed me with turmeric. If they saw my red-rimmed eyes or mussed hair, they made no comment. They bathed my limbs in milk and nettle, applied henna in intricate designs of mango blossoms and flowers, threaded golden ornaments through my waist-length hair. I bit my lip when they plunged amethyst earrings through my lobes and cuffed my wrists with bangles. They looked just like shackles.

When I stood, the attendants tightly wound a sari around my body. It was red, like the wedding saris worn by all the half-sisters before me. A bitter smile crossed my face. Red was supposed to ward off death on happy occasions.

In quick, methodical succession, the guards emptied my room of its things. Too soon, all that remained was my empty bed and the small nightstand. Over and over, my eyes returned to the small purple vial now tucked in the space between my wrist and bangles. It was cool against my skin.

I walked around the room—memorizing corners, touching edges. Above and around me, gossamer curtains wavered, bright green tiles twinkled and the golden concentric circles of the ceiling gleamed.

The door quaked.

"Princess, we must leave," called the guards.

I wished I could sink into the ground or disappear into the ether like my assailant. Now the door was opening, shadows leaking inside and, still, I was here. I cast a glance at the pillar of Narasimha in my room, wishing it would spring free and protect me. But in the end, it stayed silent as stone.

"Come, Princess," said a guard, leading me by the elbow in a less-than-gentle grip.

A final fragment of sunshine spilled across my foot before the door closed with a resounding thud. Silence pressed against me, pushing me forward.

As I walked, none of the harem women moved to embrace me. None whispered the customary blessings of fertility and love into my ears. From the shadows, Mother Shastri watched me coldly. Their daughters stood in the shadow of another pillar, their expressions unreadable. Only Gauri ran to me, led by a reluctant Mother Dhina.

"When are you coming back?" she asked, beaming.

I paused, on the verge of embracing Gauri, when I felt the vial of poison pressing against my wrist, staying my hand. An image flashed in my mind—foreign soldiers breaking through the harem walls. Stealing Gauri. Or worse.

Numbly, I unclasped my mother's necklace and slipped it into Gauri's palm.

"I don't know. But will you look after this for me until I return?"

Gauri took the necklace reverently and nodded. I straightened my back, resolution knotting my stomach. I would do as Father asked. Not for him, but for Gauri. For Bharata. Before I walked away, Mother Dhina caught my arm. Her face was tight, kohl pooled in the puffy skin around her eyes. She looked like she was fighting the urge to speak. But in the end, her words won out:

"Keep some secrets to yourself, girl," she said quietly.

Not to worry, I wanted to say. *Soon, only the ground will know my secrets.*

After that, time moved far too quickly. All too soon, I was crossing from the grounds to the Raja's welcoming hall. Any time I wanted to wait, to pause, to touch anything, the guards pulled me forward. Even the sun had renounced me, disappearing behind the clouds and withholding its warmth. A numb furor sucked the air.

Marigolds and roses adorned the entrance to the Raja's welcoming hall, and bright petals carpeted the path. Inside, the din of men's voices and the cloying smell of betel nut hit me instantly. Through my veil, I could see the suitors and their attendants. Some stood short, others stretched tall. Some wore crowns of horns, others diadems of gold. All fifteen wore garlands of red carnations.

In front of each suitor lay a clawed basin filled with fire. Behind them, the pillars of the Raja's hall bloomed into coronets of marble and vines of emerald. I glanced at the ceiling, palms sweating at the sight of the narrow rafters. How many times had I spied from that very spot?

Officially speaking, this was my first time inside the hall. Though it looked small from above, down here the chamber swelled in size.

The court notary handed me a garland of white blossoms. Whoever I chose to place the white garland upon would be my husband, if only for a moment.

"Noble visitors," the Raja said in his booming voice, "I give you my daughter, the Princess Mayavati. May her choices in life be filled with honor and grace."

As he spoke, anger flickered on the suitors' faces and their personal guards clutched their weapons. The Raja's words from last night rang true. No matter which of the fifteen I chose, the others would see the rejection as an affront. I glanced at my father. My strand of sapphires was gone from his neck. I was already dead to him.

One by one, the court archivist read the suitors' names, and one by one, each prince or Raja threw a handful of rice into the fire before him.

"The Prince of Karusha," announced the court archivist.

An old man with a silvery mustache stepped forward.

"The Raja of Gandhara."

A boy who looked hardly thirteen years of age stepped nervously into the middle of the two rows and bowed.

"The Emperor of Odra."

A middle-aged man with a henna-stained beard inclined his head.

The archivist continued rattling off the names of foreign princes and rajas until I counted exactly fifteen. My breath gathered and I held it for as long as I could, not wanting to waste a single exhale.

"Now the time has arrived for the Princess Mayavati to make

her choice," said the archivist, rolling up the parchment. "As tradition dictates, she shall make this choice alone."

The archivist blew a small horn and I bit back a cry. Sweat beaded along my temples, mingling with the tinny scent of incense and henna. As the suitors and their guards filed out of the room, the Raja gave a tight nod in my direction.

Soon I was alone. Already, the fire in the basins had begun to shrink. I had mere minutes left. Slats of sunshine broke through the gauzy curtains. I walked, dream-like, to stand in the streak of light.

What would the suitors think when they saw my body sprawled on the floor? I imagined their expressions turning from horror to dread, their eyes wild when they realized the deception. Would they fight where I lay? Trample my body like the instrument it was? Or would someone move me aside, my duty done, my life spent?

The horoscope loomed in my thoughts. Perhaps it had been right all this time. A marriage that partnered me with death. My wedding, sham though it was, *would* bring more than just my end. I breathed deeply and a calm spiraled through me.

This was my final taste: a helix of air, smacking of burnt things and bright leaves. I pulled the vial from my bangles, fingers shaking.

This was my last sight: purling fire and windows that soared out of reach. I raised the vial to my lips. My chest was tight, silk clinging damply to my back, my legs.

This was my last sound: the cadence of a heart still beating.

"May Gauri live a long life," I mouthed.

The poison trickled thickly from the rim and I tilted my head back, eyes on the verge of shutting—

And then: a shatter.

My eyes opened to empty hands clutching nothing.

Spilled poison seeped into the rug and shards of glass glinted on the floor, but all of that was obscured by the shadow of a stranger.

"There's no need for that," said the stranger.

He wiped his hands on the front of his charcoal *kurta,* his face partially obscured by a sable hood studded with small diamonds. All I could see was his tapered jaw, the serpentine curve of his smile and the straight bridge of his nose. Like the suitors, he wore a garland of red flowers. And yet, all of that I could have forgotten.

Except his voice . . .

It drilled through the gloaming of my thoughts, pulled at me in the same way the mysterious intruder's voice had tugged. But where the woman's voice brought fury, this was different. The hollow inside me shifted, humming a reply in melted song. I could have been verse made flesh or compressed moonlight. Anything other than who I was now.

A second passed before I spoke. By then, the stranger's lips had bent into a grin.

"Who are you?"

"One of your suitors," he said, not missing a beat. He adjusted his garland.

I backed away, body tensing. I had never seen him before. I knew that with utmost certainty. Did he mean to harm me?

"That's not an answer."

"And that wasn't a thank you," he said. "Before you scold me for interrupting your martyrdom, you should look outside. Particularly at the chariots."

I stole a glance at the door to the antechamber. The suitors and attendants would return at any moment. Keeping my distance from the stranger, I focused on the underside of the chariots and froze. What I had mistaken for wheel spokes were spears covered in gold paint. And hiding beneath the false chariots were soldiers. *Hundreds* of soldiers. I backed away from the window, heart beating wildly. How many men were hidden beneath the carriages? Worse, how many soldiers had Bharata unwittingly admitted? The neighboring kings could have snuck in half their militias through the open gates. I scanned the chariots. My father's army easily outnumbered them, but the suitors had the advantage of surprise.

I wheeled around. "Did you plan this attack?"

"No."

Grabbing a sharp pin from my hair, I held it toward him like a blade.

"Then why won't you tell me your name?"

He bowed. "I'm the Raja of Akaran. But you may call me Amar."

Akaran? I had never heard of such a place and I had extensively studied the geography of Bharata's surrounding kingdoms. Before I could say anything, Amar snatched the pin from my hand.

"You may threaten me later. For now, your concern should be the men outside. They know of your father's plan for a siege and they've come prepared."

My lips parted. "But how did you know—"

"My own spies informed me."

"Does the Raja know?" I thought of Gauri playing in her room, completely unaware of danger.

"Yes."

A flurry of questions rose to my mind. "But—?"

"I sent my messenger to alert him."

"I have to get to the harem. My sister isn't safe."

Picking up the ends of my sari, I turned toward the door, but then a rumble shuddered through the kingdom. The chariots had overturned. I could picture the soldiers beneath the wheels—unfurling from those crouched positions like nightmares made flesh. Thunderous footfall pounded the earth, gates creaked open and screaming ripped through the air.

"I have to go," I said, my voice rising. "I have to warn them."

Amar grabbed my arm.

"It's too late for that," he said. "They're already fighting."

I paused, straining to hear anything other than blood rushing in my ears. Distantly, I heard iron against iron, the sound of clashing shields, and the roar of screams pitted against each other. Outside the window, the chariots lay overturned, split open like hollow shells.

"There's no time," he said, releasing his grip on my arm. "The Raja himself asked me to deliver you from this."

"He did?"

Amar nodded. Outside, the sounds of fighting grew closer and the parapets of the harem gleamed impassively.

"The women will be fine. Those generals only want one war. They won't attack your sisters. If they do, they'll have to answer to the kingdoms of their betrothed. As we speak, soldiers are guarding the harem." His voice cut through my thoughts. "Who will guard you if you stay behind?"

I had no answer, stunned by what was happening outside the window.

"We must go," he insisted.

If I stayed, I would die anyway. But if I went, at least I could live . . .

A flutter of hope beat soft wings in my chest. How long had I wanted to escape these walls? And now, on the brink of drowning that hope with poison, it was *here*. The past seventeen years could have been breath held solely for this moment. Something caught inside me, as sharp as a wound. I almost didn't recognize the feeling—it was *relief*. Incandescent and glittering relief. Giddiness swept through me, leaving my hands trembling.

"Well?" pressed Amar. "Are we going or not?"

We? I looked him over. The garland of red carnations hung limply around his neck. He held out his hand like a casual invitation, indifferent to the tumult outside the chambers. How could I trust him? What if he sold me to the enemies? He had no reason to protect me . . . unless I meant something to him.

Something else guided my hands. Images flashing sideways—a different hand, a samite curtain. I was convinced that we owned this single moment, this sphere of breath, this heartbeat shared like a secret. I don't know what possessed me, but I took the white garland and threw it around his neck.

I stared at my hands, not quite believing what they'd done:

With one throw, I had married him. Amar lifted the garland of white flowers and grinned. "I hoped you'd choose me."

The right corner of his lips curled faster than the left. It was such a small movement, but I couldn't look away from it. His smile was disjointed, like he was out of practice.

The doors of the chamber burst open. The fighting that was already churning in the halls now pooled into the inner sanctum. Guards and enemy soldiers spilled inside with spears raised.

The smell of burning rice filled the room, acrid and bitter. I grabbed the edges of my sari, feet pounding against the silk of the floor. My run was frenzied. Blind. In the adjacent hall, I tripped over abandoned swords and shields, slipping over puddles far too warm and far too red to be water or oil. My heartbeat roared in my ears, pushing out the sounds of fists connecting with flesh and the echoing trill of locked swords. All the fatigue, ache and grief lifted from me, dissolving in the air. Energy snaked through my bones. A fierce, almost painful desire to live pushed me toward the door, taunting me with the promise of the sun searing my skin, of clear air rushing into my lungs.

A soldier's hand grasped for me, but Amar pulled me away. Arrows zoomed past, but each time one came near, he would whirl me out of the way. Amar never shouted. He didn't even speak. He moved fluidly, dodging javelins, always a few steps behind me, a living shield. His hood never budged and revealed nothing more than the bottom half of his face.

The doors began to open, creaking like broken bones. Blinding light spilled into the room. I squinted against the brightness, but my feet never stopped. Hot, dry air filled my lungs and left them aching. The second I slowed, I felt a cool hand on my wrist—

"My mount is this way," said Amar, pulling me away from the road.

I was too out of breath to protest as his hands circled my waist and lifted me onto the richly outfitted saddle of a water buffalo. The moment I found my grip, Amar leapt onto the animal's back and, with a sharp whistle, sent dust flying around us. The water buffalo charged through the jungle. Sounds bled one into the other—crashing iron to thundering hooves, gurgling fountains to colliding branches.

At first, I sat still, not wanting to disturb a thing in case this was a death-dream, some final taunt of escape. But then I saw the jungle arcing above me. My nose filled with the musk of damp, *alive* things. The numb evanesced.

I was free.

•» 7 «•

THE NIGHT BAZAAR

I tilted my head back, letting the wind sting my eyes. Every now and then, my hand crept to my heart, reassuring me that there was a heartbeat. Freedom was bittersweet. I would never spend another afternoon drawing beside Gauri. I would never lose hours in the honeycomb rooms of Bharata's archives. The future was blank and the weight of everything unknown left me dizzy and grounded.

We rode beneath a canopy of golden trees. I glanced behind me. We had long since left the road and no ghost of its existence loomed on the horizon. The jungle had swallowed it whole.

"Where are we going?" I asked. "The main road leads to all of the major kingdoms."

"Not all of them," said Amar.

The water buffalo ambled toward a cave matted with black

vines. Compressed earth formed the walls, and veins of quartz ran through the cave.

"To get to Akaran, we must first go through the Night Bazaar."

I nearly choked. Maybe there was such a thing as magic, but the Night Bazaar was fantasy. Its provenance lay in childhood, in dreams. Amar was teasing me. I raised an eyebrow, thinking back to Yudhistira's bullying incident and the cloud of bees that chased him into a puddle.

"Just because I was raised behind thick walls does not make me—"

The dark tunnel gave way to light.

A divided sky illuminated an unearthly city. To the left, the moon bathed small shops and twisting plants in a pearly light. To the right, the sun beamed and soft sunshine fell over strange trees shaped like human limbs and animals. The sky, ever divided by day and night, blended into a spectrum of rainbow.

Creatures both impossibly tall and short slipped between shadow and light. An ethereal elephant whose hide shimmered pearlescent dipped its trunk into the pocket of a tall mouse. Twelve birds with comely female faces batted their eyelashes at a group of *naga* men who slithered closer, their scales flashing emerald. A child with the hunched wings and crumpled beak of a vulture pouted beside his mother, who had neither wings nor beak, but the sweeping train of a peacock . . .

The last of my taunt died in my chest and I sat there, gaping at the world around me.

This *was* the Night Bazaar.

All of my calm slipped away. In my head, I pictured royal maidens dragged off to serve potbellied *rakshas* or princesses turned scullery maids in the bowels of the Night Bazaar. I scrambled off the water buffalo, biting back a wince as I struggled for some balance. Catching my breath, I backed away from Amar. In the shadows, the hood over his face glinted sinister.

"Do not come near me!" I hissed.

Amar halted.

"Let me explain," he began. "I understand that this is not—"

I lunged for a stick and brandished it at him.

"Who are you?"

Amar laughed. "A stick? I've brought you to the Night Bazaar; do you really think a stick would protect you?" I gripped the stick harder. "Not that you need protection from me," he added quickly.

"*Who are you?*"

"Amar."

"Where are you from?"

"Akaran."

I gave him a hard look, but I wasn't sure how much he could see through his covering. "*What* are you?"

He drew himself up. "A raja and your husband."

There was no hesitation in his voice.

"Why have you brought me here?" My voice shook. I couldn't stop staring at the Night Bazaar. There it was. And here *I* was. Standing on the same plot of land shared with beings that—until now—had only existed in stories. "What do you want from me?"

He stopped. The smile was gone from his lips.

"I want your perspective and honesty," he said, before adding in a softer voice, "I want to be humbled by you."

Heat flared in my cheeks. I paused, the stick in my hand falling a fraction. Perspective and honesty? Humbled by me? Rajas never asked for anything other than sons from their consorts.

"My kingdom needs a queen," he said. "It needs someone with fury in her heart and shadows in her smile. It needs someone restless and clever. It needs you."

"You know nothing about me."

"I know your soul. Everything else is an ornament."

His voice wrapped around me, lustrous and dark. It was the kind of voice that could soothe you to sleep in the same moment that it slit your throat. Still, I leaned toward it.

"Come with me," he said. "You would never be content in that world. They would cage you. They would give you playthings of silver and silk."

His teeth burned white when he smiled. "I could give you whole worlds."

Something tugged at me. The pull was far stronger than fear or attraction—it was ambition. The court of Bharata didn't expect me to be anything other than a pawn. But Amar was asking for more. He wanted my opinions, my thoughts. He wasn't offering me a prized seat among his wives. He was asking me to rule.

I knew my father. He would have already announced that I was dead, and the kingdom would ask no questions. It might even be better for me to stay away from the palace and let them grieve me falsely, rather than hate me openly. There was nothing left for me in Bharata.

Even with his eyes concealed, I sensed Amar's gaze. "What

world do *you* belong to? Theirs?" I pointed at an Otherworldly being sharpening his horns.

"No. My kingdom is neither among humans nor Otherworldly beings. It is between."

"Why did you come to Bharata?" I asked. "The invitation to my *swayamvara* was issued only to the nations we're at war with."

"Everyone is at war with my nation," he said with a smile.

"How did you even know about me?"

"Akaran has its eyes and ears."

He could have been lying. Nothing escaped me from the rafters where I had spied for years. But my father had other meetings . . . and he was not always in Bharata.

I hesitated. "How can I trust someone who won't even reveal their face?"

"It's far too easy to be recognized here."

He drew the cloak closer and the gesture was so final, so closed off and unwelcoming, that I stepped back, chastened. Amar removed the wedding garland from around his neck. From the sleeves of his jacket, he withdrew a small knife. Before I could react, he swiped the knife across his palm. Small beads of blood welled to the surface. He held his palm out to me like a perverse offering.

"I make this bond to you in blood, not flowers," he said. "Come with me and you shall be an empress with the moon for your throne and constellations to wear in your hair. Come with me and I promise you that we will always be equals."

My mouth went dry. A blood oath was no trifling undertaking.

Vassals swore it to lords, priests to the gods. But husbands to wives? Unthinkable.

Still, Bharata's court had taught me one thing: the greater the offer, the greater the compromise. And I had neither dowry nor influence from Bharata, nothing to give but the jewels I wore.

"You're offering me the world, and you ask for nothing in return."

"I ask only for your trust and patience."

"Trust?" I repeated. "Trust is won in years. Not words. And I don't know anything about you—"

"I will tell you everything," he cut in, his voice fierce. "But we must wait until the new moon. The kingdom's close ties to the Otherworld make it dangerous grounds for the curious."

In my stories to Gauri, the new moon weakened the other realms. Starlight thinned their borders and the inhabitants lay glutted and sleepy on moonbeams. The thing is, I had always made that part up.

"Why that long?"

"Because that is when my realm is at its weakest," said Amar, confirming my imagination and sending shivers across my arms. "Until then, the hold of the other realms binds me into silence."

The night before the wedding ceremony, there was no moon in the sky. I would have to wait a whole cycle.

"And in the meantime, you expect me to go away with you?"

"Yes," he said, matter-of-factly. "Do you accept me?"

He held out his hand to me, the cut on his palm bright and swollen. Against the glow of the bazaar, Amar's form cut a silhouette of night.

I looked past him to the glittering secrets of the Otherworld. The Night Bazaar gleamed beneath its split sky—an invitation to be more than what Bharata expected, a challenge to rise beyond the ranks of the nameless, dreamless harem women. All I needed to do was slip my hand in his. I was reaching for him before I knew it and the warmth of his hands jolted me.

"I accept."

The Night Bazaar unfurled before us in a spectrum of color and life. Carts bearing persimmons and custard apples weaved between the crowds. Stores hopped across streets to greet likely customers. Other shops shrank to the size of thimbles, fit only for clientele no wider than a mouse. The Night Bazaar was filled with the sound of reedy flutes and the rill of haggling tongues.

I kept turning around, practically spinning as I walked. Twice, I just barely avoided careening straight into a band of animated *sitaars* and drums. It was a world already vivid with my dreams and each time I blinked and opened my eyes anew, something warm spread slowly across my chest. To see the Night Bazaar before me, to feel its warm and irregular ground beneath my feet and let my fingers trail against the licorice teak of its balustrades, lulled me into a stupefied walk. I never wanted to blink again, as if in a second, this whole fragile secret would crumble out of sight. But it was there. It was solid. And I, against everything I had believed only the night before, was *here*.

The scent of fresh berries, ripe fruit and the smokiness of roasted nuts and salted corn wafted around me. I could feel it tangling in my hair. Every sound was a new song expanding in my chest and imprinting onto my memory.

The inhabitants of the Otherworld moved airily through the Night Bazaar, sidestepping dancing conch shells and examining iridescent fruits. With their long limbs, stark cheekbones and symmetrical features, they were too perfect to be mistaken as human. They walked with a lope and glide so graceful, it would've made Bharata's *devadasi* dancers look like broken dolls.

Wherever I moved, my skin prickled under the weight of watchful eyes. Everywhere we walked, the inhabitants bowed their heads in polite acknowledgment.

"You seem quite popular. I suppose your cloak is failing its camouflaging purpose." I hoped the last part would have needled him into drawing the hood from his face, but it remained stubbornly pulled over him.

He shrugged. "They recognize and appreciate our duty to keep them safe."

Our duty, I repeated silently, a tendril of warmth coiling in my stomach. "I didn't realize the Otherworld needed protecting. Are you . . . some kind of guardian?"

Amar moved like a weighty shadow. A not-unpleasant chill emanated from him. Even the Night Bazaar inhabitants who greeted him did so with a touch of franticness in their eyes.

"I prefer that term, but I think others see my occupation as something that takes rather than protects." No sooner had he spoken than his hand flew to his throat. For a panic-stricken moment, I thought he would collapse. But a moment later, he relaxed, swallowing a mouthful of air. "I apologize," he rasped.

"I was not lying when I said I could not reveal Akaran's secrets. Not yet, anyway."

A guardian, then, I mused. But of what? None of the folktales I had read made any mention of wardens straddling the divide of human and Otherworldly beings. Just then, a herd of dark-eyed *kinnara* children rushed past me, their cheeks rosy and their legs and feet clawed like birds. The sight of them made me ache for Gauri. Was she safe? What had happened to Bharata? I comforted myself with those images of the guards marching toward the harem and Amar's assurances. Still, a twinge of guilt nettled me. I wanted to believe that I had fled Bharata because I had no choice, but the thought that I had abandoned Gauri continued to bite.

I was still thinking of Gauri as we wandered into the thicket of the Night Bazaar. There, the sound of shopkeepers haggling and screaming—sometimes in languages that only registered as sharp whistles—enveloped us.

Amar hung back some distance behind me as I stopped by strange tents and vendors. The first tent was draped in a black velvet cloth that giggled at the touch of my hand. Small glass ornaments hung from its awnings, little spinning planets that emitted a drowsy song.

"Place one beneath your claw or foot or what have you and I guarantee a restful sleep!"

The owner—a bull-headed being—immediately began tearing them from the tassels, rolling them in front of me like glittering dice.

"I'll give you five for the price of three! And all it will cost is the sound of your voice for a week."

"No, thank you . . . I was just looking," I said apologetically.

The owner harrumphed, gathered his nights of restful sleep and hung them back on the tent with a glare on his face. I walked quickly to the next table, where the owner, smoking a pipe of rose quartz, fanned her hand indifferently around her wares.

"A snarl of nightmares," she said, gesturing to blinking, fanged wisps of smoke, "or a tangle of daydreams. Your choice. I could care less."

I reached out to hold a daydream. They looked like they were spun from glass and yet their touch was silk-soft. As they drifted between my fingers, I *felt* them—a nap in the sleepy sunshine of a winter afternoon, a reverie where a sea alight with flowers and bright candles washed over my ankles.

The next table was crowded with animal bones. I picked one up lightly before shivering and hurriedly putting it down. It felt like the bone was *reading* me.

"Those are for auguring, *dikri*, for scrying futures," wheedled a matronly looking being. She had wings pinioned to her back that were dull gold and edged in fire.

"I'm not interested," I said, thinking of my own horoscope.

"What about a love charm, then?" persisted the owner, pushing a flower carved of pearl to me. "To awaken your lover's interest," she added with a wink.

At this, Amar walked to the table and slid the flower rather ungently back toward the owner.

"I am her husband. She needs no charm to hold my interest."

At the sight of Amar, the shopkeeper grabbed the flower and bowed repeatedly. We continued walking through the market when I saw a being with arms banded like a snake holding a platter of carrot *halwa* high above his head. It was Gauri's favorite dish. The longer I looked at the *halwa,* the more I couldn't remember the last time I had eaten.

I was *desperately* hungry. I fought the knee-jerk urge to swipe something off one of the hundred platters of food. I was a queen now, or something like that. I had to show composure. Calm. My stomach betrayed with me a loud grumble and Amar's lips quirked in a smile.

"Have you had anything to eat all day?"

The reek of mandrake poison stirred in my memory. Somewhere between thinking I was about to die and fleeing for my life, eating hadn't factored into my plans.

"It seemed unnecessary," I said drily.

"After your brush with death, your first taste should be sweet and bitter. Like freedom itself."

I glanced back to the carrot *halwa*. "It's too late for bittersweet food."

"I can change that."

•» 8 «•

THE PALACE BETWEEN WORLDS

Trees like cursive script stretched above dark plots of earth, entwining against pale beams of ivy and sprouting flowers that turned their heads to watch us pass.

"This way," said Amar, lifting a cluster of branches.

An orchard festooned with silver trees greeted us. Amar walked through them, leading me toward a grove of five trees. The first had emerald bark, the second sapphire, the third ruby, the fourth quartz and the fifth pearl. Sparkling fruits hung beneath their dark branches.

"Pick one," said Amar, plucking a shining sapphire.

I winced, waiting for his teeth to chip and clang against the rind. But his teeth sank into the sapphire fruit and juice dribbled between his fingers. I was still suspicious, but I reached into the pearl tree and pulled out a fat fruit with spherical markings. It was light in my hands, as if hollow. Slowly, I bit into it. The pearl fruit tasted like warm chestnut, ripe pears and rich honey. I sighed, devouring it core and stem before eyeing the other trees.

Just as I was reaching back into the pearl tree, a ruff of feathers brushed against my fingertips followed by an indignant *hoot!* I barely had time to jump back when Amar's shadow fell over me and his hand encircled the small of my back.

"They're just *chakara* birds," he said in a low voice, close to my neck, close enough to drink in the scent of him—mint and smoke, cardamom and wood.

He stepped toward the tree, lifting the branches to reveal four pairs of narrowed orange eyes.

"Rather grumpy birds. They think the moon belongs to them," said Amar. "But, irritable or not, they're harmless. Not like some of the other things here."

I turned to look into his face, but he quickly stepped away, revealing the awning dark behind him. No silvery branches arced in those shadows. The tangle of brambles and fallen stones had the unmistakable gloom of something avoided. And for good reason. The dark was more than impenetrable, it was *sticky*, as if it would devour whatever fell into its path. Something swayed in the distance, catching in the darkness. And though I wanted to convince myself otherwise, whatever hung beneath the disquieting trees looked an awful lot like . . . bodies.

"Not everything wants the boundaries of the Otherworld and human realm maintained."

"Why not?"

He was silent and I wondered whether the pull of the Otherworld kept him from responding. Finally, he said, "Because not everything respects balance. Not everything wants to be contained to one side or the other. Some things crave the chaos."

I thought back to the woman in my room, the way the darkness glommed around her, choking off all the light. Her voice needled at the back of my mind—*I need you to lead me.*

"We must leave," said Amar, his voice cutting through my thoughts.

We left behind the sparkling fruits and yawning shadows and traveled back to the Night Bazaar's slice of day. The water buffalo lumbered to Amar's side, pushing its nose into the palm of his hand.

"Are you ready?" asked Amar.

I took in one last glance. The Night Bazaar had ensnared me. I could smell its perfume on my skin—of stories and secrets, flashing teeth and slow smiles. In this land, I was no stronger than a calf in a lion's jaws. But I liked it. Even though I couldn't admit it aloud, even though I comforted myself that I had no choice but to go with him, the truth was that I *wanted* this. I yearned to draw breath beneath a split-sky leaking with magic. And not just live within one of the other realms' strange kingdoms, but *rule* it. Without answering, I lifted myself onto the water buffalo's back. Amar bowed his head, another ghost of a smile at his lips. The animal took off at a brisk pace and my heart raced.

My head bowed against the harsh wind as we sped down the same tunnel we used to reach the Night Bazaar. When the wind died down, I turned, expecting to see the ghost-lights of its torn sky. Instead, there was only a gnarled *parijaat* tree. Its thick trunk clung to the hill and sparse branches twisted into the sky like wrought iron.

"Welcome to Akaran," said Amar as the water buffalo moved down the hill and the palace came into view.

This was Akaran? After seeing the Night Bazaar, I'd expected another crowded city filled with thin Otherworldly beings and strange shops. But Akaran was empty. The hill sloped into a huge, flat gray valley. As far as I could see, there was nothing but scrubland and rock. I stared around me, but the emptiness was almost solid. There was so much *space*.

Akaran was a world completely alone. Elegant fountains and handsome statues paved the path to Amar's kingdom, a sprawling palace adorned with ivory spires and silvery arches. Spirals of reflection pools next to stone sculptures of acacia trees fell on either side of us as we approached the entrance.

"This is now yours as much as it is mine," said Amar.

Mine?

I breathed deeply, closing my eyes, stilling the tremble in my fingers. Every now and again I glanced at Amar, waiting for him to talk about the richness of his grounds or the costliness of his palace. Whenever I'd spied on a foreign royal's introduction to the Raja's court, the wealth of the foreigner's palace, beauty of his queens and plumpness of his livestock always preceded his name. But Amar was different. He had said his name first and nothing after.

Once we were inside the courtyard, Amar leapt from the water buffalo. I tried to do the same, but my legs felt clumsy. Amar lifted me gently, his hands lingering at my waist a moment too long before he drew them away. My face warmed, and I was glad when someone stepped out of the shadows.

A clean-shaven man with a bulbous nose bowed to us. He was richly dressed, his brocade *sherwani* a gleaming silver next to Amar's black robes. His arms were full of scrolls that he clutched at with ink-stained fingers. He looked like the studious court archivists. I looked at him intently, waiting for something inevitably strange to happen. What was he hiding? A tail? Clawed feet?

His eyes were fixed on the ground and he lifted them slowly, as if he was fighting the moment when he finally looked at me. When our eyes met, his smile faltered. He made a strangled sound, a weird mix of surprise and disbelief. I ventured a smile, but that seemed to make things worse. The man swallowed air, his grip on the parchments tightening.

"May I present Gupta, my councilor and dearest friend."

Gupta cleared his throat, staring at the ground. "Welcome to Akaran, Rani."

Rani, I repeated in my head. I really was queen. Gupta spoke softly, his voice trailing into a nervous stuttering. It was the kind of tone Ajeet had used when he disagreed with the Raja. *Does he think I shouldn't be here?* Walking to him, Amar clapped a hand against his back. Gupta stared back, his expression a mask of hesitation and wonder.

"Gupta is indispensable to the realm."

"Not nearly as indispensable as some," he said, not meeting my gaze. He rocked on his heels, examining the scrolls in his arms. "I must excuse myself. I have matters to attend to."

"Join us for dinner," said Amar. "You've never shied from eating with me before." He smiled, before adding jokingly, "No one will judge you for trying to organize your grains of rice."

A smile flashed on Gupta's face. "You could learn a thing or two from me the way you carry on with a plate." But then he turned to me and the smile slid off his face. He shook his head.

"Another time, my friend."

All of Bharata's court archivists were arrogant, but Gupta's cagey responses and narrowed glances bordered on insult. I was a princess of Bharata, not some foundling Amar rescued by a roadside. The next time he met my gaze, I raised my chin, my ears turning hot. For the first time, Gupta grinned.

"I hope you will not mind the silence of our halls, Rani."

The memory of clashing iron rang in my ears. I could still see the lips of the soldiers as they shaped their mouths around a scream.

"I've had my fill of noise," I said.

Gupta tilted his head. "Then again, perhaps our halls will no longer be silent. The Raja has waited a long time for you."

I frowned. "He waited a long time to marry?"

"No," said Gupta. "He waited a long time for you. I look forward to discussing your duties tomorrow morning, Rani."

He flourished a bow to me and nodded at Amar. And then he disappeared behind a pillar. Amar sighed, rubbing his temples through the fabric of his hood. He still hadn't taken off the garment.

"Gupta is not used to company," he said. "I hope he did not offend you. He can hold a conversation for hours about sentient underwater creatures, but protocol and etiquette are beyond him."

"Perhaps that's a good thing."

"You don't care for councilors and their flowery speeches?"

"They make me suspicious. In my experience, big words ornament bad news."

"A fair observation," said Amar with a smile. "Please, follow me."

Amar led me from the antechamber to a large room filled with low-hanging lanterns. A panel of ornate mirrors covered the wall on the right, while windows filled the left. The open windows revealed a stretch of nighttime. Lanterns illuminated the room to a pale gold. In the middle of the room were two saffron-colored cushions, along with a score of small plates piled high with steaming rice cakes, bowls of hot dal and buttery slices of naan. I stepped inside, my gaze falling on the elaborate rug wrought with the image of a huge *makara*. Purling emerald silk formed its serpent body, shimmering beneath the lights, so that for a moment, the sea dragon almost looked real. Gauri filled my head once more, and I remembered the last night we spent together. *We could have been twin stars or* makaras *with tails long enough to wrap around the ocean twice.*

Amar leaned against one of the cushions.

"Please," he said, pushing a golden plate toward me.

My half-sisters had always feigned a poor appetite, but the naan looked too good to waste on modesty. For the next hour, I ate with happy abandon, my stomach warmed with dal and bursting with fullness. When we finished, a glass tray of mint tea and a bowl of candied fennel seeds appeared on the table.

"What do you think of your kingdom?"

"It's beautiful," I said. *And very empty. Where is everyone?* "It might even be dangerous to live in such luxury and repose."

"This is no place of repose." Amar glanced outside where a sliver of moon glimmered behind clouds. "I am at the mercy of the moon to reveal the secrets of this kingdom. Until then, you must practice what it means to rule. I will test you, as this palace will, in its own way."

I straightened in my seat. "On what?"

"Familiarity, you might say." His voice was low. "All the usual aspects of ruling. I'll test your fangs and claws and bloodlust." He stopped to trace the inside of my wrist, and my pulse leapt to meet his touch. I scowled and grabbed my hand back. Treacherous blood. "I'll test your eyes and ears and thoughts."

"Not geography, then?" I asked, half joking.

"It's useless here." He shrugged. "You'll see."

"History?"

"Written by the victors," he said with a dismissive wave of his hand. "I'm not interested in one-sided tales."

"Legends? Folktales?"

This time, Amar grinned. "Perhaps. Do you have a favorite tale?"

My throat tightened and I thought of Gauri standing outside my door and demanding a story. "Many . . . And you?"

"All of them. Except for tragedies. I cannot abide those."

In the harem, all the wives preferred tragedies. They wanted stories of star-crossed lovers. They wanted betrayal and declarations of love that ended with the speaker dying at their feet.

"You don't find them romantic?"

"No," he said, an edge to his voice. "There is no romance in real grief. Only longing and fury."

He rose to his feet. "Tomorrow, you can tour the palace fully. It's yours now."

His words echoed in my head. All of Akaran—its cavernous space, lush splendor and enchanted aura—was *mine*. Even though I had walked through the Night Bazaar and tasted its fruit, my soul staggered. My joy was ghostly, like something not quite realized. I kept thinking back to the moment where I had stood with poison against my palm, where I had owned nothing, been nothing and almost . . . was nothing. Even with this new kingdom, my heart still focused on the one I knew before.

"My kingdom—" I started, hesitating, "is it unharmed? Do you know what happened to my sister Gauri?"

Amar's hands tightened at his sides. "Your sister is safe. Now, come, let me show you our chamber."

Every bone in my body ached, but my nerves made me feel tense and awake. Wordlessly, Amar led me from the golden dining room through a series of hallways. I squinted into the darkness, trying to make out details or edges. But shadows concealed everything.

Finally, we reached a marble door that could only be the bedroom. My pulse quickened, and for a moment, I thought my nerves might make me retch the contents of my rich meal. Amar pushed open the door, revealing a room with a high ceiling and a circular bed. A translucent gossamer canopy fell from the ceiling, rippling in silken pools. Handsome borders gleamed along the edges of the wall. The rooms in Bharata's palace could've been a pauper's hovel compared to this.

"The adjoining room should have anything you may need,"

said Amar, pointing at a tucked-away door. He then inclined his head politely and entered a private chamber.

He said nothing about sharing a room.

Maybe he was too tired or too full. Or not interested. A flicker of disappointment shot through me. I didn't have Parvati's milky complexion or Jaya's thick-lashed gaze, but I wasn't revolting. In the imposing room, I felt small and ridiculous. No servant appeared to help me with my garments, but I did not mind. I was used to taking care of myself in Bharata. Strangely, there were no mirrors inside the bedroom, but one swipe of my hand across my face was enough to know how I looked. Smudges of kohl had left my eyes and pooled against my temples. Groaning, I splashed my face with water and began the tedious task of removing my sari and jewelry.

I felt blindly at my face, poking at my nose and stretching my cheeks taut. After seventeen years, I still hadn't grown into my nose. My skin felt shiny, and irritated bumps trailed across my forehead. I glanced down, taking stock of my narrow shoulders, sharp collarbones and straight waist. I looked boyish. Maybe that's why he showed no interest.

I walked back into the bedroom. Amar was standing by the foot of the bed, playing lazily with the cuffs of his sleeves. I tensed. That foolish disappointment was gone.

"Are you frightened?" he asked.

Don't cower. I straightened my back. I would've stared him in the eyes if I could. "Should I be?"

"I should hope there are more frightening things than sharing a bed with me," he said. He flourished a bow. "Did I not promise you that we would be equals? Your will is where I lay my head. I will not touch you without your permission."

I moved to the bed, taking stock of the unnecessary amount of cushions. I could feel Amar's gaze on me and rather than tossing the cushions to the ground, I stacked them in the middle of the bed. Amar followed me and slid onto the opposite side. The fire in the *diyas* collapsed with the faintest of sighs.

"A daunting fortress," he said lazily, prodding one of the pillows. "Have you so little faith in me?"

"Yes."

He laughed and the sound was unexpectedly . . . musical.

"The dark is a lovely thing, is it not? It lets us speak in blindness. No scowls or smiles or stares clouding our words."

I lay in bed, my body taut. Amar continued:

"I spoke no falsehoods in the Night Bazaar," he said. "I would rip the stars from the sky if you wished it. Anything for you. But remember to trust me. Remember your promise."

I fell quiet for a moment. "I remember my promise."

After that, I said nothing.

The air between us could have been whittled in steel. An hour passed before I ventured a glance at Amar. His face was turned from me, leaving only dark curls half visible in the light. Moonlight had limned his silhouette silver. The longer I stared at him, the more something sharp stirred within me and I was reminded of that strange ache in my head, where forgotten dreams jostled for remembrance.

I stared at the ceiling, fighting the giddiness dancing in my chest. I replayed the day slowly, languorously, reliving every detail—from the Night Bazaar's sky seamed with light and the sensation of my teeth sinking into the fragrant rind of fairy fruit, to the splendid emptiness of Akaran. I rehashed the day again and again, wearing down the memory like a river pebble, until I had convinced my own stubborn mind that everything had truly happened, that every bit was real.

Even so, what tasks did a kingdom that lay between the Otherworld and the human realm want? And why me? Already I knew that Akaran was as different from Bharata as night to day. But there was something thrilling in its differences . . . a promise of change in its stone hallways.

•» 9 «•

A TURN OF THE MOON

When I woke up the next morning, Amar was gone. I stretched my hand across the bed, pressing my fingers into the side where he had slept. It was cool to the touch—he'd been gone for some time. Not a good sign for the first day as queen. I pulled at my hair, biting back a groan and hoping he'd left while the room was still dark. My hair fell in knotted waves around me. I probably looked feral.

Gray daylight puddled onto the floor, illuminating the room's golden borders and carven doors. I tilted my head up, eyes still disbelieving. Yesterday morning, I thought I would be wandering the halls of the dead. But instead, I was here.

"Rani?" came a voice from outside.

I recognized the voice. Gupta.

"Please dress at your leisure. I'll wait outside to escort you to the dining hall, where we can go through your engagements for the day."

Escorted? Engagements? In Bharata, I'd never lived by a schedule.

"Good, thank you," I said, my voice wavering.

In the adjoining room, steam curled around water basins. I stared at my hair, pulling at some of the dirty strands. I might as well have never left the jungle.

By the time I had washed and returned to the room, the bed had been fixed and a brilliant green silk sari was spread across the sheets. There were heavy rings piled in a quartz bowl, a handful of bangles in another and dainty anklets fashioned with dangling nightingales in a third.

I wrapped the silk around me slowly, savoring its length across my body. I was almost too scared to move around in it, convinced it would tear. But it didn't. My hands drifted across the heavy jewelry, but in the end I couldn't wear anything. The hollow of my throat felt cold and empty in the absence of my mother's necklace. None of this finery compared.

When I walked outside, Gupta flashed the bare bones of a smile before nodding and starting off down one of the halls. Despite Akaran's coldness, the pallid corridors and mirror-paneled foyers sang to me. The same dining room from before had been laid out with a placemat set with rich foods, fruits and water. I drew my chair to the table, stealing glances out the window toward Akaran's barren landscape. Loneliness in Akaran was worse than being stared at by the Raja's harem. At least I knew *who* was doing the watching. Here, even the walls were leering, weighing and examining me.

"I trust you slept well," said Gupta.

"Yes, thank you." I glanced around the wide dining room. "Will you be joining me?"

He hesitated. Like yesterday, he didn't meet my gaze.

"I suppose that will be agreeable."

I stopped myself from joking. *I don't bite . . . often.*

The moment Gupta sat down, he began to rub at the table, inspecting an invisible speck of dust.

"I hear Amar apologized on my behalf." This time his voice was softer, hesitant.

I froze. He had referred to Amar by his first name. I'd never once heard a councilor or adviser—no matter how close he was—call my father by his first name. They'd sooner behead themselves. Gupta's gaze was shy, perhaps curious about what I'd make of his familiarity. When I said nothing, he noticeably relaxed.

"He did, but there was no need," I said. "I think it's . . . refreshing, that you grew up away from the protocols of court speech and etiquette."

Gupta itched his hawkish nose, his eyes widening. "You do?"

I smiled. "It doesn't matter to me."

Gupta grinned back and his nose spread impishly across his face. "I'm glad to hear that, Rani."

I chewed my cheek. I didn't want to be locked in by invisible rules of caste or rank. My father's words echoed in my head: Immortality lay in emotions. If this was going to be my kingdom as much as Amar's, I needed to prove it. And that meant knowing Gupta the way Amar did. Not as a councilor or an adviser, but as a friend.

"Call me Maya."

Gupta's hands clenched and he quickly looked away. I thought I saw tears glittering in his eyes, but instead of facing me, he rubbed at a spot on the table.

"I detest dirt. Did you know there are at least five thousand different kinds of tiny beasts in a unit of dirt? It's appalling. You can't clean it properly," he said, crinkling his nose.

"How do you know that?" I asked, torn between disbelief and laughing.

"I am the scribe of this kingdom," he said, drawing himself up. "I make it a point to know as much as I can. For instance, I once interviewed a snail that had slept for three years. I have also detailed the song of sunbears and translated the treaties of autumn trees. Absolutely critical things to know."

"I see. Well, I hope . . . I hope we can be friends."

He stared at his lap. "Once a friend, always a friend."

A sound spidered through the floor. A laugh, a trill. The ghost of another's voice. I spun around, expecting someone standing behind me, but there was no one. Nothing but empty space and gleaming walls.

"What was that?"

"Or who," said Gupta casually.

"Who?"

"I'm not sure . . . it could be anyone. Or anything. It could be a wind angry with its lover and dreaming of revenge. It could be the voice of a *nagini* remembering her first kiss. Akaran's strange position makes it a home for a thousand voices."

I remembered Amar's words from yesterday.

"Is it because Akaran lies in between the human and Otherworld?"

"Precisely," said Gupta. "There's all kinds of hidey-holes dotted about. There are places where you can jump and find yourself buried beneath the earth. There are pools of glass that you can swim through and find lost monsters with no names. In Akaran, things just *are*."

"Could I see these places?"

"Eventually," said Gupta. "But all things must wait. For the right time, for the moment when—" His eyes suddenly bulged as he clawed at his throat.

The moon, I thought. Gupta must be bound into silence by it too.

"I apologize," he gasped. "I—"

"I know," I cut in. My hands balled into fists in my lap. I felt helpless. I could feel magic coating the air around me. It felt like starlight and a swoop in my stomach, something heatless and bright and extraordinary. And yet I couldn't *know* it. A mere turn of the moon, I reminded myself.

"But, Maya," said Gupta, leaning forward. His eyes gleamed. "Be careful not to follow the sounds of the palace. It is a tricky thing. It will test you. It is fine to explore. The doors that cannot open to you will not do so."

He pulled aside one flap of his jacket where a thousand keys—of horn and bone, metal and pearl—jangled.

"Look around," he said. "Akaran is a land that is, by nature, easily accessible."

He stood up, pointing to the barren expanse around us. It hadn't changed. Not a single cloud drifted across its sky. No bird trailed its shadow on the ground. A world draped in silence.

"There are places behind our doors that must never be opened. Cunning, dark things. They can sense an invitation by something as small as another person's breath in the same room."

I shivered. "The most minor acts can herald destruction?"

"Well, only if you get behind the doors," he said, patting the jacket flap. "Those places are locked away. I doubt you'll ever find them. But you shouldn't go looking either. Sometimes the palace sings and murmurs. Bored and tricky thing."

Gupta glanced at the scrolls on the table and his face paled. "Amar!" he exclaimed suddenly. "We must go. He won't forgive me if I don't take you to the throne room in time."

When Amar wasn't there in the morning, I assumed he'd left Akaran entirely. The thought of seeing him again sent a rush of heat to my cheeks. I looked at my lap, tamping down my eagerness. I'd seen enough of the harem women begging for scraps of the Raja's attention that my mind revolted against it.

"Is that where he is?"

Gupta nodded. "Yes, he's waiting for you."

Waiting. For *me*. I smiled to myself as Gupta led me through the empty corridors. Doors of all shapes and sizes dotted the halls, some of them carved and inlaid with ivory and gems, others plain slabs of dark wood. Rich rugs sprawled out beneath my feet, softer than silk and festooned with more detail and beauty than all of Bharata's paintings combined.

All along the hallway, hundreds of mirrors caught the light, but as I stood before them they did not twin my image. One mirror boasted a plain wooden frame, splintered at the edges. When I looked through it, I saw the sands of a desert piddling out beneath an ochre sun. Another mirror studded with sapphire showed the reflection of a glittering port city, heavy boats with ivory prows gently rocking on a gray sea.

Mirror after mirror . . . giving way to countries spiked with spires, turrets bursting with small ivy flowers, cities awash in color, and a thousand skies painted in vespertine violets of anxious nightfall waiting for stars, dawns just barely blooming pink and orange with new light, afternoons presiding over sleeping towns . . . it was all *here*. I could have stared through those mirrors for hours if Gupta hadn't kept marching forward.

"You see?" said Gupta smugly. "Lovely, aren't they?"

"And you can get to any of these places?" I breathed.

"Oh yes."

"Could I go?"

"Soon enough."

We passed the mirrors, and the corridor gave way to a stone archway.

"May I ask you something?" I said suddenly.

"You may, but I cannot guarantee I can answer it."

"Why does the Raja of Akaran hide his face? Is he . . . disfigured?"

"So many of us hide behind our glazed words and practiced expressions. Amar is not like that. His expression leaves no room for mistake. Around you, let us say his expression would make his feelings too obvious. Give him time."

Gupta threw open a pair of doors. "This is the throne room," he said, quickly blocking my path. "Gaze lightly. This kingdom is magnificent, but its power is old and runs deep and will not hesitate to test you."

I nodded uncertainly before walking past him, my eyes widening as I took in the stark and imposing room. But what stole my breath was the tapestry covering the wall beside the dais. On the left wall, obsidian threads shimmered, forming a tempestuous ocean streaked with foamy white waves; rose-gold filaments arced into a bulbous lotus and silken veins stretched into gnarled orchards.

Across the tapestry's middle stretched a terrible seam, rent apart on either side like the scalloped edges of a flesh wound. Something about the tear struck me, I could feel the rip *inside* me, forcing me to glance down and lightly tap my wrist to make sure that it was flesh that met my fingers and not a thousand threads. The tapestry stretched far beyond the walls of the throne room. I could feel it like a cloak around my heart.

"We'll meet again in the evening," said Gupta.

"Anything else I should know before you leave?"

Gupta grinned. "Amar is terrible at flattery."

I smiled, but I couldn't help but wonder who had been the last person he had attempted to flatter. The thought bothered me.

"I was never wooed by courtly speech anyway."

As Gupta closed the door behind him I heard a soft laugh by my side.

"Is that so?"

Amar.

I turned to face him, my gaze tracing the emerald robes that matched my sari perfectly. Like yesterday, he wore a hood that left only the lower half of his face in view. I looked at him, and even if it was only a moment, he eclipsed the staggering pull of the tapestry.

"I'm not swayed by flattery," I said. "I think a woman could feel insulted by a compliment. But I suppose that depends on the delivery."

"I think it depends on the *sincerity*. If you tell a woman she sings beautifully when she knows the sound of her voice might as well drop a slab of stone on the person next to her, then a compliment would be insulting."

I crossed my arms. "She could think you're blinded by love."

"Or deafened."

"You seem quite learned in the art of giving compliments," I countered. "Do you give them often?"

"No. Gupta was telling the truth. I've forgotten how to pay courtly compliments," said Amar. "For instance, etiquette demands I tell you that you look lovely and compliment your demure. But that wouldn't be the truth."

Heat rose to my cheeks and I narrowed my eyes. "What, then, would be the truth?"

"The truth," said Amar, taking a step closer to me, "is that you look neither lovely nor demure. You look like edges and thunderstorms. And I would not have you any other way."

My breath gathered in a tight knot and I looked away, only to catch sight of the tapestry. The threads throbbed behind my eyes, sharp as any headache. My vision blurred, swallowing the room around me. I blinked rapidly, squinting at the threads.

All I could see were that all the threads were out of place. Some had either skipped a stitch or poked out altogether. I walked toward the tapestry in a daze, my hands outstretched.

I could feel the tapestry's pull, sharp as hunger, dry as thirst. Nothing would sate or slake me. All I wanted was to adjust the threads, tuck them back into place. There was an order, a pattern, like a stitching trick. I could feel it like a word balancing on the tip of my tongue and all I had to do was—

Amar's hand closed around my wrist. He moved before me, blocking the tapestry.

"Stop!"

I blinked, my head woolly. His hands were around my shoulders, drawing me to a wobbly stand.

"Did I fall?"

"That sounds ungraceful," he said, a smile playing at his lips. He was trying to joke with me, to ward off whatever happened as though it were nothing. But his hands were tight at my shoulders and there was the slightest tremble in his fingers.

"A graceful tumble, then?" I suggested, stepping out of the circle of his arms.

I didn't need any help keeping myself upright.

"I should've explained the tapestry before showing it to you. It can be overwhelming."

Amar led me to the throne and I sank into it wearily. There was a new ache tethered inside my bones. In the haze, the pressure of Amar's hand against my arm was warm, comforting even. I closed my eyes, concentrating on the warm pulse in his fingers.

When I finally felt strong enough to speak, I opened my eyes to find Amar's face mere inches from mine. I could count the immaculate stitching of his emerald hood, the stubble along his chin and the veins raised along his hand. His eyes, as always, lay hidden. But he was so close that if I wanted, and I did, I might be able to peek—

Amar jerked backward, his jaw tightening. "The tapestry is how we keep the borders between the Otherworld and human realms safe."

He walked to the tapestry and ran his hands over the flickering threads. "Each of these threads is a person."

"The threads represent *people?*" I repeated, sure I had misheard him. "And the entire tapestry . . . ?"

"It's what keeps everything in order."

"Everything?" My brows drew together. "As in—"

"As in the movements of fate."

"Fate is in the purview of the stars," I quipped, not without some bitterness. I had been fed that line my whole life. It was hard to forget my blind jailers in the sky, shackling me to a fate I didn't even believe. Not that it changed anyone else's mind.

"Fate and order are entirely different. And one cannot rely on stars for order. Some of the threads represent the people who have fallen accidentally into the Otherworld," said Amar, pointing at a darkened section near the corner. "Our task is deciding which people should be allowed in, and which ones shouldn't."

"Why not just keep everyone out?"

"Some people are bound to fall into the Otherworld. Their fate is fixed. All we can do is move between its fixed rules and change what we can to maintain a balance. Let me show you," he said. I rose to my feet, masking a sigh of relief that my legs wouldn't give out from under me.

"Touch the thread."

10

THE BOY WITH TWO THREADS

The thick silver thread resonated warmly against my fingers. I felt a tug inside my body. The next time I opened my eyes, a forest filled with tall pines vaulted above us, their shadows crisscrossing the earth in black nets. Sweet, smoky resin filled my lungs. In the distance, the fading sun silhouetted the leaves a bloody red. My heart sank. The sight of trees usually filled me with happiness. But these trees were different. Their tragedy was tangible.

"Where are we?"

I was still trying to find my bearings in the strange woods. Amar stood by my side, his hands clasped behind his back. He raised a finger to his lips, nodding toward the outlines of two people in the forest—a mother and son. The mother's hair fell about her shoulders and sweat gleamed on her brow. She looked feverish. Beside her, the boy jumped along the leaves and kicked over rocks.

"Is the silver thread hers? Can they see us?"

"Yes, the silver thread belongs to the mother. And no, they can't. This is simply the projection of the thread. Nothing we do here affects them."

He picked up a rock and hurtled it against the tree. But no sooner had he thrown it into the air than it reappeared by his feet.

"This moment in time is fixed."

"Fixed? So it's already happened?"

"In a way, everything has already happened and every option has already run its course. But those multiple fates are contained in the tapestry. Our challenge is selecting the best fate to maintain a balance of peace and letting the other outcomes fall away. Time runs differently in Akaran."

"But if we can't change anything about this moment, then why are we here?"

Amar held a finger to his lips and pointed at the woman.

She was leaning against a pair of twisted trees. With their outstretched limbs and arched trunks, the trees reminded me of someone in the act of falling. I looked at the other trees and a shiver ran down my spine. Each of the trees looked . . . human. And they were all in various shapes of collapse—mossy knolls for braced knees, spindly twigs for overextended arms, the language of a fall.

"What do you see?"

I tore away my gaze. "The tree reminded me of something."

"A person?"

"But that's—"

"—exactly what they are," finished Amar. "This is a twilight grove, a place where the lines between the Otherworld and human realm are blurred."

"What happened to all those people?" I asked, looking at the trees in new horror.

"They got stuck in the Otherworld."

"Did they ever leave?"

"In a way. But by the time they were freed, they were no longer the same people and they could never return to the life they left behind."

I watched the little boy pluck a handful of flowers for his mother.

"Then why are we here? Clearly, the mother shouldn't leave her child behind." My jaw clenched, my thoughts flitting to the mother I never knew, but had always wanted. Instinctively, my hand flew to my throat, fingers searching for the sapphire necklace. I kept forgetting it was gone. "Why does this need any more discussion?" I bit out.

"I'll show you."

Amar held out his hand. I looked once more at the little boy before slipping my hand in his. The moment we touched, the forest sank away, replaced once more with the throne room. This time I was prepared for the dizziness and I ground my heels into the floor to keep from swaying. Amar pulled at a dark green thread next to the silver one.

"This belongs to the boy."

I looked at the thread; it was split at the end, diverging into two frays that entwined with different spectrums of color.

"Two outcomes?"

"Two fates. Let me show you the first one."

Amar took my hand in his. I blinked once, and we were back inside the forest. But this time, the boy was alone. My heart ached just looking at him. He stood barefoot in the woods, his hands at his sides and his eyes glistening. Tears had left wet tracks along his cheeks and he wiped his eyes.

"*Amma?*" cried the boy.

"No," I said, steeling my voice. "I don't like this outcome at all."

Amar's hand steadied me. "Don't be impulsive."

Scolded, I forced myself to stare at the impassive outline of Amar's hooded face, my cheeks flushing. It was the closest I could get to staring him in the eye, trying to show him that I wasn't faint of heart. That I could, even if it hurt, witness this.

"The boy has two paths before him. Both are great in their own way. And both depend on when his mother enters the Otherworld." Amar pointed to a white flag waving near the horizon. "Do you recognize that sigil?"

I scrutinized the flag—a red crocodile against a white background. It was the symbol of the Ujijain Empire.

"Yes."

"The Emperor will come this way. He will see the boy and raise him as his own. He will be a hero among his people, a warrior both cunning and compassionate."

As Amar spoke, my eyes fluttered shut. I breathed deeply and saw everything come to pass. I saw the boy training, his eyes battle hardened. I saw him grow strong, settle disputes between neighbors, win the affection of his countrymen. I saw how each night he peered at the moon, his handsome face drawn. His mother's loss clung to him, a constant memory to live with kindness, with love. The vision sped up. I watched the boy age, listened to him tirelessly advocate for his country to choose peace instead of war. But all the while, the war dragged on.

Bodies piled up in the Ujijain Empire and my heart clenched. It was not just Ujijain that suffered. On the fallen soldiers, I recognized Bharata's crest—a lion and an eagle, both with one eye closed. My people were dying at the cost of this slow reconciliation. Only when he lay on his deathbed, his hands pallid and wrinkled, did peace heal the fractured empire. I watched his final smile fade, his eyes still gleaming hopefully before the vision faded.

When I opened my eyes, my cheeks were wet with tears.

"Was what I saw real?"

"Yes and no," said Amar softly. "It's a fate hanging in the ether, merely an option and a thread that's already run its course."

"And this outcome of"—I hesitated, remembering the people strewn on the battlefields, the ones bearing my father's symbol—". . . peace . . . only happens if his mother slips into the Otherworld?"

"Not if. When."

"When?" I echoed.

Amar lifted my hand and spun me in a quick circle. I blinked and found myself facing an entirely different landscape. Before me lay a village razed to the ground. I recognized the landscape; I had seen it in the tomes of the palace archives a hundred times. This was part of Bharata's territory. Unattended fires dotted the horizon. My hand flew to my nose, but nothing softened the stench of war. A sharp sound caught my attention and I turned to see the same boy, now grown up, pushing his horse at a breakneck speed over the burning land, rallying the surviving villagers together and spearing Ujijain's flag into the charred soil.

The vision sped up. Bharata was no more. Hammers were taken to its parapets. Sledges to its ancient monuments. It was like my father's reign had never existed. Everything had been swallowed up by the grown boy and the blazing war. Yet . . . even with my father's legacy completely erased, there was one thing I noticed: no bodies.

The scores of dead from the previous vision were gone. They had survived. Revulsion twisted in my stomach. I saw the choice before me, only it didn't feel like a choice at all. Either way I looked, it was an execution. No matter what, Bharata would pay the price.

"In this fate, the boy becomes a mercenary. The king never raises him. Instead, he must fight to survive. But the peace he fought so hard for in the other life is much more easily accomplished in this outcome."

I closed my eyes, watching this version of the boy's life unwind behind my eyes. Instead of words to unite a kingdom, he used war. He had his peace, but it was a fragile thing, born of blood and at the cost of an entire country's legacy.

"And his mother?"

"She slips into the Otherworld a mere year later."

"Why isn't there an option where she avoids the Otherworld altogether?"

"There are some pulls of fate that no one can alter," said Amar, his voice worn. "While our kingdom has great power, some fates are fixed. All we can do is move in the spaces left ambiguous. Thankfully, fate leaves most things ambiguous."

The village fire heated my face and I turned away from the flames.

"Get me away from here," I said hoarsely.

My throat tightened. So this is what maintaining the borders of the realms meant. It was a cruel duty. Amar's cloak fell across my eyes. I breathed deeply, letting the black silk cut off my sight.

When I opened my eyes, we were standing in the throne room. Amar drew the cloak away slowly, his fingers grazing my arms so lightly it might have been unintentional. That familiar warmth jolted in my stomach and I stepped back.

Beside me, the tapestry was dormant. Although it unfurled into beautiful pictures of the sky, sea and land, my eyes kept returning to its torn seam. It looked like a wound.

"What happened there?" I asked, pointing at the tear.

He stilled, refusing to turn in the tear's direction. Finally, he spoke.

"Sometimes, a great trauma in the worlds can untether the threads. Hopefully, the tear will never concern us again." His voice was quiet, dream-like, as if the tapestry were a sleeping thing he couldn't bear to awaken. "But enough of that. Only one of the boy's thread outcomes may survive. It is your decision."

"Does the mother die when she enters the Otherworld?"

I pictured the Dharma Raja, the lord of justice in the Afterlife, riding toward the boy's mother, swinging his noose to collect her soul and taking her to his bleak kingdom to await reincarnation.

Amar's lips pressed into a thin line. "No one really dies. Death is just another state of life."

"What's the boy's name?"

"Why do you ask?"

"Why wouldn't I?" I said. "Each thread has a color and each color belongs to a person. If I'm going to make such a decision, I don't want a nameless person on my conscience."

"Wouldn't it be easier keep your victim faceless?"

I shuddered. "Not a victim."

"What else do you call one hemmed in by fate?"

"Human," I said, bitterness creeping into my voice.

"What about guilt, then? Why open yourself to pain?"

"Guilt is what makes you accountable."

Amar smiled and I sensed that I had passed some test. "His name is Vikram." I repeated the name in my head. "You need not make your decisions now. That moment takes practice. But if the time comes and you cannot perform—"

"No," I said, a little too quickly. This was what I had wanted all these years, hadn't I? The chance to demonstrate that I was worthy of power? I couldn't back down now. "I can do it."

"I never doubted you."

My anger wilted.

"Last night, I told you I would test you," said Amar, stretching his hands. "Consider this our first lesson."

•» 11 «•

A BLOOM OF MARBLE

He walked to the center of the room, his hand hovering over the marble tiles. The space around him shimmered. Enchantment suffused the room. The floor trembled and in the next instant, a dusky pillar shot out from the ground. Its column ended in a delicate marble bud fashioned like an unopened flower bloom. He lay one hand against the bloom of stone, tapping his fingers against it expectantly.

"Ruling Akaran is a strange task. In many ways, it is like balancing an illusion. You must separate the illusion of what you see and the reality of its consequences," he said. "Tell me, my queen, are you ready to play with fate?"

The light in the room dimmed so that the tapestry's glittering threads were all but faint shimmers.

"Is that necessary?" I asked, waving my hand around the darkened room.

"You will learn to appreciate the shadows here. Better that you become accustomed to them now. The dark is more than just the absence of light. Think of it as a space for your thoughts."

"My thoughts prefer sunlit spaces."

"Then your thoughts need an education," said Amar. "Allow me to enlighten them."

He thudded his palm against the stone blossom. With a quiver, the marble petals uncurled. At the center crouched a marble bird. Amar tapped the bird once and it trembled, shaking its wings of stone and turning its head to glare at me. A small chain wrapped around its claws, rooting it to the slab.

"How did you—" I started, stretching a finger toward the animated bird when I felt a sudden heaviness in my arm. I turned to see a long sword in my grip. A flash of cold shot through me.

"Go on," said Amar, gesturing at the stone bird in a bored voice. "It is a mere illusion of marble. Use your sword."

"And do what with it?"

"What do you *think* swords are used for?" he asked drily.

I glanced between the bird and the sword. His words were as good as an execution. I cringed. Even though it was stone, a sense of wrongness crept through me. It looked so *alive*.

"How is this a test?"

"That remains to be seen. Now do as you will." Amar unfolded his arms and his voice was a dark purr in my ear. "What's this, my queen? All your vicious speech and you are moved to mercy by a stone bird?"

My grip tightened on the stone. The stone bird hopped a pace. Heat coursed through my veins. I didn't even feel the weight of the sword in my arm. I raised it over my head and brought it down. Metal crunched into stone and bile rose into my throat. I dropped the sword, shaking. I couldn't bring myself to look at the remains of the stone bird, but I glimpsed it from the corner of my eye—shards of marble like bone slivers.

"There," I bit out. "I performed your test."

Amar considered me for a moment, arms crossed, lips pursed into a thin line.

"No. You *failed* my test. You sacrificed an innocent thing."

Nausea roiled in my stomach. "But you said it was an illusion."

"It is." He picked up a piece of what once was the stone bird. "Nothing more than stone." He snapped his fingers and the bird reappeared—whole and animated. Its wings shivered behind its body and it fixed an irritated gaze on me.

"The bird was not the innocent thing. It's the feeling," said Amar, dusting his palms. "Preservation is an innocent desire. And you let arrogance compromise that."

"Arrogance?" I returned, my cheeks burning. "I was showing strength. Strength that I could be—"

"—merciless and thoughtless?" returned Amar. He flashed a vulpine grin. "Kill, if you must. String a garland of severed heads around your waist if you want. I would take you in my arms if you were drenched in blood or dressed in rubies . . . but *think*. Impulsiveness is a dangerous thing."

"You gave me no choice—"

"I merely gave a command. 'Use your sword.' You were the one who thought there was only one choice."

"When I asked what you wanted me to do with it, you . . . you asked me what swords are for . . ." I finished quietly. He hadn't actually *said* what to do.

Amar picked up the sword from the ground and twirled it against the marble.

"Swords could also be used for freeing. You could've cut through the chain around the bird's foot and set it free. Swords could be used for killing. But it needn't be the bird. Wouldn't the more merciful choice have been to use the sword against the oppressor?"

"So run the sword through you?"

"Why not? Everything is a matter of interpretation. And that is how you will rule," he said, before handing the sword's hilt to me. "Think on what you've seen today. But do not let me influence you. Your will is yours alone."

I stared at the sword in my hand, still gleaming despite the dark. "I can promise you I won't forget."

Amar paused, his voice soft. "Memory is a riddled thing. I would caution you from making promises you cannot keep."

I moved toward the door, but Amar stopped me with a shake of his head. "Gupta will arrive in a moment to escort you." He straightened the cuffs of his *sherwani* jacket. "I myself have a number of duties to attend to, so I must leave."

Before I could stop myself, I blurted out, "Why?"

He paused and took a step to me. Darkness, soft-edged and

heavy, clung to the room. In the shadows, his smile held all the lazy grace of a cat.

"Would you miss me?"

"Curiosity inspired my question. Nothing more," I said, but even my voice was unconvinced.

"Even so, there's no greater temptation than to stay by your side."

The door swung open and a chorus of voices trickled into the room—silvery and indistinct, like whispers released through clenched teeth. Amar lingered for a moment, his lips tight as though he wanted to say something.

Then, he cupped his palms together and blew into them. When he opened his hands, a bloom of light shaped like an unopened flower bud lifted off his palm and floated into the room. Brightness drenched away the shadows.

"I will never leave you in the dark."

And with that, he left.

I waited for the door to shut before I sank against the throne. I buried my face in my hands, squeezing my eyes shut. When Amar promised me the power of a hundred kings, this wasn't what I had in mind. It felt wrong. My duty was to tweak people's fortunes like they were designs gone awry instead of lives filled with dreams, quirks and ambitions. A knock at the door pulled me out of my thoughts.

"Are you ready to change for dinner?" asked Gupta.

I frowned, turning to the windows of the throne room. When

I had stepped inside, I was sure it had been broad daylight. Now, wispy clouds like ghost skins streaked a crimson sky.

"Yes," I called back, still trying to work out the time I had lost.

Gupta said nothing as he led me from the throne room back to the bedroom, but there was nothing stiff or awkward in his silence. He was grinning to himself and every now and then when he caught my eye, he beamed.

"I will wait for you out here."

"There's no need, I remember my way back to the dining room."

Gupta shook his head. "I insist."

"If you insist," I said stiffly, annoyance prickling inside.

I entered the room and immediately noticed a new sari folded delicately on the bed—yards of dove-gray silk strewn with pearls. I dressed quickly before meeting Gupta outside and we walked through the halls. The mirror portals paneling the walls glittered strange reflections. Lush hills carpeted in small blue flowers, a forest tangled with lights and a bone white temple balanced between the tips of a craggy mountainside flashed past me. But something else caught my eye, tucked away in a corner of the hall that I hadn't seen before: a door, charred at the edges, lengths of iron wrapping it round and round.

Something about the door twisted my heart. A voice, a mere scratch in the silence, began to sing:

I've never tasted dreams so sweet
Such pearly flesh and tender meat
Oh queen, if you only knew
You'd gladly rip your heart in two

I stopped. "Gupta, what door is that?"

He frowned. "Door? What door?" He turned around and then asked sharply, "What did it look like?"

I hesitated. Mother Dhina's words echoed . . . *keep some secrets for yourself.* The words caught in my throat. This secret, just this one, I would keep to myself until I understood it. I had barely been in Akaran for a day. I couldn't let my guard down entirely. And that voice . . . it felt like it had been sung to me alone.

"I can't remember," I lied.

Gupta shrugged. As we walked, I kept turning around, half expecting a door strung with chains to glitter just out of sight. But it never appeared.

The dining room had changed since yesterday. Today its rug showed a herd of elephants moving through the jungle. And instead of golden platters piled high with food and saffron cushions placed around the table, there were silver platters and mother-of-pearl cushions. Akaran's riches lay unfurled at my feet. But even with all that wonder, I sensed a chill in the room. I pulled my sari closer. There was something else *here*. I could feel it like breath against my neck.

Amar was nowhere in sight. Instead, Gupta pulled out a chair for me.

"Please, have a seat," he said. "Amar won't be able to dine with you this evening."

"Oh." A twinge of disappointment ran through me. "Why not?"

"He had to attend to an urgent matter of retrieval."

"Retrieval of what?"

Gupta stiffened and his voice came out in a wheeze. When he

caught his breath, he merely pointed to the night sky, where the moon was a ghostly crescent.

"Right," I said, deflating a little. I kept forgetting the rules of the Otherworld. Not a word could be spoken about Akaran's secrets until the new moon.

I glared at the moon.

Gupta shook his head apologetically and pointed at the food. "Please, eat."

As I ate, I watched Gupta from the corner of my eye. He was writing furiously, quill rapping against the wood as he filled the page with line after line of ink.

"What are you doing?"

He looked up, quill half suspended in the air before he tapped the scroll. "Record keeping. Nothing is certain until the ink dries."

"What's not certain?"

"Life," said Gupta matter-of-factly.

The half-eaten platters of food stared back at me glumly. I was, against all experience, strangely without an appetite.

"When you finish, you have the evening to yourself," said Gupta, scrutinizing the scrolls before him. "I would be happy to show you my collection of record keeping on the distribution of leaves per branch. It's one of my more noteworthy accomplishments."

I glanced down the halls. Again, that voice from the charred door rustled against me. The air prickled with invisible heat and magic. Gupta continued talking, but his voice ebbed in and out, splashing against a rhyme I couldn't catch no matter how hard I strained—

Oh, the treacherous moon, dear queen, please—

"Did I ever tell you about the time I interviewed a mollusk? Fascinating—"

—free me, find me, hidden in the tree, if you—

"—hungry more often than naught, which is—"

My pulse slowed. A sharp pain turned the colors bright and sickening. I couldn't even feel the rugs beneath my feet. My toes felt like they were sinking into damp, gritty sand. Water lapping at my ankles. A name crouched in my throat. A name I should have been screaming, but couldn't recall. The voice from the charred door was a plea and all I knew was that I had to leave this room. *I had to find the door.*

I stood up, knocking my chair over behind me.

Whatever spell of pain had clung to me broke instantly. I looked down and saw the silk rug. Gupta stared, a little confused. I needed to get out. I needed to distract him.

"Why don't we play a game of riddles?" I said suddenly. "I'll stand outside and let you think. When you're ready, call my name. Yes?"

Gupta sat up straighter, his head tilting bird-like to one side. "What riddle?"

"I'll give you three. You seem like you'd be very good at them."

Gupta beamed. "I have been known—"

"Excellent," I said quickly. "I am a nightmare to most, and a dream for the broken; who am I? Next riddle. I am your future, who am I?"

Gupta silently repeated them. "And the last?"

"I hide the stars but am frightened by the sun. I am not the night, who am I?"

"Delightful!" said Gupta, clapping his hands. "You'll stay outside?"

I smiled. "Of course."

He gave a distracted nod, and I slipped out of the dining room.

Curiosity sharp as frissons of heat ran up my spine. I tried calling out to the voice, but there was nothing. Alone, I was beginning to think it was nothing more than the palace's quirks. Both Amar and Gupta had said the palace would test me. Perhaps this was nothing more.

I looked around. The great corridors of Akaran unfurled before me like a stone maze and I took off down one of the paths, fingers trailing along the walls and murals. Moonlight flooded the palace, wiping away its solemnity and filling it with a cold, twinkling beauty.

Gupta had been right yesterday. I did mind the silence. It felt too controlled. When he spoke of the palace, he made it sound like it was a sentient being, something that could hop and shuffle, talk back and frown. I hadn't believed him, but I was beginning to. Everything about the palace felt deliberate.

Some of the mirrors around me were lit up with life. A few of the cities inside them were deep in sleep, with a slim moon keeping vigil over their slumber. And then there were the mirrors with darker scenes . . .

Wars and flags of countries I didn't recognize. A burning smell, as if it could stretch through the silvery portals and spill into Akaran. I never saw anyone in these reflections; the portals were like a bird's-eye view looking down. But I still saw the fires. I still saw the horses pounding the ground beneath them, moving out of sight, far beyond the edges of the mirrors.

Up ahead, the white marble floors of the palace had given way to shiny lacquered wood. I walked forward, sure that I could hear Gupta's voice if he called. Unlike the bare stone walls of the throne room or main hallways, these walls were giant mirrors, darkened with time and peeling to reveal the silver beneath them.

Beneath the shadow of a large arch, something glittered. I stared into the darkness, but saw nothing but a pale wooden door cracked open. The stone was cool beneath my feet and tendrils of light snaked past me, pooling into silver puddles before bringing the room into full view. My eyes widened—

Before me was a twinkling garden. But instead of potted plants and wilting flowers, every piece of this garden was bright and translucent, like it had been carved from glass. I leaned forward . . . it *was* carved of glass. From the stately banyan tree with its ropy leaves to the *ashwagandha* shrub and its bright red fruit, everything was glass and crystal. I walked in a daze through the labyrinth of crystal plants and lightly touched the cool stems. I stroked the glassy tendrils of an *amla* plant and laughed as emerald vines glittered and brushed against my skin.

But not even the crystal plants were as lovely as the soft blooms of light winking and disappearing into the translucent vines and petals. Thousands of lights blinked in and out, whooshing and whirling around the plants so that everything seemed wrought of light and glass. It was beautiful. I turned around, taking in the full view of the garden. Moonlight had teased away the shadows and my world had become dream-soft and slicked in glass. For the first time since coming to Akaran, I felt at peace.

"What are you doing here?" thundered a voice behind me.

I nearly jumped. Even without turning, I knew who the voice belonged to:

Amar.

•» 12 «•

THE GARDEN OF GLASS

I raised my chin and stared back at him. I had no reason to feel embarrassed. After all, he was the one who said Akaran was just as much mine as it was his. The door *had* been open. And yet, a flush still crept up the back of my neck.

"I was taking a walk," I said weakly.

"Where's Gupta?"

"The dining room," I said before adding defensively, "I only walked a little down the halls."

His jaw tightened. "I told you that the kingdom's location makes it dangerous."

"Gupta told me that anyplace that might hold danger would be locked up," I retorted. "The door to this room was not locked."

"Even so," said Amar. "They might sing through their bindings. It's better to have an escort."

"As you can see, I am unscathed from my walk from one hall to the next."

"Today," cut in Amar tightly. "*Today* you are unscathed. Tomorrow is unknown. As is the next day and the day after that. Never make light of your life."

"I never do."

The vial of mandrake poison flashed in my mind. Life led me here. Life and the desire to *live* it.

Gupta burst into the room.

"Oh, good!" he breathed, hands pushing against his knees. He looked like he'd just run from one side of a country to the next. Guilt heated my face. He turned to Amar. "I apologize. I lost track with the riddles."

"You can leave, my friend," said Amar. "She is safe with me."

Gupta looked between us, started to say something and thought better of it. There was a touch of pity in his expression as he looked at the winking lights around us. With one last glance at the garden, Gupta left.

Amar loosed a breath. "I understand, you know."

I looked up.

"The forced silence . . . the voices of this palace."

We stood there, not saying anything. I felt too aware of the space between us. Even with Akaran's secrets spiraling in the shadows of my head, I couldn't ignore the weightless feeling that had gripped me. Standing beside Amar *did* something to me. Like my center had shifted to make room for him.

"You do not trust me, do you?"

"No," I said. I had no reason to lie. "I told you in the Night Bazaar that trust is won in actions and time. Not words."

"I wish you trusted me."

"I don't place my faith in wishes," I said. "How can I? I can't even—"

I bit back the rest of my words. *I can't even see your face.* Perhaps Gupta was lying and he really did have a disfiguring scar. Amar moved closer until we were only a hand space apart.

"What?" he coaxed, his voice hovering between a growl and a question.

"I can't even see your face."

A strange chill still curled off of him like smoke and even though the glass garden was teeming with little lights, shades veiled him.

"Is that what you want?" he said. "Would it make you trust me?"

"It would be a start."

"You are impossible to please."

I said nothing. Amar leaned forward, and I felt the silken trails of his hood brush across my neck. My breath constricted. "Is that what you want? An unguarded gaze can spill a thousand secrets."

"I would know them anyway," I said evenly.

I waited for him to dissuade me, but when he remained silent, I reached out. Amar stood still, lean muscles tensed beneath his clothes. I could hear his breathing, see his chest rising and falling, smell that particular scent of mint and smoke that hung around him. Slowly, I untied the ends of the dove-gray hood. Small pearls snagged against the silk of his covering.

Suddenly, his hands reached around my wrist.

"I trust you," he said.

The hood fell to the ground, a mere rustle of silk against glass. I lifted my gaze, searching Amar's face. He was young, and yet there was something worn about his features.

I took in the stern line of his nose and the smooth expanse of tawny skin. His features possessed a lethal kind of elegance, like a predator at rest—bronzed jaw tapering to a knife's point, lips curled in the faintest of grins and heavy brows casting dusky shadows over his eyes.

When I looked at him, something stirred inside me. It felt like recognition sifted through dreams; like the moment before waking—when sleep blurred the true world, when beasts with sharp teeth and beautiful, winged things flew along the edges of your mind.

Amar met my gaze and his eyes were raw. Burning.

"Well?" he asked. There was no rebuke in his voice, only curiosity.

"I see no secrets in your gaze," I said. *I see only night and smoke, dreams and glass, embers and wings. And I would not have you any other way.*

"You have made your request, what about mine?"

"I am not the one withholding secrets."

He smiled and I stared at him for a moment. When he smiled, his severe face softened into something beautiful. I wanted to see it again.

"On the contrary, I am the one who has no choice. You, on the other hand, do."

"What do you want from me?"

He reached out, fingers sliding across the length of my hair. "Some strands of your hair."

Some of the courtiers in Bharata used to tie their wives' hair around their wrists when they traveled. It was a sign of love and faith. To remain connected to the person you love, even if it was just by a circlet of hair.

"May I?" asked Amar.

I nodded. With a small knife, Amar deftly clipped a number of strands. Quickly, he twirled them into a bracelet and slipped it onto his wrist. There was another bracelet on his hand that I had not noticed until now. A simple strap of black leather tied into an elegant knot.

"Thank you for this," he said, pulling his sleeve over the other strap.

"It's nothing," I said, trying for lightness.

"And yet I would trade everything for it," he said. There was no tease in his voice. Nothing but a strange straightforwardness, like he'd never said anything more honest in his entire life.

"Then you must be relieved I gave it willingly."

"Astounded," he murmured, still tracing the circlet. He looked at me and something light fluttered in my stomach. "Not relieved. Relief is when you want something to stop."

A small light floated between us, only to vanish in an instant. "What are those?"

Amar followed my gaze. "Wishes."

My eyes widened. "They *grant* wishes?"

"Sadly, no. They're wishes already made."

"Of what?"

"Or who?" countered Amar.

"Is this another secret the moon keeps from me?"

"No," said Amar with a grin. "It is a secret that *I* choose to keep from you."

"Why won't you tell me?"

"Because then this would lose all its fun."

I rolled my eyes and turned away from him when he caught me around the wrist.

"Don't you want to know what I wished for?" he said, his breath against my neck.

"No," I said, but my gaze was fixed on all the blinking lights. There were so many. And why did he say *or who?* when it came to his wishes?

"I can't stand deception."

"Then stop flattering yourself."

He laughed and released me. "I'll tell you what I wished for if you give me a kiss."

I turned to face him. "Even if I did, you might lie. There's no way to prove that you wished for what you said you did."

He smiled. "Clever as ever."

"Or unwilling to kiss you."

"Another lie," he said, grinning.

Amar reached into the air and a handful of lights danced on his palms. "Kiss me and you'll know I'm telling the truth."

He leaned forward, the small lights illuminating his face. In the light, he looked honey drenched. But I wasn't going to give him a victory so easily. I quickly pecked his cheek and stepped back. Amar was still tipped toward me, his eyes a little wide before he started laughing.

"Foolish optimism."

I ignored him. "And those wishes?"

"See for yourself," he said, opening his palm.

There was nothing in his hands. Around us, a third of the lights had disappeared. I stared into the dark, waiting for them to flare into being. But they were gone.

"Once a wish comes true, it disappears for good."

"*That's* what you wished for?" I asked, incredulous. "A peck on the cheek?"

"No."

"Then what?"

"This," said Amar, gesturing to the space between us, "the chance to be this close to you."

We looked at one another in silence. There was something new between us. Fragile and thrumming. I didn't know what to do. Nothing I had learned in Bharata's sanctum had taught me this. Nothing I had seen in the harem came close to what I felt. There was an undercurrent of depth, of something hard-won and dangerous. I couldn't treat it with lightness . . . and I didn't want to.

"Maya, I—" he started, when another voice cut him off.

Gupta stood in the arch of the doorway, his face twisted in apology. "I tried to contain it as much as I could."

Amar stepped away from me, his face stony. "I'll be there in a moment. Take her back to the room."

Something cold thudded in my stomach. A reminder to rein in how I felt and keep him at a distance.

"I'm sorry," said Amar.

But he wouldn't look me in the eye. And before I had a chance to speak, he had left.

That night, I tried to enter a peaceful dream of nothingness, but I kept waking. Each lapse of restful sleep slipped into a gray and distorted vision of the glass garden. In my dream, a monster wearing five blurred faces turned to me:

"Did you notice nothing strange about your garden?"

Separate voices sprang from the mouths. Panic turned my skin cold. I could think of a number of strange things, not the least of which was the animated split personality accosting my dreams, but I kept my mouth shut. The creature leered its split face at me.

"There's not a living thing in this court, is there?"

•» 13 «•

A ROOM FULL OF STARS

I woke with a start. The nightmare's words burned in my mind like a flame. Not a single flower or tree filled Akaran's marble halls. Even its garden was glass. I thought of what I had seen of the Night Bazaar. It was magical, undeniably beautiful. But it was also dangerous. Coaxing. The star-bright loam where jewel fruit swung beneath silver trees hadn't been the only thing I saw. Something else had moved in that sticky darkness.

Flurried sounds of movements quickened outside and I closed my eyes, feigning sleep. The bed sank as Amar sat beside me. Warm fingertips trailed across my cheek, brushing the hair from my forehead and sending sparks of light up my spine. His lips grazed my temples.

"Soon, *jaani*."

I waited until his footsteps echoed outside before squinting around the room. Without him, it seemed colder. I retraced his touch lightly, careful to avoid smudging the imprint of his lips against my skin. He had called me *jaani*—"my life." I stared at the closed door. Where his skin touched mine felt burnished, hallowed by the words he left hanging in the air. *Jaani jaani jaani.* I wanted him to say it again. I wanted him to say it closer to my ear, my neck . . . my lips.

But the surge of warmth faded as the memory of my dream prickled behind my eyes.

Magic was not the only coaxing, dangerous thing around me.

Like yesterday, when I returned after washing up, the bed had been made, and a new sari was waiting for me. This time it was a rich amber, studded with topaz stones and small mirrors so that when I wrapped it around me, the colors shimmered as if they had borrowed some of their brilliance from the sun. A similar set of matching jewels lay in piles on the bed.

Something about wearing a necklace other than my mother's felt wrong. Inevitably, my thoughts turned to Gauri. Who was telling her stories in the dark?

When I stepped outside my room, Gupta was already standing there. The air felt tense. As if someone had smothered the palace into silence so that it could watch . . . and wait. I paused outside the door. I thought I heard something. A voice? My name?

Shaking my head, I walked down the familiar hall toward the dining room, but my glance kept darting from the walls and doors, ignoring the beautiful sights flashing in the mirrors. What had happened to that door from before? Around me, muddled voices filled the palace.

Sometimes the voices were incoherent, but today, I heard a sound sonorous and riven as an ancient stream:

You can have him, but not hold him
He gives you gold, but your bed is cold
You've seen his eyes, but not his spies
Who is he?

"Amar," I breathed.

Gupta looked up. "Did you say something?"

"The riddle you asked," I said, a little dazed.

"I didn't say anything."

A chill shot through me. There was no one in the hall but us. I said nothing, and walked quickly down the halls, trying to shake the doubt and fear that kept creeping up my arms.

When we got to the dining room, it was decorated in a sun-drenched yellow. Carven statues of mynah birds with ruffs of silk around their stone necks dotted the room. Outside, there was no flash of the sun. No hint of clouds.

Gupta pulled out a chair for me.

"I figured out your riddles from yesterday."

I looked at him, my mind still twisting around the words I heard in the hallway.

"And?"

"Your first one was, 'I am a nightmare to most, and a dream for the broken; who am I?' and the answer to that is death."

"Correct."

"Your second riddle was, 'I am your future, who am I?'"

"And?"

"The answer to that is ash."

"Again, correct. And the last?"

"'I hide the stars but am frightened by the sun. I am not the night; who am I?' The answer is darkness."

I smiled. "All three are correct."

He stared at me. There were dark circles beneath his eyes. He looked aged in the space of a day. "You ran off last night."

"I got lost."

"You're smarter than that, and so am I," said Gupta.

I looked away from him, feeling the slightest twinge of guilt.

"If I were you, I'd remember the answers to those riddles when you're walking around the palace."

"You yourself said that you held the key to anything dangerous."

"Even so," he said, mirroring Amar's response.

I tried to think of something to say, but Gupta had turned from me and the tight, closed-off expression on his face said that I shouldn't even bother trying to push the subject.

"You seem quite absorbed in your work," I said, trying to change the topic as he bent his head toward the endless scrolls.

"If only I wasn't," said Gupta.

"Can I help?"

He smiled, but it was a weary thing. "The fact that you are even here is help enough."

But I wasn't doing anything. I was wearing clothes set out for me on a bed, wandering allotted spaces of a hall, feeling around for questions they could answer. I was in a limbo of waiting.

"How did you sleep?" asked Gupta, his gaze once more fixed on the parchment.

I thought of the nightmare and masked a shudder.

"Well enough," I lied.

After breakfast, Amar stood waiting for me in the center of a marble vestibule. Around him, the mirror portals flashed through the settings—a fox napping in tall grass, a shining cave strung with ghost-lit threads and a cliff jutting a stony chin to the sea. Amar grinned and once more, I was transfixed by the way a small smile could soften the stern angles of his jaw and the haunted look in his eyes.

"Are we going to the tapestry room?"

He shook his head. "Not yet. Those decisions take time. There are other things to see and know here."

I shivered at the thought of yanking the threads. I was in no rush to condemn someone. Amar stepped toward a door I hadn't noticed until now, inky black and studded with pearls and moonstone. He pushed it open and a chilly gust kissed my face.

"I promised you the moon for your throne and stars to wear in your hair," said Amar, gesturing inside. "And I always keep my promises."

Infinite. That's how it felt to stand there in a realm, a field . . . a marvel . . . of stars. Cold light spangled the space around us. Darkness so old that the shadows felt like relics twisted between the lights. The air was scentless, laced with frost. We stood on nothing but air and yet it was solid. In the half-light, Amar's face glittered and starlight clung to his hair. I stared around me, my heart skidding. The things I had called bright and blind enemies shimmered all around me. How many times had I cursed them? And now I was in their world.

Amar reached for my hand and put something in my palm. I looked down: string.

"For conquering," he said.

I stretched the string into a taut line.

"Conquering what? Insects?"

"No. Your enemies."

The stars. Fate.

The string drooped in my fingers.

"Why do you hate them?" he asked.

"If Akaran has its eyes and ears in Bharata, then you already know," I said darkly, thinking of the horoscope that had shadowed the past seventeen years.

"Do you believe the horoscope?"

"No."

I meant it. There was no proof. Sometimes, I still thought it was a hateful rumor born of Mother Dhina's jealousy.

"Then why hate the stars?"

"For what they did. Or, I guess, what they made other people do," I said softly. "For making me hated without reason and without evidence. Wouldn't you hate distant jailers?"

"I don't believe they're jailers. I believe the stars."

"Then you're a fool to marry me."

He laughed. "I believe them, but I choose to read them differently."

"I don't see any happy way to explain death and destruction."

"Doesn't death make room for life? Autumn trees die to make room for new shoots. And destruction is part of that cycle. After all, a devastating forest fire lets the ground start anew."

I stared at him. No one had *ever* said anything like that in Bharata. No one had ever challenged the stars. And yet, the light contoured him, clung to him, like the stars knew and believed everything he said. Maybe I believed him too. All I had done was curse the stars from a distance. I'd never thought to reinterpret what they meant. I turned around, as if seeing the night sky for the first time.

Gently, Amar placed the string back in my hand. He pointed at three stars: one on my right, one in front and one on my left.

"Bind them. Conquer them."

The stars were on completely different sides of the room. One, with blue edges, dangled above me; the other had a core of fire and the last was nothing more than tendrils of bright smoke.

"They're too far apart," I said, holding up the small piece of string. "That's impossible."

"Then make it possible. Reinterpret them. The room will answer."

"It's not even a room—" I started, gesturing across the vast expanse of sky.

And then I stopped.

It wasn't a room.

. . . *yet.*

As if answering my thoughts, the space around us shrank, dragging the stars together so that their celestial glimmer was lost and they looked like little more than shining cuts. Light still seeped out, but the room felt brighter. The three stars were closer, but still not close enough to tie with a foot of string.

I reached out, my thoughts whirring. *Reinterpret them.* I used to think of the stars as cruel and fixed ornaments, but what about the sky that held them aloft? Could I . . . touch it? Push past it?

My fingers grazed the night—cool and sweet-smelling, perfumed with the scent of vespertine flowers that only opened their blossoms to the moon. And then I stepped forward. I gasped. I could *move* in the night gaps, like they were hallways themselves. Quickly, I slid into the rifts between stars. I imagined the space as a sphere bedizened with little astral ornaments, and soon those heavy celestial bodies became small as candies held in one's palms. The thread easily looped them together.

I grinned, turning to Amar. Between us was a sphere thick with stars and around us twined soft shadows like cats weaving between ankles.

"Magnificent," he said.

His gaze was full of awe, but I saw something else in his eyes. *Longing.* Then, he reached into the sphere, drawing out the string with the three stars. He twisted them between his hands, fashioning a constellation no larger than a sparrow. Amar stepped forward, sliding the stars above my ear. It cast a glow that turned his face silvery and beautiful.

"There, my queen," he said. "A constellation to wear in your hair."

We spent the rest of the day lost in that room of old planets and forgotten meteors. I stepped across flattened comets and spilled haloes of things that may have burned for centuries or may have always been illusions. It didn't matter. For the first time, I felt like I was seeing things differently. Amar kept testing my perspective. He clasped nebulas in my hands and told me to think of them as fate.

Being with him was like seeing for the first time. I even started to think differently about the horoscope. Could I see a glimmer of silver in all that darkness? I wanted to. And now, I almost did.

When we had closed the door to the star room, Amar reached up to brush his fingers against the constellation in my hair.

"It suits you," he said.

Warmth crept to my cheeks. For a long moment, we stood in that alcove. The mirror portals faintly shimmered. In the distance, I could see the lines of cities and flush of daybreaks, but everything felt dim compared to the space between us. It felt so charged it could have been alive.

Amar moved closer to me, but a sudden howl across the palace sprang us apart. Amar's eyes snapped to a distant hall and his mouth, just a moment ago curved in a smile, was now a tight cut.

"Come, Maya. It's not safe for you to be out here."

"Why?" I said, following his gaze.

Were my eyes fooling me or did the shadow of a beast just cross the vestibule? Something dank overwhelmed my senses. Wet fur. Salt-crusted claws. That sound of the howling slid under my skin, conjuring something horrifying and nameless in my mind: faceless bodies falling to the floor, the frantic spurt of blood leaving a vein.

Amar half pulled, half ran me to the dining room. Inside, the room was lit up and lanterns of cut topaz hung suspended from the ceiling. Gupta ran to meet me, his gaze shadowed as he and Amar exchanged some silent conversation.

"I am sorry," Amar said quickly, before running out of the room.

I stood there, unable to shake off the sound of the hounds. Gupta flashed a mournful expression.

"What was that?"

"I—" Gupta started before shaking his head, his face pained. "I cannot say. I am sorry."

My hands clenched into fists. "The moon?"

He nodded.

"Were those hunting hounds in the palace?"

Gupta paused and nodded.

My skin crawled. "What were they hunting?"

"You know I cannot answer that."

I sat stiffly in my chair, sparing a single glance to the taunting half-moon outside. There was still time before Akaran would make itself fully known to me. Until then, I had to endure. I tried to pretend that the sound was a warning. That there was a reasonable explanation behind it. But I couldn't forget the horrible, stomach-churning feeling it rent through me. And when I bent my head to eat, the constellation of stars fell onto my lap.

Dull and silver. But sharp as teeth.

14

THE LION IN THE PILLAR

For three days I did not see Amar. The only sign of him was the sleep-mussed side of the bed. Always, it was cold to the touch. I wandered the halls alone, exploring the doors of Akaran that would open to me. Many of them were bolted shut, but some were not. One door in particular kept flickering to my mind—the charred one, with chains wrapped around it. But I never saw it, despite looking.

On the first day, I found a room where snowdrifts floated upside down in soft, swirling eddies. Once the snow had piled onto the ceiling, it fell in ribbons of translucent silk before sinking into the floor, for the snow-silk cycle to start anew. On the second day, I found a sweltering hot room behind a door that bore a shifting pattern of sand dunes. Inside, sinuous shadows danced across the floor. Curious, I reached down to touch the pattern and the dark puddled into my hands, wet as ink. On the third day, I found a door carved with feathers. Carven niches filled with eggs covered the walls. Behind the shelves of eggs, someone had painted beautiful renderings of rain quails and white-eared pheasants, jungle fowl and storm petrels, ibis and osprey. When I stepped inside, the painted birds cocked their heads, chirruping and crooning to themselves. The eggs became seamed with light and soft birdsong filled the air.

On the fourth day, I found a pale white courtyard with a single huge pillar in the middle. The ceiling above was a soft twilight, burnt copper edging a smoky blue. It was a strange place. The air smelled damp and furious.

I ran my fingers across the pillar before snatching my hand back. A crack had split the pillar. The hairs on the back of my neck rose. A hideous roar growled from within the pillar and I jumped back.

"It's only an illusion," came a voice near the door.

I spun around to see Amar slouched against the doorway. He looked gaunt; shadows creased the skin under his eyes and his hair was mussed. Still, he smiled to see me and I couldn't help but smile back. Until now, I didn't realize that the listlessness I had felt was because of him. I had missed his presence, his speech. Next to him, I felt more alive.

"What is this?" I asked, gesturing to the growling pillar.

Amar sank into an onyx chair that he had conjured from thin air. He tilted his head back and took a deep breath.

"Are you well?"

"Soon enough." His smile didn't meet his eyes. "That," he said, "is a reminder that none can escape death. I am fond of the legend."

The moment he said that I knew exactly who was in the pillar, and with a strange ache I remembered the harem of Bharata.

"Narasimha," I breathed. "I have always liked that tale."

His eyes widened in surprise. "You are familiar with it?"

I nodded. It was the one tale I never told Gauri. Too gory. But for some reason, strangely comforting to me. The pillar quivered behind us, as if it was waiting for me to tell the tale myself. Amar leaned forward, his broad shoulders hunched around him like a predator in wait.

"Tell it to me."

"Why? We both know the tale."

"Even so. I want to hear it from your lips. Tell the tale. The room will keep rhythm."

Tell the tale. My heart clenched. *I miss you, Gauri.* Sinking into my old habit was easy enough. I sat on the floor, crossing my legs in front of me, my gaze flickering between Amar and the pillar. Amar's eyes were closed, his head tilted back to expose his bronzed throat. I spun my tale and the sky shimmered with images. I told Amar of the demon king who wished to escape death so he performed the most severe penances until he was granted a boon by the gods.

"He prayed that he would not die inside or outside his home. He prayed that he would die neither at night or day nor in the ground or in the sky. He prayed that neither man nor beast could kill him. He prayed no weapon could harm him."

Amar's head snapped up. He looked at the pillar with a wicked smile.

"And yet death found its way to him."

I nodded. "One day, the god appeared as part-man, part-lion and burst forth from the pillar."

A being of shadow tore through the pillar. A lion's mane cast a torn shadow across the marble. Fangs lengthened in its mouth.

"He came upon the demon king at twilight—"

"—which is neither night nor day," said Amar.

"And he appeared on the threshold of a courtyard—"

"Neither indoors nor out."

"And he spread the king across his lap."

"Neither above nor below ground."

The shadow story played out in front of us, a tusked hulking man dragged to his knees and then lifted onto the thighs of the beast god.

"And he used his fingernails."

"Not a true weapon."

The shadow being lifted muscled arms above his head and claws erupted from his fingers. Amar grinned.

"And then death took him," I said.

"Yes," finished Amar. "He did."

The shadow beast tore its claws into the demon king. Blood spattered across the walls. Within seconds, the images collapsed and the beast god slunk back into the pillar, one eye slit to the outside world before the marble folded up and swallowed him. I stood up, my hands shaking for no reason.

"Beautiful," said Amar.

"I found it gruesome," I said, shivering.

Amar rose and walked to where I stood.

"I was not talking about the story."

"Oh."

"Why do you like such a gruesome tale?"

In Bharata, we were taught that it was a tale of the god's might. But I saw another story within it: the play of interpretation that turned something terrifying and iron-clad into something that could be conquered. I was reminded of the star room where Amar had taken me only days ago. The story was like a different way of seeing.

"It gave me hope . . . that maybe there was some way around the horoscope. It was a lesson in language too, almost like a riddle . . ."

Amar stared at me and then he laughed.

"Only my queen would find hope in horror." He took my hand in his and his gaze was burning. "You are my hope and more."

"What does that make you? My horror?"

"And more," he said.

All I saw were his eyes. Velvet dark. The kind of umbra that shadows envy. Amar stared at me and his gaze was desperate with hope. Reckless. I should've stopped. I should've stepped away. But I didn't. I leaned forward, and a soft growl—like surrender—escaped his throat. He dug his fingers into my back and pulled me into a kiss.

Amar's kiss was furious. No heat. Just lightning. Or maybe

that was what his touch teased out of me—vivid streaks of light, dusk and all her violent glory. I was lost. I leaned into his kiss and the world around us peeled into nothing. I felt like I could stand over chasms empty of time, and this moment, like a chain of soft-blooming stars, would still be *ours*.

We kissed until we couldn't breathe. And then we kissed until we needed the touch of one another like breath itself.

I never glanced at the moon for the next week. I knew, buried beneath my happiness, that it was temporary and that sooner or later I would have to pull Vikram's thread, but I ignored it. I was too lost in the magic of Akaran and Amar.

Akaran had no seasons, so we spent our days trying to find them. Amar led me to a summer hall, where the sky was dim and lovely, bleached of its blue by the heat. Squalls gusted in the corners and above us hung lush glass vines where crystal mangoes swayed. In the monsoon room, we fashioned small enamel elephants and sent them trumpeting across the liquid, stormy floors. Amar blew on them and small coronets of clouds hovered above their heads. In the summer hall's heat I told him stories and in the ruthless rainstorms of the monsoon room, he kissed me. Beside him, the world was a soft, pulsing and bright thing, alive with hidden angles that we could uncover one by one. It was more than magic. It was life turned relentless and astral. And I reveled in it.

But even in this happiness, my bed was always cold. He would leave before dinner and return while I slept. Sometimes his face was more gaunt than lovely, but he smiled anyway each time that he saw me. Sometimes, at night, I heard the echo of hounds baying and my skin would crawl, but I would forget it, choosing bliss over burden. Sometimes, I looked behind me, certain I had seen a glimpse of that charred door wrapped in chains. But it always danced out of sight.

And then one night, Amar appeared for dinner. He sat across from Gupta, not meeting my gaze. Outside, the moon waned to a paring. Just two more days.

"Tomorrow, you must make your decision," said Amar quietly.

He left abruptly after that, hardly touching his food, hardly saying a word. Worry bit at me. What if I made the wrong choice?

When I walked back to the room, I heard a soft song calling out to me for the first time in days.

You are running out of moon time
Listen to my warning rhyme
I know you hear me in your head
I know the monster in your bed

I shook off the voice and shut the bedroom door behind me. I felt like insects made of ice had crawled under my skin. The palace was filled with riddling voices. It was nothing. It meant nothing. Maybe tomorrow I would find a room playing out a skit where one character said those words to another. My heart calmed, but my mind wasn't convinced.

That night, I dreamed of locked doors and baying hounds, rooms that were night-dark and a beast-king that smiled and laughed around a mouthful of broken stars to sing one phrase over and over: *I know the monster in your bed.*

15

VEINS OF MAGIC

I stood before the tapestry. Sweat stamped my palms. Even now, the threads dazzled—shifting, coiling, breathing, pulsing. Impossible to tame, like the sea in a storm. Amar faced me. He looked *haunted*. His hair was mussed and when he finally turned to look at me, it was with a mix of hope and fear.

"What have you decided?"

I tried to think about a decision, but each time, I was struck by the memory of the helmets piling up in my father's inner sanctum. I forced myself to look at the tapestry. I already knew what it would show me. The bodies of my father's people being dragged through a foreign empire that would herald peace but at a deadly cost. A future of fragile peace won more quickly, with less bloodshed, but with no memory of Bharata's great legacy. Worse, its people would lose all their sovereignty and identity. Some might even be forced into slavery, but all would be forced to obey a new ruler.

"Why do we need to make this decision now?"

Amar's hands tightened, but he relaxed them almost immediately. He was quiet for a moment and I colored from his silence.

"The longer you wait, the more the threads unravel," he said. "See?"

Amar was right. Several of the glittering threads had begun to fray. My fingers hovered over them—the white one gleamed with Vikram's potential as a leader, the red one shone with Vikram's potential as a warrior. Both threads held the promise of peace and both came with a different cost. And yet, with either path, it seemed like Bharata would pay the price.

Amar circled me, his hands clasped behind his back. "You *have* to make this decision."

I could feel his gaze on me—sharp, unrelenting and also . . . desperate.

"We must choose the thread that affords the best outcome for the most people, thus maintaining a balance of peace," he said. "You see, though, how it draws on so many different aspects. It is not just one person. They are all interconnected."

I stared up at him. For a moment, his eyes searched mine and in the depths of his gaze, I felt a swell of sorrow. He turned sharply from me and I forced myself to summon the most diplomatic tone I could.

"The red thread carries too much risk," I said. "The peace was accomplished more easily, but who's to say that the peace will hold long after Vikram dies? The risk is far greater. What is lost is more than just lives. It's an entire city. I think a peace that is won through words and advocated tirelessly will hold better than an alliance of bloodshed even if . . . even if it means at the price of more blood."

Tears burned behind my eyes. How many people had I doomed?

"Then your decision is made. Rip the thread."

I brought my hands slowly to the tapestry and wound my fingers around the red thread. It pulsed, struggling against me. I searched myself for the nerve to pull, but when I closed my eyes, all I saw were my people burning and bleeding.

I drew my hand away, scalded.

"I can't." I dropped the thread, backing away from the tapestry.

Sweat coated my palms. I didn't feel solid. I felt as limp and soft as a pile of threads. I fixed my eyes on the floor. More than anything, I had wanted to prove that I was more than a sheltered princess of Bharata. I wanted to show that I could handle this enormous task and not fail.

"Weakness is a luxury you can no longer afford," said Amar.

"Compassion isn't weakness."

"It is here."

"When you took me to the Night Bazaar, you said you wanted my perspective and my honesty," I said, facing him. "I've given both."

"You knew the decision the moment you saw the outcomes. I know it," challenged Amar. "Now you have to follow through."

The accusation in his voice taunted me. Where the throne room had once filled me with possibility, now I felt small.

Amar grasped my hands. "I know you're not comfortable with this."

I clenched my jaw. No matter what I said, he would think less of me. And all too often, I found myself caring about what he thought.

"It feels wrong. What if—"

"Never let your doubts cripple you." He stepped back, his arms raised in a surrender that made me feel anything but victorious. "I leave this to you. I trust your instincts, Maya. As should you. Trust yourself. Trust *who* you are."

The door closed with a soft thud and I stood still, letting the silence twist around me. The tapestry hummed. I turned my back to it, letting it guide my hands as my fingers hovered over the thread. The words of my horoscope needled in the back of my conscience. *A marriage that only brings death and destruction.* Destruction was letting Vikram become a ruthless warrior who would raze villages to the ground and hoard power in the name of "peace." I wouldn't let that happen. I gathered my strength and held on to my breath as though it were an anchor linking me to a thousand places at once.

And then . . . I pulled.

Nothing.

I opened my eyes. The thread wouldn't budge. Like someone digging his heels into the ground. I focused on the thread and yanked again, trying to wrap around its root, its length—but it would not yield.

My heart slammed. It wasn't the thread . . . it was *me*. I wasn't strong enough. The tapestry and the palace had judged and deemed me unworthy. Weak.

Amar had said to trust myself. I had, hadn't I? But other thoughts had crowded my mind. Thoughts of Bharata, thoughts of what I was doing. Where I was . . . who I was. All my doubts and insecurities. I dropped the thread and it fluttered softly against the others. I spread my fingers across the tapestry, as if I could will it to listen. To give me another chance. Or, barring that, the strength just to move one of its pieces.

In response, the tapestry quivered, a glistening ichor seeping through the threads, dampening them. Light wavered from the dangling thread and a high-pitched hum settled over the tapestry. I stepped back, heart racing. What was happening? Had the fact that I couldn't even move a single thread broken the whole thing?

Light burst through the threads, dazzling me with a thousand streams of color so vivid that I could feel it seeping warmly across my fingers—shards of evening sky, the cool frost of lonely mornings, drenching nectar-sticky heat. I could feel the color as if it were a dimension of time and space, heavy and solid, full of flavor, of *life*. It snuck under my tongue like a bright candy, and voices—loud and soft, whispers and howls, of passion so grand that it tottered on the edge of mythic and sorrows so plangent they trailed their own shadows. I couldn't take it. I stumbled backward.

The light draped around me, murmuring, muttering. It pushed against my closed eyes, like it was trying to pry my sight open, to show me something. But I already guessed what it would show and I hated it. No matter how badly I wanted to belong, how dearly I wanted to draw breath beneath split skies leaking magic and pretend like I had some claim to it, it wasn't for me.

I didn't belong here.

In a blink, the pull of the tapestry was gone, like it had withheld all of its magic and transformed into an ordinary skein of silk. The threads fell flat, all their enigmatic song sewn silent. I dropped my hands uselessly, watching dull light from the window spill onto the floor. The weight of the decision settled across my shoulders like a thorny mantle. My hands clenched, frustration gathering steam and fury inside me.

What would I tell Amar? That no matter how much I tried, I couldn't do the one thing he asked? I felt so caged and foolish that I slammed my palms into the tapestry.

A clap of thunder rattled the sky. I jerked my head up. Thunder? It was hardly overcast a moment ago. As if answering my thoughts, the bruise-colored storm clouds melted away.

I stepped back, cold clattering over my skin. The change in the clouds felt . . . *deliberate,* as if in response to me. That couldn't be right. Nature didn't hear thoughts and adjust itself accordingly. Did it?

Facing the open sky, I thought of rain, and a drizzle started to fall softly. I imagined a blazing hot sun, and rays fractured the sheets of lightning. I gasped, stumbling backward.

What was happening?

The weather was becoming more erratic by the second, fumbling from storm to sunshine, from clear to chaos. Outside, the sky swelled, looming and crackling like some disjointed beast, melding against the palace, spreading blackened veins across the marble in an attempt to reach *me*.

My skin prickled. The air was clammy and heavy, suffused with magic. Alive. Possessive. I felt like all of the palace's watchfulness had ended and now it was turning on me, eager to swallow me whole within its walls.

My heartbeat quickened and I ran from the throne room. But the magic followed, unrelenting. The floor gathered around me, shifting beneath my feet into small hillocks, slick puddles. The balustrades of the palace creaked into life, bending and snapping into trees of ivory and alabaster.

All around me, the doors swung open. Doors that had never once budged when I had tried to open them. Doors that revealed human and animal skins hanging from glinting hooks in the wall. Doors that had nothing behind them but fire unending.

I ran so fast, I almost careened straight into the double doors of the glass garden. Pushing them open, I ran through the crystalline plants until I got to the banyan tree. I tried to clear my head, but my thoughts were no clearer than wisps of smoke.

"Maya—" called a voice in the distance.

The voice was distorted. I flattened myself against the banyan tree. A figure approached me, its edges blurred. I screamed, tripping over a quartet of glass roses, shattering them. Spikes of glass dug into my heels, and a howl ripped from my throat. Hands reached for me, but I fought them off. Desperate. Clawing against the stranger, but the hold was firm. And soon, my vision faded to black.

Voices broke through my foggy dreams.

"She's not ready—" came Gupta's voice from both near and far away.

A crashing sound, of anger and temper, filled the vacuum of silence as I pulled myself out of the fog. I shifted my weight, wincing from a sudden jab of pain. I could still hear Amar and Gupta talking, their words harried and rushed. I lay still, trying to hear more.

"Yes, she is. You've seen what's happening outside." Amar. His voice was so weary. He nearly croaked out his words. "I am always traveling. Always moving. And even then, even being in a thousand places at once, it's not enough."

"She *knows*," said Gupta. "I don't know how, but she's hunting, like she's caught a scent."

Another jab in my side wrenched a gasp from me and I inwardly cursed. If I didn't wake up now, they'd know I was eavesdropping. Carefully, I opened my eyes to a slit, and the gilded ceiling of the bedroom beamed back. I propped myself up, rubbing at my temples as I looked around and caught sight of Amar. Gupta had disappeared.

From the edges of the bed, Amar turned to me. Despite his exhaustion, a smile creased his face.

"Wonderful performance, though misdirected in the end. What do you remember?"

I strained to remember anything . . . but all I saw were flashes. Vikram's dormant red thread, a glint of lightning and the surge of something nameless and powerful snaking through my veins. The tapestry loomed in my mind. A taunt. And then, with the full force of fresh shame, I remembered my failure. The thread wouldn't move.

"What happened?" I asked, my voice barely above a whisper.

Amar sat up and began pacing the room. "Something wonderful."

He grinned and I flinched. His smile was far too knowing to be mistaken as comforting.

"You're beginning to show a sense of power and ability that has always been yours," he said in his silky voice. "It's why I came to Bharata in the first place. To free you. This awakening is what makes you a true ruler of Akaran, it's what lets you control the tapestry."

Nausea roiled in my stomach. The choices I'd made—throwing the wedding garland around his neck, agreeing to flee Bharata—were they ever mine to begin with? In the grand tapestry of Akaran, everything and *everyone* had a thread. Including me. My stomach turned.

What control did I have? The tapestry had rejected me. Perhaps he knew that and that's why he chose me. I would be malleable to his will. But I was done. Done being treated like a child, done being left in the dark, done being instructed. Fury rent through me.

"You know just as well as I do that Vikram's thread never budged," I said stonily.

Amar bowed his head. *Good,* I thought. At least he could fake some guilt.

"I know."

"Why couldn't I? Why did you made it sound like I could? All this talk about being a true ruler here, this . . . awakening of power. Or control. I had no control over that thread. I couldn't even pull it from one side to another."

"It takes time. But it's a start. It's a new beginning," he said. A chill ran up my spine. "For you and me."

He braced his elbows against his knees, the sleeves revealing the bracelet of my hair around his wrist. He had tethered a part of me to him, but I had nothing of his. He kept all his secrets from me.

"Trust me," said Amar. "And tonight, we shall celebrate. Where shall I take you, my queen? Your will is where I lay my head."

My mind twisted into a snarl.

"How can I trust you?"

Amar's grin slipped off his face and his eyes narrowed. "Have I not proven myself? I rescued you from death—"

"You don't know that," I retorted, my voice raising. "Perhaps I would've made a last-minute escape. Perhaps the kingdom would've changed its mind."

"But they didn't, did they?" said Amar coldly. "I'm the one who took you to safety. I'm the one who made you a queen."

"*Queen*? I'm no better than a caged bird," I bit out. The words tasted like bile.

"What would that make me? An owner? You have free rein, as always, over this kingdom. Much more freedom than any caged bird. Think on that. All I ask, for now, is that you don't—"

"Walk alone? Question you? Breathe without your permission?" I offered, knowing what he would say. "I have free rein except when I don't."

I pushed aside the covers, ready to storm out when the silk sheet in my hand *changed*. The entire night sky had become our bed, stars glinted in and out, comets zinging across the part where I had clutched a corner of the sheet. I pushed my hands into the fabric, but they seemed to fall through and through, as if this really was the night sky . . .

The floor had changed too. Deep teal and translucent, the waters of a hundred seas. Beneath the waves, something turned a sightless eye toward me. A *makara* with a tail gleaming long and emerald. The salt smell of the ocean burned my nose. I felt overwhelmed with awe, fright . . . envy. Is *this* what I was capable of? Could I *trust* the person who could do this?

I blinked and the images were gone.

"A strange illusion," I murmured shakily.

"Not an illusion," said Amar. His voice was brittle. "Didn't I promise you the power of a thousand kings?" He crossed the marble floor that had once been an ocean. Water glistened on his feet and a gray fish flopped helplessly in a corner.

He stood in front of me, his eyes hectic and alive. Even through my fury, I couldn't look away from him.

"You and I are the ground and ceiling of our empire," he said, his voice harsh and desperate, pleading and ruthless at once. "You and I can carve lines into the universe and claim all that we want. We need only share between ourselves. Don't you see?"

"All I see is your power," I said. "None of my own. All I see are my words and expectations thrown up against whatever it is that you choose to tell me—"

"—whatever I *can* tell you," finished Amar. "And as for your power, I was hoping you would ask that. It's time to practice."

"Leave me alone," I hissed.

"Your duties in Akaran will pay no heed to the whims of its empress."

I bared my teeth at Amar and he returned it with a half-grin.

"From now on, whatever concentration you use is yours alone. It is your power. Not mine."

"How would I know?"

"You'll feel it in your bones. Like blood singing to marrow."

I slid off the bed and when my feet hit the floor, something silvery trilled through my body, like light had seeped in and was rediscovering me. It was like being full for the first time. Like being weighed and made whole.

"Power needs balance," said Amar. "Our game today, as our reign, is simply a matter of reaction. What can we do when chaos is flung into our face?"

A sound sliced through the air. I looked up just in time to see an arrow heading straight for me.

"What will you do?" asked Amar. His voice was everywhere at once.

I felt a tug in my hands, a strange itch and restlessness. Without thinking, I threw up my hands, all my attention focused on the arrow. It stopped midair. I flicked my hand and it whirled to charge at Amar. He snapped his fingers and the arrow shivered, paled and turned into a blossom of ice.

"I take it you're angry," said Amar. The brittleness from his voice wasn't gone; if anything it seemed more pronounced. "Only two more days until the full moon. Then, if you want, you may certainly fling arrows into my back. Until then, try for more creativity. We cannot just spin problems back. We must do more."

More, I thought. *I could do that.*

I don't know how much time passed while we danced, spinning power between us like it was just another game. He tossed the ball of ice my way and I shattered it.

"What were you thinking when you broke that?" he asked. Even though I saw him across the room, I could feel his voice at my ear, low and burning.

"You."

He laughed and continued to conjure things out of the air and throw them to me. Amar's movements were graceful, spinning. All his power seemed concentrated and sinewy as the muscle that corded his arms and shoulders. Mine felt strange. Lumbering. But instinctual all the same. I'd never felt this way before, as if there was an unexplored dimension in my body full of silver light, ready to be devastating. The power in my veins terrified me. Not just because I knew it was real, but because I wanted it. I reveled in it even as I glared at Amar across the room.

He must have known because he grinned each time we sparred. He flung a chakra of flames in my direction and I turned it to a great wave of water to rush at him. Without blinking, he flattened the whole wave to a plane of ice and slid forward, graceful and serpentine.

"You enjoy it, don't you?"

"You know the answer."

"I want to hear it from your lips."

"We don't always get what we want," I said. "Tell me, this ability of mine was not something the moon prevented you from revealing, was it?"

This time, he had the grace to look guilty.

"No. But such things need a foundation before they can be known. I thought it was best for you. It was a protective measure too. Untested power is a dangerous thing."

Another flash of fury shot through me. *I thought it was best for you.* The light in our room clung to him in silver wisps. Amar pushed his hands through the curls of his hair and in that moment, he looked so . . . lost. In spite of myself, I wanted to ease that pain from his face. To make him smile. I was weak before him.

"This is why you couldn't move the thread," he said. "You need to believe in it. Believe in *you*."

Amar twisted his fingers and the silk of my sari changed . . . from yellow to deepest blue, flecked with stars.

"My star-touched queen," he said softly, as if he was remembering something from long ago. "I would break the world to give you what you want."

I touched my sari and the stars faded.

"I want you to leave," I said, not looking at him.

When I looked up, he was gone.

I stared at the closed door before sinking to my knees. I had been a fool to fall so quickly for Amar's gift: the most beautiful illusion of *independence*. It had felt so real that I thought it hummed in my bones. Now it was gone. Even our kisses felt like treachery. All that was left was the unending and infinite niggling of something that didn't quite fit together—his words, his promises . . . my powers.

I wrapped my arms around my knees. If this power was truly something that was in me all along, why would my mind keep it a secret? A familiar pang struck me. The absence of something unnamed fluttered just beneath the surface of my skin, a secret hovering within reach.

Outside my room, a slamming sound echoed, raising goose bumps along my skin. *What door was that?*

I paused. *The doors.* I remembered them flinging open, all their locks and bindings forgotten. With a lurch, I remembered what lay behind them—swaying bodies, the fug of decay. Fires to drown out worlds.

They had opened to my power. Responded to it like a song.

Guilt tugged at me. In the shadows of the Night Bazaar, I had pledged Amar my trust, my patience. But this was not Amar's secret to keep from me. It was mine. The warning rhyme flashed through my head. Perhaps it was not some aimless trick of the palace. I needed to find the door.

I just had to figure out how.

•» 16 «•

THE MEMORY TREE

A knock at the door pulled me from my thoughts. I opened it, expecting to see Gupta, but it was Amar. His expression looked carved in stone and his lips were set in a grim line. But the moment we held each other's gaze, something in him relented. His hands tightened at his side.

"I would never want to cause you pain."

I flinched. "I am not in pain."

Lie.

"I am not some animal you wounded," I added.

Truth.

"It is only a night longer," he said.

The warning voice from the halls echoed back to me: *You are running out of moon time. Listen to my warning rhyme.* What would happen tomorrow?

Amar hesitated, before reaching out to hold my hand. I stared at the circlet of my hair around his wrist. Bitterness rose in my throat. I glanced from my bracelet to the other one on his wrist—black leather and knotted—dull and malevolent.

"Do these past days mean nothing?" he asked, so gently that my weak self curled around his words.

But I would no longer be weak. I tapped into that power in my veins and a shimmering wall of flames sprang up between us. Amar jumped back, shocked and then . . . amused.

"A little ruthlessness is to be admired, but it's cruel to play with a powerless heart."

"Crueler still to promise equality and hide a person's true self."

"I thought it was best for you," he repeated.

"Strange how something that only affected *me* was decided by *you*."

Amar's smile turned cold. "My promises were true. You seek to punish an illusion without fully knowing. What were your kisses, then? Vengeance?"

The wall of flames shimmered away. Anger still flared inside me, but now it was mixed with something else. Something I couldn't push away, despite fury. *Want.*

"They were nothing," I lied. "They meant nothing."

I didn't look at him. And then, a bloom of cold erupted beside me and Amar was at my side. His fingers traced a secret calligraphy along my arms.

"Nothing at all?"

My heart twisted. I reached forward, my hands tangling in his hair as I kissed him. It was a kiss meant to devour, to summon war. And when I broke it, my voice was harsh:

"My kisses mean nothing."

"Cruel queen," he murmured, tilting my head back. His lips skimmed down my neck. Amar's hands gripped my waist, before tracing the outline of my hips. Heat flared through my body. But just as I pulled him closer, a sudden clash echoed in the hallway, and we sprang apart.

Gupta's screams thundered through the walls, lingered in the air. In an instant, small lanterns sprung up on the blank walls. Amar took off at a run, following the path of light, and I chased after him.

At the end of the row of lanterns, Gupta lay half slumped on the floor. He was shaking violently. His clothes were singed. I looked around, but there was no fire, no scorch marks on the ground or the walls. The only thing that bore signs of damage was Gupta. For all I knew, he might have spontaneously combusted where he stood.

I moved toward him, but Amar blocked me.

"He'll be fine," he said coolly.

I stared at him. Danger had unleashed itself from this very spot and we were standing around like nothing was the matter.

"If there's danger, I should know," I protested.

"Your intentions are admirable, but let me handle this."

"You haven't answered my question," I said in a steely voice.

Gupta's gaze never wavered from Amar. "There was an accident."

"How?" I nearly yelled, pointing to the emptiness of the room, the vast, leering space of the palace.

"Maya," said Amar through clenched teeth. "Return to the room. Immediately. It is not safe."

I stepped back, scolded. Here I was, a child playing queen. Anger flashed through me. I turned on my heel, marching down the halls as shame lit up my cheeks. I stood before my bedroom door, but I refused to enter. If the doors responded to power, then power is what I'd use. I concentrated, curling my power in my palms like a handful of dust, and blew, seeking all the time for one thing—the charred door wrapped in chains. The door with the voice.

The door did not take long to find. I felt like it had been waiting for me and had only made itself known when it sensed my power fluttering against it like the lightest of knocks. Despite the chains and charred frame, it looked oddly ordinary. Just a slab of wood, as any other. At first, the chains wouldn't budge, so I gathered my will and imagined it melting the metal. Like the weather that had bent to my will, the chains wilted beneath my hands. Soon, they were nothing more than a pile at my feet.

I pushed open the door.

Inside, a gigantic tree stood in the middle of the empty room. Unlike the slim trees of my father's court, gnarled trunks and twisted roots swelled this tree to an impossible size. Nestled in its branches and obscuring its leaves were thousands of small candles enclosed in glass cylinders. From a distance, it looked like a tree with stars caught in its limbs.

I rested my hand on the trunk but immediately yanked it away. The tree had a heartbeat. It should have been impossible. Then again, many things that should have been impossible were possible in Akaran. The pulsing light of the tree beckoned me, singing with familiarity. How would it feel to cup the smooth glass against my palm, bathe my face in the candles' light? But I couldn't. This was the first place in Akaran that felt holy. Even the silence was hallowed.

A length of obsidian mirror shined against the wall. I walked toward it, expecting it to be like the other mirrors of Akaran—windows into different worlds—but this showed nothing but an expanse of black space.

Turning back to the tree, I walked around it in circles, staring at the limbs that spun out dark and forbidding, sharp as arrows. But also familiar. Like a beast tamed to know my hand. I reached for the trunk, shocked by its warmth. Slowly, I started to scale the trunk, my hands gripping the smooth dark wood until I was balancing on a tree limb. Out of breath, I leaned against the tree. Below me, the floor gleamed with silver veins.

Reaching for one of the candles, I took it slowly from its niche. It gave way easily. Only when I brought it to my eyes did I see that it wasn't even a flame. It was little more than a slice of bright mirror. And there was something inside . . . an image. A *face*. Startled, I nearly dropped the candle, but the image had taken hold. It spread over me, slipping behind my eyes. In the candle, I saw a girl whose face glowed with the kind of beauty and slow smile that can make a man believe in magic. She spun happily in a grove of trees, her hands pulling someone along . . . another girl, whose face was obscured by a curtain of black hair. I leaned closer. And I knew who she was even before the other girl turned around.

It was me.

I saw myself laughing, calling to the other girl, "Nritti! Slow down!"

My mind was grasping, carding through years of memory, trying to sieve through every moment to explain the impossible: I knew that would be her name. And it wasn't a guess. It was a knee-jerk reaction in my soul.

I stared at myself spinning on a hill. My skin echoed the night sky, velvet black and spangled with diamonds that matched the stars above. Even if we didn't look the same, I knew it was me. There was something more in the image that I couldn't ignore. The pulse of friendship, of warmth. Of memory.

I placed the candle back, my heart thrumming as I stared around me. Every single one of these memories was *mine*. Why would Amar have all of this locked inside a tree? I pulled my sari closer around me, as if it could ward off the chill under my skin.

Then, I reached for another candle and saw the girl I had called Nritti, but this time . . . she was screaming. Her roar was a hideous, heartbroken bellow. She was in the orchard of the Night Bazaar, tears coursing down her face and clutching her heart, her legs crossed beneath her as she rocked back and forth. The image filled me with a strange ache . . . *guilt*. Like it was my fault Nritti was screaming. The image faded. My hands trembled as I put the candle back in its niche, and fumbled for another candle.

. . . This time, Nritti was wandering through the Night

Bazaar, a sunken look in her eyes. Mud and dust caked her feet. Her beautiful clothes were torn and her gaze was searching. Gupta's words rippled through my thoughts. I remembered his exchange with Amar, the worried sound in his voice: *She knows . . . I don't know how, but she's hunting, like she's caught a scent.* I couldn't shake the sense that she was looking for me.

A low sound drifted through the room. Up ahead, the ivory door gleamed brightly and Amar's voice called to me from outside. I froze. I couldn't let him catch me here. There was still so much I had to understand, so much I needed to know.

"Maya?" called Amar again. He was getting closer.

I rushed through the door, murmuring a plea for silence to mute the jangling of my anklets as I tore down the hallways, nearly skidding into the bedroom. I opened the door just in time to see Amar striding toward me. His jacket flashed a fiery red, the light from lanterns throwing his figure into relief. My heart was beating so loudly, I was convinced he would be able to hear it through the silk of my sari.

"I am glad you stayed here," he said, taking my hands in his.

There was that same flitting in my stomach. But I couldn't forget the memories in the tree. I couldn't forget that it was *Amar* who had kept them from me, who had chained them behind iron and consigned them to silence. Amar who had lied. There was no danger behind the doors, only the danger of knowing myself.

"I will come back later. I only wanted to see that you were safe."

"Where are you going?"

Amar's jaw tightened. "I cannot say."

I was tired of this answer. I could *feel* something nameless and evil blooming in every shadow. It wasn't paranoia. I knew it with the certainty of daytime.

Lightly, Amar traced my jaw, his gaze lingering at my lips. Then, he turned on his heel and disappeared behind the halls. I blinked. For a moment, I thought I had seen the snaky tendrils of a noose unraveling from the second bracelet on his wrist.

Where was he going? And if he thought I would stay behind like some petulant child, he was wrong. I waited a few moments and then slipped down the same hallways Amar had entered. As I crossed the halls, a second shadow nearly crossed mine.

A woman's shadow.

My heart clenched. Who was she? I'd never seen another soul in the palace aside from Amar and Gupta. Her clothes were tattered and she moved with a strange, labored effort. Like she was in pain. I crept out of the hall, following the woman down the darkened hallway. I followed her around another corner and this time saw an impossible sight—

Hundreds of people were walking through Akaran's halls.

I flattened myself against the wall, eyeing the crowds who wound through the halls like a great serpent. They were tall, short, fat, skinny, dark, light, young and old. And then I noticed stranger details: a woman with a black and blue neck, a man who looked distinctly gray, a child with something sharp protruding from her side and another man covered in blood. I clapped my hand over my mouth, my throat dry as I sank to my knees.

They were all dead.

The dead walked in droves. Crouching in the shadows, I searched their drained expressions. There was no light in their eyes as they queued outside a wall of scarlet and silver flames.

In the distance, four massive hounds—two pairs of eyes on each side of their heads—kept appearing and disappearing. Their mouths were full of something wet and silvery. Each time they snorted and dropped open their jaws, a soul dropped onto the floor. Hellhounds. I shuddered. Their coats of fur were close cropped, brindled like emerald and diamond.

Gupta stood at the front of the line, a heavy bound book in his arms. "Go quickly to the south wing and await judgment from the Dharma Raja."

The south wing. I paled, turning slowly to a door made of nothing but pale beams of smoke. I recognized the arch beside it—the entrance to the glass garden.

I tried to grab something solid and only vaguely felt a stone pillar against my palm. My knees buckled. I thought of Amar's promise outside the Night Bazaar . . . a kingdom of impossible power. A kingdom that all nations feared.

No wonder I'd never heard of Akaran . . . there was no such thing. I had always been in Naraka—the realm of the dead. Which made Amar the Dharma Raja, the lord of justice in the afterlife. A harsh laugh escaped me.

Partnered with Death.

Death shackled all fates. It was fixed. And all I could do was modify the ambiguities left between. No wonder Amar looked disturbed when I asked whether those who entered the Otherworld died. He knew, and he didn't tell me. Gupta knew too.

I looked around, disoriented as the shadows of the dead striped the white marble of the floors. I was about to leave when a familiar woman caught my eye. Vikram's mother. Her brow still gleamed with sweat and in her hands she carried a bundle of wilting flowers. Her neck was bent too sharply and bits of mountain gravel clung to her hair. She must have fallen.

I retched onto the marble, my body shaking. Amar must have pulled the thread. What outcome was there for the boy? I was disgusted with myself. I wanted to fling myself at the woman's feet, and beg her for forgiveness.

Someone marched beside her. A figure silhouetted in metal, a limp crest of scarlet on its helmet. I remembered the stomping gait, the familiar vermillion sash now tattered and trailing blood. Memory clamped its jaws into my chest: he was a soldier of Bharata. But far, far worse than that—

He was a harem guard.

I remembered taunting him on the day my father told me of his plans. The young guard whom I had never bothered apologizing to. He looked *aged*. Or perhaps it was the cold lights of Naraka slowly teasing out his youth. My heart slammed against my ribs as I watched the line of the dead. Who had he died protecting? And where was he going? Who else would I recognize in these halls?

I wandered far into the line of the dead, pushing past them, refusing to shudder when my skin came away clammy at the contact. By the time I was sure there was no one else from Bharata, I couldn't find my way back to the south wing. The halls skipped around me.

I was losing my way through the palace, but there was nothing I could do. The palace thrummed with its own magic, its own plans. Each step was a small battle against the draining energy of the dead. My skin shifted taut and stretched, as though I were turning skeletal with every movement, weighed down by the pull of magic and spent lives. I found myself at the threshold of the throne room. The doors were flung open and as I stumbled past the entrance, I saw Amar bent over the tapestry. A crown of blackbuck horns gleamed on his head, cruel and slick. In the dark, they looked blood-tinged. His hands roamed over the threads, fingers flicking, yanking, snarled in strands that he pulled out in swift, merciless strokes like he was tearing throats instead of threads.

The threads—whole entire lives—fell noiselessly to the ground. It was a slaughter.

I moved faster, heart racing. I couldn't be caught. Years could have passed by the time I found myself outside the doors of our bedroom. *Our bedroom.* The weight of it sent a stab of pain inside me. I had slept beside him. I had kissed him. I had even . . . begun to feel something for him.

I sank to my knees. I had never escaped my horoscope. I had only been blind to its meaning until now. A wave of revulsion rushed over me as I glanced at the bed we had shared. He had concealed the consequences of my judgments and made me an accomplice to death. He had asked me for patience—for *trust*—but he had betrayed both.

Shadow and light danced across the floor through a sliver in the door frame. What did he want from me? What would happen when the moon had run its course? Outside my window, an ochre glow crept up a nearly dying moon. I shuddered. The warning rhyme flickered in my heart, dredging up old nightmares: *I know the monster in your bed.*

So did I—

Death.

»» 17 ««

A FINE LEGACY

As dawn crept slowly along the floor, my eyes flew open. The memory of my nightmares clamored for attention—dreams of trees incinerating, of silent chasms deep in palaces, of threads being ripped savagely from their place.

Beside me, the weight of the bed shifted. I squeezed my eyes shut, only to feel the brush of Amar's lips against my cheek, the rough stroke of his fingers at my forehead. A humming trilled in my body, but I clenched my fists, waiting for him to leave.

Ache and unrest flooded my bones as I pinched myself to alertness. The room was silent. Amar had left. Pinned to the cushion beside me was a note that said I should rest until the evening. I crumpled the letter. I was done doing what Amar wanted. Ignoring the peacock blue sari on the bed, I smoothed down my silk nightclothes, fixed my hair in a braid and crept outside.

A Bharata soldier had walked these halls. And he had disappeared into them too. Even now, I could picture the dead. I could see Amar ripping out the threads in a bloodless slaughter. The images scalded me. Every time I blinked, all I saw was the deceit that I had welcomed so openly, mistaking it for magic, for power . . . for something deeper.

I willed the shadows to swirl around my feet, mute the jangling of my anklets and conceal me in case the walls were watching. Though the dead had long since passed into the south wing, their echoes lit up the walls, as if the wisps of their lives had stamped burning footprints into the floor.

Slowly, I wound my way through the palace until I stood at the entrance to the glass garden. Behind me, the windows leaked blurry sunlight onto the ground. There was no sign of the smoke and glass door from yesterday. The stonework had swallowed it whole, but even so I could feel it, like a cold shadow. It was hidden somewhere in front of me, wedged between some slice of air. I pressed my hands against the wall, searching inside myself for that spiral of power, that weird sense of calm . . . of *summoning* . . . and the door of the south wing shimmered.

Vast and transient. That is death. I knew because I stood on the other side, peering through a tear in the frame, and all I saw was light. All I heard was my heartbeat's echo fluttering softly, sleepily against my ribs. All I tasted was smoke on my tongue. A dry wind carried pale ashes across my feet and the particles were so fine, it might have been like stepping over pulverized sugarcane.

I could have turned around, but I didn't. Guilt stilled me. Who had I left behind when I fled Bharata? What had I done to them?

Life and death surged from behind the smoky portal, calling me from beyond the door.

Breathing deeply, I pushed open the door. Heat seeped through my skin and I shivered. Cold sludge moved through my veins instead of blood. I turned around the room, my ears straining to hear the whisper of a voice, but only silence met me. There were no exits in the south wing and the only entrance had already closed.

The moment my foot touched the gray floor, lanterns sprung up along the dark halls. Their light was as silvery as moonshine, but cast no shadows. They were only beacons in a haze, like thousands of unblinking eyes. My breath came in ragged heaves, and the straight walk forward felt like an uphill battle. My muscles ached and my head was dizzy, but I pushed through. Eventually, the floor ended, melting into a steep cliff with soft sloping sides of ash. The smell made me nauseated. I could taste funerary ash on my tongue and quickly clasped the end of the sari to my nose. Once more, lanterns lit my way along the edge of the cliff. All along the walls, sheaves of parchment covered in Gupta's neat handwriting fluttered in the windless air. I leaned closer and saw that they were the records of the dead. They stretched in infinite directions.

The sides of the cliff revealed jagged steps leading to the edge of a strange body of water. Sounds bubbled from below. Human ones. Goose bumps erupted along my arms. With one hand touching the craggy slopes, I descended into the depths of Naraka. At the base of the cliffs, a silver pool lapped at the stone. Something about the pool kept teasing my mind, as if there was some reason why I should know about it. From where I stood, the pale moon-bright water looked like a mirror. I leaned over the water's edge and what twisted in its reflection sent me reeling back—

Spectral bodies writhed beneath, turned over and over by invisible mechanics. In its waters, luminous souls were being sheathed with new skins and new identities. Something in the water fitted a silvery lion pelt over transparent shapes; affixed tusks to a humanoid snout; braceleted a dancer's *ghungroo* bells around the ghost of an ankle. This was the reincarnation pool. The place for remaking souls.

I stumbled backward, flailing a hand behind me until it hit rock. Something seared my skin and I turned, eyes widening as the wall of rock shimmered and revealed a thousand rooms sprawled behind it—some filled with ice, others with flame. At first I thought the rooms were empty, but then I saw the souls toiling in the flickering light. Some were digging holes, sweat glittering thickly on their necks. Others hung suspended by chains, their groans echoing in their cells. I knew why they were there. Before passing to the next life, the soul must atone for sins of the past life.

I walked past the sea of cells, relief flooding me each time I didn't recognize someone.

"Mayavati?" called a voice.

I halted in my tracks. Turning to the sound, a cry escaped my lips—the Raja. My father walked toward me, pressing his palms against the wall of glass separating us. Instead of his familiar *kurta*, he wore armor, his worn battle helmet tucked beneath his arm. Chain mail peeled off his body, revealing a dark gash near his rib cage.

"No," I whispered.

I stretched out my hand, but retracted it suddenly and wrapped my arms around myself. The last time I saw him, he wanted me dead. Anger should have welled in my heart. But all I could see was a man wearing the wounds of his death day. A man who had once left me gifts of poetry and knew my name when he could barely recall his number of offspring. A man with regret printed on his features.

I tried to control my breathing, but it came in unsteady halts. His chain mail glinted as he moved toward me, throwing his wounds in stark relief. In Bharata, modesty would demand that I cover my head, avert my eyes and wait for him to speak. But death left no room for formality.

"Were you in pain?" I asked, my voice barely above a whisper.

The Raja shrugged and I winced as the gash on his collarbones widened.

"It was fast," he said, looking away from me.

I knew he was lying, but didn't press him. For the first time, I noticed that the lines of worry from his face were gone. He was calm, even in this glass dungeon. And he smiled at me, a smile filled with unguarded relief, even joy, to see me once more.

He cleared his throat. "My accommodations are not nearly as grand as the palace. But it is better than most. A sin of selfishness demands a penance of introspection, not labor."

I nodded numbly.

"You look well," he said, tilting his head to one side. "I am glad you escaped before they descended on us."

His eyes shone with tears and I wished there was no glass to separate us. I wanted to press my forehead against the lattice of his armor, tell him I forgave him. But he guessed all that I wished to say because he shook his head with a sad smile.

"We lost the war?" I ventured.

The Raja paused. "Bharata won the war. But I am the one who lost. *I* led people to death. *I* allowed my halls to be swallowed by fire. But Bharata survived."

He leaned against a wall of mirror, rubbing his temples. His hair had grayed considerably since the wedding. How was that possible? Had time tricked me as well? And then another wrenching thought went through me. The lack of mirrors in Akaran that showed the viewer. There was a puddle beside my feet, no larger than a palmful of water. But I recognized myself. Perhaps a little lovelier, a little more regal. But still seventeen.

"How long did the war last?" I asked, my voice hoarse.

The Raja blinked at me.

"It was ten years ago," he said slowly. "Surely you've seen your countrymen in these halls?"

I suddenly felt dizzy. *Ten years* had passed since I was in Bharata? When Amar asked me to wait until the full moon, he had spoken of a matter of days, not years. Fresh fury poured through my veins. I hated him.

If I'd seen Bharata's citizens, could I have saved them? I looked up to see the Raja considering me from the wall of his cell. "I never saw them," I said quietly.

He was silent for a moment. "At first I thought you were your mother, come to free me from my hell. Like an angel. You take after her, though you are as young as I remember."

I stared at my ash-covered feet, and the hair that fell in a mussed braid by my side. I thought of Bharata's dead walking past my bedroom while I slept. I thought of Vikram weeping for his dead mother while I kissed the Dharma Raja in a winter room. I was no angel.

"Who rules in your stead?"

"The *yuvuraja,* Skanda," said the Raja, thoughtfully tugging on his beard. Death had not relieved him of all his habits. I almost smiled to see the familiar gesture. "I hope he remembers all I have said. Sometimes I expect to see him across my cell. And I do not know if he will be young as I remember him, or old because time has passed and I am here." He looked at the ground. "Do not pity me, daughter. Everyone comes here. Some merely stay longer than others."

We stared at each other through the glass. I could feel his eyes searching me, trying to match up the memory of when he had last seen me to the person who stood before him now.

"Partnered with Death itself," he said, repeating a part of my horoscope. A harsh laugh escaped him. "I understand now." The Raja moved away from his mirror wall, his eyes twinkling as he bowed low.

The gesture was wrong. My cheeks flared with heat.

"No," I said, "please don't do that."

Pressing my palms against the glass, I willed it away, and slowly, it became thinner and thinner until it disappeared. The Raja, still bent in a bow, looked up in surprise as I walked into his cell. I lifted him up by the shoulders, not letting myself flinch when my fingers brushed against the blood on his armor.

"You do not need to bow to me, Father."

The Raja smiled. "Your forgiveness makes my hell easier to bear."

This conversation, this air of ease unshackled from courtly posturing, struck me. It was so natural. We might have even been close in another lifetime.

"I do not know how you became a princess of Bharata," he said. "Who knows how our last lives slip into the ones we live in now. I will never know those memories. And perhaps that is for the best."

A lump rose in my throat. *I will never know those memories.* The tree behind the chained door . . . it had so *many* memories. All of which, I was convinced, belonged to me. Nritti's image flashed in my head, bright as a flame. I didn't know her from this life, but I must have known her from before.

My father must have seen a look cross over my face because he stepped away from me. "You do not belong here, daughter. Go. Be who you will be. Do not waste your life mourning the dead."

I nodded tightly, my throat thick with so many things left unsaid. "I will not forget you, Father."

He smiled. "That pleases me. A memory is a fine legacy to leave behind."

I stood before the tree filled with memories. My feet still bore the signs of the south wing. Gritty bits of ash clung to my ankles. Each time I blinked, I saw the sea of cells stretched out in front of me like waves.

My father's words echoed in my thoughts. In death, he found

what he could not in life—peace. Even then, my hands curled into fists. A single door, not a thousand miles, had separated me from my father. And Amar had known the whole time. He had gathered the souls of my countrymen, shepherded them to their next lives without once telling me what was happening outside my very door.

On the far side of the wall, the obsidian mirror glittered. It was still a blank expanse of black, but there was something else there . . . a warmth. Like it was awake.

Turning from it, I circled the tree trunk before climbing into the hulking branches, ignoring the snags of boughs that pulled at my hair as I reached higher and higher. When I reached the middle, I caught my breath and grabbed one of the candles. It trembled in my cupped palms and light spilled over my fingers, stealing my vision . . .

I saw Amar bent over the reincarnation pool, his knuckles gripping the water's pebbled edges. There was something in his hand, an amethyst crown. I couldn't tell what he saw in the pool, but whatever it was, it twisted his face in anguish. In fury. In another candle-flame, Amar was cradling a tree limb that held a single flame green as new jealousy. I couldn't understand it. What was he doing? I reached for a final candle and something in my chest splintered—

When I opened my eyes, I was inside Bharata.

To the right were the familiar honeysuckle vines and the copse of trees. On the left was a statue covered in jasmine, where I had once hid Mother Dhina's slippers. My smile faltered.

A sound in the vision caught my attention, and I turned to see three girls standing in front of a decorated tent. I frowned. I knew that tent. It was the snake singers' tent from my tenth Age Day. The two girls had to be Jaya and Malika; therefore, the girl beside them had to be . . . *me*.

The vision changed.

Now I was inside the snake singers' tent, standing before a basket of cobras. Amar stroked the inky creatures, patting their heads. His hands twitched at the defiant, tremulous sound of a voice in the distance. My stomach flipped at the memory—this was the moment I lost the argument against my half-sisters. Any minute now my younger self would be thrust inside the tent.

The vision spun and from the shadows of the tent, I saw myself lying facedown in the dirt. My half-sisters had upturned the baskets of snakes. I watched myself anticipate the cobra's bite, my hands clenched and my eyes squeezed shut as the same snake that Amar had stroked slithered toward me . . . only to flick its tongue playfully around my ears. In the vision, I heard Amar sigh with relief.

And then the image faded, the halo surrounding the flame receding into a miniscule glow. I slumped against the tree. Amar had been there on the eve of my tenth Age Day. He had watched me from the sidelines the entire time.

He had protected me.

I reached for another candle, and this time when the vision took, I froze. I saw the profile of an unfamiliar woman. The vision broadened, revealing the glass garden. The woman bent over a shrub of crystal roses, her hair neatly obscuring her face as she slipped a ruby blossom into Amar's palm.

There was a quiet love in the way the woman gave Amar the

crystal rose; it was a promise and a declaration contained in scarlet fractals. My limbs felt leaden. Over and over, I watched the woman slip the ruby blossom into his waiting palm.

An ache gripped me. He had fooled me into thinking I was anything more than a slighted princess of Bharata. For a second, I wished I had swallowed the poison. At least then I could have felt a semblance of control over my own life. Instead, I was left with the sinking knowledge that nothing had fooled me more than myself. I had been so lonely before that I had mistaken our connection for something other than what it was: betrayal. But then . . . why had he protected me if he loved another?

I yanked my face away from the flame, gasping for air. Resting my forehead against the tree trunk, I breathed in the heady scent of fresh dirt and cloves. I was about to reach for another candle, when I heard a voice below me—

I spun around. There, in the length of obsidian mirror, the image of a girl flickered in and out. I knew her instantly. Nritti. Even in the reflection of the mirror, she was lovely. Her hair fell in black sheets around her, nothing like my own black hair, so erratic the waves looked more like snarls than curls. Her skin was incandescent, a soft shade of honey, the very opposite of my dusky complexion.

"It's really you," she breathed, wavering in the reflection.

She was only a flimsy version of herself, but she seemed trapped behind that portal, flung back behind an obsidian veil. Even now, her voice was intensely familiar and warm.

"Nritti?" I ventured.

She nodded and smiled. "Do you remember me?"

"I—" I faltered. I *knew* her. But I didn't remember her. Not really. I knew her in blips of memory.

"I've been waiting," she said, tears shining in her eyes. "I have been looking for you for centuries. Ever since you were taken and scurried away into that *awful* palace, I knew I would find you. But then all of that"—she stopped, breaking off into a sob—"but then everything changed," she said through gasps of pain.

"Where are you?" I asked. "How did you even . . . know . . . where I was?"

"The mirrors," said Nritti, tapping the black veil. "I knew there was a portal leading from the Otherworld to *his* palace." She snarled *his*, refusing to say Amar's name. "I knew it would be a matter of time and now you're here! The moment you stepped into the room, I could feel it. My own mirror lit up."

I said nothing, words failing me. Distantly, I heard Gupta's voice in the back of my mind, shining like a warning.

There are places behind our doors that must never be opened because of what they hide . . . They can sense an invitation by something as small as another person's lungs filling with air in the same room and it's like a lightning bolt, like a conduit of destruction.

"So you know now . . . you know what he's capable of," said Nritti through the mirror. She pressed her hands against the glass, like she was desperate to be free. "We have to get you out."

I nodded, still numb. All those threads being pulled from the tapestry. All those people wandering the halls close by where I slept. Oblivious. All those promises and dreams he had kindled in my head.

I looked at Nritti. "Where have you been? Why now?"

She gave me a pitiful expression and I felt chastened beneath her stare. "It's hard work to get into this part of Naraka. And harder to stay."

"Tell me everything," I said. "How do we know each other?"

"We grew up together," said Nritti. She pointed vaguely at the memories above. "Our story is somewhere in that tree. We were like sisters, you and me."

I frowned. But what about the memory of Amar and the other woman? That had been his, hadn't it?

"There was someone else," I began, "a woman, she—"

"There's always a woman," said Nritti, with a flippant wave of her hand. "He traps them here. He finds one girl, lovely or not, it doesn't matter. And he feeds off of them. He is Death, he can do anything he wants."

"But why was it in my memory?"

"You must have found out what he was up to," said Nritti in a rushed voice. There was sweat gleaming on her brow. And a smell, like metal, perfumed the air. "I am sure you figured out in the end what he had planned. Perhaps you found the other girl's memory tree and that's why it's there."

I felt a leaden pit in my stomach. "There's more?"

"Oh yes," said Nritti. "Hundreds of trees, hundreds of girls. Just like you."

I fell silent. Had I been wrong the whole time? I thought I had seen an expression of love between the woman in the flame and Amar. But he was ancient and deathless. Perhaps he had just learned how to cull a heart, like he had a soul.

"But how do you know?"

Nritti flashed a thin, pitiful smile, like she was explaining a child's redundant question. "Was your horoscope something horribly grim?" asked Nritti.

I nodded.

"All of them are," said Nritti with a sigh. Her words were so casual, but they slid into me, sharp as knives. *He finds one girl, lovely or not, it doesn't matter.* I didn't matter. "And then he seduces them, tricks them with power, makes them think that it's real . . ."

I remembered how the weather had changed outside the throne room. How the floor had shifted beneath my feet, and at the end of it, I had collapsed in the glass garden, falling straight into his arms. He had planned all of it. My hands curled into fists, and I pressed them against my chest. In Bharata, at least I had the solace of holding my mother's necklace. But I had nothing to hold on to, nothing but words and thin air and false hope.

"Last time, you got away," said Nritti, her voice dropping to a whisper. "I don't know how, but you did it. And I thought," she stammered, "I thought you were dead. But something led me back to you." She smiled, but it was a cold thing, feverish and burning.

"What was it?"

"Oh, I don't know," she said. Another smile. Another burst of cold. "Maybe it was something in the wind or a change in my heart." She brought her fingers to her heart, her beautiful eyes cast downward. There was so much desperation in her eyes. I felt heartless for not trusting her. "But I knew I only had a number of days before I could get to you."

"The new moon?" I guessed.

Her head snapped up, and something dark flared in her lovely eyes.

"Yes," she said. "Why? Has it already happened?"

"No, I don't think so," I murmured. "I just remember that that's when—"

"That's when he'll *kill* you," said Nritti. "You've seen him. He cannot stand being crossed. The first time you were here, you got away. Somehow you must have gotten to the reincarnation pool to escape him. It must have taken him years to find you again. But he locked away all those old memories. He would never want you to find out who you had been. His arrogance couldn't stand that a girl escaped his grasp."

I thought of those oaths Amar had promised. The beads of blood brimming on his palm. That kiss. Even the memory of him saving me. He was keeping me alive to kill me for later. I scolded myself. My own foolishness was looking for scraps to grasp at, something that would validate all of the poor decisions I had made. How weak I had sounded. I clenched my teeth. I wouldn't be weak for him.

Something splintered inside me. Nritti had to be right. No wonder Gupta and Amar had warned me away from all the hidden doors in Akaran. No doubt, they didn't want me to find out. All those voices I had heard. Who did they belong to? Girls trapped inside of trees? Or were they the plaintive voices of the dead, calling to me. Warning me.

"Who was I in my last life, then?"

Nritti smiled. "You were my friend. I am an *apsara,* but I left all of that behind the moment I lost you. I don't know why you went away with him. But I can see why you were seduced . . . a powerful kingdom . . . leaving behind a place of obscurity."

An *apsara*? That made her a heavenly nymph. I wasn't surprised. She was easily the most beautiful person I had ever seen. And as for the reason why I would be seduced to follow Amar . . . even that made sense. It was the same in Bharata. That constant need to leave, to prove myself, to rise above the nameless, dreamless ranks of the harem women.

"You meant so much to me," said Nritti, tears shining in her eyes. "You still do. I would've done anything to keep you safe. I know you would have done the same for me. I just needed you to lead me."

"Was I, also, an *apsara*?"

I felt stupid asking such a question. Of course I wasn't. Nritti flashed a sympathetic smile.

"No. You were a forest *yakshini* and you knew those woods so well."

I nodded, trying to wrap my mind around this version of myself that she was telling me. I sounded like a cowering thing, resigned to silence and shadows. But maybe that was the way it was always supposed to be. Here, I was nothing more than an imposter playing at power and failing miserably.

Nritti placed her hand against the glass. "I don't know how much longer I can stay at this portal. I'm risking my life for you with every passing minute, but I won't let you be unsafe. There's something you need to do. To be free."

"What?"

"Bring me his noose and destroy the tree. He'll never find you again after that. And then you and I can escape. We can go back to the Otherworld. We can free all the other girls trapped in this kingdom."

All the other girls. My throat tightened and I nodded tersely.

"Where does he keep the noose?"

"It is always on his person. Perhaps not in the same form."

My heart clenched. The black strip of leather around his wrist. Right next to my own circlet of hair. It had to be the noose. The source of his power. The noose was how the Dharma Raja dragged the souls to his dread kingdom before they were assigned to a new life.

"The tree *needs* to be destroyed. Do you understand?" Her reflection wavered and her voice was strangely harsh. "He will kill you if you give him the chance."

Before I could say anything, the door glowed blue. Someone was near.

"I have to go."

"Are you ready for this, sister?" asked Nritti.

I nodded. "I'm ready."

Footsteps echoed outside the door. I clambered down the tree, throwing one last glance at Nritti's waning reflection in the obsidian mirror before running out into the hall. The door closed with a soft thud behind me, the glowing blue of its walls fading and melding back into white. I breathed a sigh of relief, my hands still pressed against the wood.

Voices snaked through the halls, hushed and urgent. I was still reeling from Nritti's words. *He will kill you if you give him the chance.* I knew I had to be on guard. I'd only seen a few of the memories in the tree, but they had all the intimacy of realness. My friendship with Nritti, even the way my instincts told me to trust her. That she wouldn't hurt me. Even then, I clasped the memory of the days Amar and I had spent together close to my chest. The way he looked at me, an amazed smile turning his face incandescently beautiful. The embraces of fire and starlight when he kissed me. How could they be false?

But then I heard Gupta's voice in the hallway . . . his words reached me. Roped around me.

"Tomorrow is the new moon. You need not worry any longer. Everything you've done, saving her life and bringing her here . . . it will all be worth it," he said. "Now that she's here, we can get rid of her the way you always wanted. I am confident of it."

I backed against the wall. In that second, every space was too tight and each light glinted with malice. *Here* was the reason. He had been waiting for the right time to get rid of me, the right way to exact vengeance. Nritti was right.

He would kill me if I gave him the chance.

·» 18 «·

THE TRUTH, AT LAST

I stayed in the shadows, waiting for their footsteps.

"There is still much to do before then," said Gupta. "You must anticipate her response."

"She's ready," said Amar impatiently. "I have waited long enough and I will not be denied."

I pressed myself against the wall, praying I wouldn't be caught. I thought back to Amar's words in the tapestry room. *Weakness is a luxury you can no longer afford*. How right he had been. Friendship had weakened me. Even Gupta's friendship had been a ruse, a means of distracting me, a blindfold as they trapped me in the halls of death.

Soon, their voices faded into the distance.

I stepped out, my breath clammy in my lungs. Outside, a hundred mirrors loomed, each displaying a picture of night. Some of these nighttime scenes looked out over lush valleys sprinkled with snow. Others stretched out over huge tracts of sea, reflecting the skies in the water so that the stars seemed endless. At the end of the hall, the door to a new room was cracked open. A strange smell unraveled from the door, heavy with the stench of blood. I felt the hairs at the back of my neck rise. Slowly, I pushed open the door and glanced inside. What I saw nearly froze my heart.

It was filled with all the objects from my father's palace.

Torn chain mail, scraps of silk, an ink-blotted scroll bearing my father's sigil. Something sparkling caught my eye and I blinked rapidly, convinced my eyes were playing tricks on me. Even before I reached the object, I knew what it was—my mother's blue sapphire necklace. The one I gave Gauri.

The invisible prospect of everything that could have—*must have*—gone wrong wrenched inside me as sharp as any dagger. I sank to the ground, refusing to touch the thing. Scuff marks framed the delicate strands of pearl, the dull pendant of sapphire. Someone had tried, and failed, to kick it out of sight.

Someone had not wanted me to see.

I pulled the sapphire necklace from its hiding place. Red and gray spots flecked the seed pearls. I traced the sapphire orb just as something crumbling and brown fell onto my fingertips. Dried blood. The whole necklace was soaked in blood.

A cold veil fell about me. Time leeched, memories heavy with Gauri's bright smile spilling behind my eyes. My shoulders caved as I clutched the necklace. My lips formed around Gauri's name, but I wouldn't speak it aloud. I refused to say a name that pulsed with life while I held this bloody necklace in my hand.

I inhaled a shuddering breath. I understood now. Amar's silence about Bharata, the fact that none of the mirror portals looked over my father's kingdom. Everything was fitting together. Horror—bright and heavy—gripped me. My mind flashed with images dredged up from the depths of my nightmares—

Gauri holding the necklace.

Gauri screaming.

Gauri bleeding to death on the harem floor.

And I knew what I had to do. No matter what it cost me. Tonight, I would steal his noose and deliver it to Nritti. Tonight, I would bring him to his knees and make him pay for all that he had done.

Tonight, I would destroy him.

The whole evening, I paced across the floor. I tried not to look at the bed we shared, but it was impossible. The light kept catching on the gossamer veils, a reminder that some terrors were silk-cloaked and lovely as a dream. I knew Amar would come. I knew what I had to do. The problem was my own weak heart, lulled by his words, his touch, his presence.

For tonight, I had slipped into a black sari. I wore no bangles or anklets. My hair was brushed away from my face and a single pearl hung from a silver circlet around my forehead. I slid my hands along the silk and small stars flickered into life against the fabric.

The door creaked open and there he was.

"My star-touched queen," he said. "I missed you."

He walked toward me. In the candle-lit glow of our bedroom,

every feature was more pronounced. The sweep of his shoulders, the short hair that curled at his neck. The glow of his skin, honey-drenched and russet. My beautiful nightmare.

I caught his hand in mine, my fingers trailing over the band of leather around his wrist. The noose. Against my skin, the noose was a cold pulse. There was a small knot at its base, lazily tied. He probably hadn't expected it was in any danger.

"We lost an entire day together," he said.

I loosened the silk around my waist and Amar raised an eyebrow. Around him, the shadows rippled silkily. I met his gaze and he stared at me, his breath shallow and waiting. The silk fell noiselessly to the floor.

"We still have the night."

The moment he touched me, my universe constricted to the space between our lips. We were a snarl of limbs and bright-burning kisses. Amar held me to him, strong hands burning against my neck and waist. And even though vengeance thrummed in my skin, a part of me drowned in the feel of him. He murmured my name with each kiss until it no longer seemed to belong to me. It was a song, a prayer, a plea.

But when I pulled him to the bed, he paused. His breathing was ragged and when he looked at me his eyes were damp with desire.

"Wait, my queen," he breathed. "I want you to know me first. I want you to know this place where you are empress."

He rubbed his thumb along my jaw and the braceleted noose around his wrist glared. Disbelief coiled sharply in my throat. I already knew about this realm. I already knew who he was. But I almost forgot when he reached out to trace my lips.

"Any farther," he started, his voice hoarse with want, "and I would not know how to stop."

We spent the evening in each other's arms. Amar plucked glass blossoms from the air and slid them one by one into a crown around my forehead. He conjured the lightest of snowfalls, each flake teasing out into gleaming feathers before melting into the silk. All through the night, he smiled daggers into my heart.

"I love you," he murmured into my hair. "You are my night and stars, the fate I would fix myself to in any life."

I had chosen vengeance and freedom. I would not back down for sweet words, no matter how much I wanted them to be true. No matter how I felt.

"I know," I said.

While he slept, I betrayed him.

I wove my own magic. A dream of sleep full of silvery spangles that I slipped over his eyes in the same moment that I stole away the noose. The noose fought against me, perhaps aware that I was not its rightful owner. I gathered Gauri's necklace from its hidden place in the corner of the bedroom and pushed open the door.

I didn't look back.

Nritti was waiting for me.

"Do you have it, sister?"

I nodded numbly. When I bit my lip, I could still taste him. Smoke and cinnamon.

"Give it to me," she said, extending a hand through the reflection.

I hesitated. "What will happen to him?"

Nritti arched an eyebrow. "What he deserves. He will be rendered powerless. Don't tell me you have grown to care for him? After all he's done? To you and to so many other women?"

Nritti stepped aside and behind her, another image wavered in the obsidian mirror. A hundred trees filled with lights. The trees of other girls. Other victims. My hands clenched around Gauri's necklace. Wordlessly, I handed over Amar's noose.

The moment I did, something sizzled and snapped through the air. My heart plummeted. Behind us, the great tree full of memories seemed to gasp and twist. The tree—once massive and stretching toward the ceiling—had begun to decay. Thick branches lay around it like bones. Its trunk was rent, entrails of wood and root rising, shattering the marble floor and uncurling toward us. My gaze trailed toward the branches—everything was on fire.

Flickering memories began to drop, falling out of the branches. I stepped back, horrified. The memories fell like a score of dying phoenixes. All around us, the air was suffused with smoke; violet-bruise flames snaked around the edges of the marble, gorging themselves on branch and root.

The blue arch of the door glowed, swinging open. I threw up my arms against the sudden wave of heat. In the doorway, cut like a silhouette of night, stood Amar. He looked between me and Nritti, his gaze fixed on the noose in her hands before he turned to stare at the great tree. Horror was etched into his face. He looked at me and I felt like collapsing. His shoulders sagged and in his expression there was more than heartbreak. It was sorrow given shape.

"No," he whispered, his face gaunt. "What have you done?"

I flinched, as though slapped.

"You lied to me. About everything."

I thought of Bharata littered with the refuse of war. I thought of Gauri. "My home . . . my people were destroyed. You knew, but refused to tell me. Do you deny it?"

My anger was an element. Heat slashed through the air between us, dragging claws of invisible flames. That nameless power growled at my heels, like a beast ready to rend flesh at my word.

I wanted to hurt Amar. I wanted my anger to bruise him, burn him, as if all that heat and fury could weld back my mangled heart. But at the sight of him . . . I hesitated. In the pale light, Amar's hands trembled.

"The deaths were fixed. There's nothing you could've done."

Behind me, Nritti let out a deranged laugh. "Lies. Oh, so many lies you spin, oh Dharma Raja. Without you, there would be no fixed death. There would be no death at all."

I shivered at the sound of her words.

He turned from me, hands raking through his hair, pacing across the marble. I shrank back. "Those memories were not to be disturbed until you were deathless! They were to protect you, Maya."

"I'm protecting her now," said Nritti.

I turned around. Nritti was no longer in the portal. She had stepped out, and behind her, there was nothing but a broken mirror. Memories exploded around her, and each time they did, I winced. Whatever secrets they held extinguished on the marble.

There was a knife in Nritti's hand, a manic glint in her eyes. Gone was the soft honey color of her skin. Even her hair seemed to pale and dull, no longer the beautiful, glossy sheets of black that had once hung around her shoulders.

Nritti looked at me, a smile of camaraderie lighting her face. She placed the knife on the floor and kicked it across the tile, where it clattered against my foot.

"Take it, sister," she crooned. Her voice sounded different. Still familiar, but there was no warmth to it, and I couldn't remember why. "Plunge it into the tree. Reclaim yourself."

"Leave us, Nritti," said Amar. His voice thundered through the room. "I will not let your chaos hurt her or come between us ever again."

"Or what?" taunted Nritti. She tilted her head to one side, like this was a game. "Will you chase me down like you've done my sister? Will you trap my memories in some dingy chamber and lord them over me?"

"That is a lie, and you know it," he growled.

"You know I tell the truth, sister," said Nritti, turning to me. "You cannot deny the memory of us in that tree. You cannot deny how familiar I am to you. Familiar as flesh. I would never hurt you. I only want to protect you. I've spent years searching for you—"

"Don't listen to her," hissed Amar. "You have to trust me, my love. There has only been you. I know who you are. You are my queen. You always have been."

I couldn't look at him, but I could feel his gaze on me. So pained and tender that I fought the need to run to him, to comfort him. But I couldn't push out the image of the woman in the glass garden. I couldn't forget Gauri's necklace encrusted with blood. I couldn't forget how he had hinted at some latent power within me, and yet I couldn't move a single thread on the tapestry.

I couldn't forget his lies.

"Go near that tree and I will lose you forever," he said fiercely. "Your memories won't keep. Your *powers* will be gone." Amar staggered toward me, and this time, I couldn't help but look at him. His eyes held mine in a firm, unyielding gaze. "*Jaani,* I put too much of myself and my own memories into the tree."

Around us, the candles sputtered, their mirror shards brightening like miniscule comets before extinguishing into smoke and ash. Each time a light went out, Amar clutched at his rib cage, as if something was tearing at his heart. By now the flames had reached the middle of the trunk, writhing golden and serpentine, spitting out ash and memory.

"You must destroy the tree now!" roared Nritti. "He lied to you. I would never lie to you. Don't let yourself be one of the many women who was fooled by him. Do not look at him, sister. Look at *me*. I am the one who came here to protect you."

Each memory roared. I could hear the fire warping the voice of my past life, turning it into shrills and bellows. Voices burst from the trunk, echoing in the room. It was fire and chaos and sound. I backed against the tree trunk, the knife gleaming with sweat in my hands.

Amar's eyes darted between me and the tree, but I refused to move. I tried to summon the tingling sensation of power, but it only buzzed weakly at my fingertips before abandoning me. The tree was beyond my control.

Amar shut his eyes. When he spoke, his voice was haggard, sweat shining on his neck. "Destroy that tree and I will be stripped of my memories. No one will remember who you are or what you mean to me," he said, his voice rasping.

"He's lying to you!" screeched Nritti. "You will not remember *yourself* if you do not destroy the tree while you have the chance. Whatever you do, do not look at him."

The tree's shadow lengthened, its limbs stretched forward in glaring whorls of branches. Everything loosened. Whole branches the size of full-grown men spluttered to the floor, splintering like glass. The room was spinning. All the smoke from the extinguishing memories wreathed my hair and filled my lungs. I tried to fight the dizziness, to focus on Amar's and Nritti's faces, but they seemed far away.

I couldn't fade away. I couldn't let myself be lulled to weakness out of false love. Tears streamed down my face, pooling on my neck. My lips were full of salt. No matter how I felt about Amar, one thing was true—

I didn't trust him.

I plunged the knife into the tree, pushing all my force, my heartbreak, my broken dreams, into the tree's thick bark. Shrieks tore through the room. I heard Nritti yelling, laughing, and it felt *wrong*. Her laugh . . . it was identical to that of the intruder in my room. Had it been *her*?

I need you to lead me . . .

Instinctively, my eyes clasped on Amar's. He was shocked, his face pale. He grabbed me; his hands entangled in my hair even as my fingers were wrapped around the hilt that destroyed him.

"I love you, *jaani*. My soul could never forget you. It would retrace every step until it found you." He looked at me, his dark eyes dulling, as if all the love that had once lit them to black mirrors was slowly disappearing. "Save me."

The glow of the candles cast pools of light onto the ground, illuminating his profile. I knew, now, why Nritti begged me not to look at him. His gaze unlocked something in me. It was both visceral and ephemeral, like heavy light. The eyes of death revealed every recess of the soul and every locked-away memory of my past and present life converged into one gaze . . .

I was weightless, my vision unfocused and hazy until the memory of the woman in the glass garden engulfed me. Slowly, the woman turned and a wave of shock shot through me—I was staring at myself.

I remembered another life . . .

Once, my skin wasn't covered in smooth snake scales like the *naga* women or striped in hide like the shape-shifting maidens. Once, my skin bled from one hue to the next, shifting to reflect the transition from evening to night. Before, I never left the riverbanks unless my skin was the cream and pink of a newborn sunset.

But something had changed . . . I had met someone. Someone who had seen me the way I was and had not sneered. He had *seen* me, reached for me when my skin was velvet black and star-speckled. I could still feel his stare—lush as obsidian, star-bright and pouring into the crevices of my dreams.

I remembered meeting the Dharma Raja's gaze and wreathing his neck with a wedding garland of sweet marigold and blood red roses. Death clung to him subtly, robbing the warmth of his eyes and silvering his beauty with a wintry touch. And yet, I saw how he was beautiful. It was his presence that conjured the brilliant peacock shades of the late-season monsoon sky. It was his aura that withered sun-ripe mangos and ushered in the lush winter fruits of custard apple and *singhora* chestnuts. And it was his stride that adorned the Kalidas Mountains with coronets of snow clouds.

His hands moved to my shoulders, warm and solid, and his arms were a universe for me alone. He had enthralled me, unwound the seams of my being until I was filled with the sight of him and still ached with *want*.

"I hoped you would choose me," he said.

I blushed, suddenly aware of my unbraceleted arms and simple sari. "I have no dowry."

He laughed, a hesitant, half-nervous sound that did not match his stern features. "I don't care."

"Then what do you want from me?"

"I want to lie beside you and know the weight of your dreams," he said, brushing his lips against my knuckles. "I want to share whole worlds with you and write your name in the stars." He moved closer and a chorus of songbirds twittered silver melodies. "I want to measure eternity with your laughter." Now, he stood inches from me; his rough hands encircled my waist. "Be my queen and I promise you a life where you will never be bored. I promise you more power than a hundred kings. And I promise you that we will always be equals."

I grinned. "Not my soul then, Dharma Raja?"

"Would you entrust me with something so precious?"

I was silent for a moment before reaching for my foot and slipping off the worn slipper. "Here, my love, the dowry of a sole."

I began to laugh, giddily, drunkenly, before he swallowed my laughter in a kiss. I melted against him, arcing into the enclosure of his arms, my breath catching as his fingers entwined in the down of my hair. The music of the songbirds could not compare to the euphony billowing inside me, pressing against my bones and manifesting in a language of gentle touch.

In Naraka, he drew me into the small universe of his embrace, laying kisses at my neck, the inside of my wrists, the dip in my abdomen. Now, the hum had settled to a lustrous melody, ribboning us like silk. And when we clung together, we drank in the other's gaze, reveling in the secret hope and happiness that blossomed in the space between our lips.

Amar wore many names. Samana, "the leveler"; Kala, "time"; Antaka, "he who puts an end to life." But I had called him *jaan*, "my life," and kissed the gloom from the tips of his fingers. Together we had sleeved souls in new bodies, slipped the soul's crux into a golden-ruffed sunbear or a handsome prince or a troublesome gnat. Together, we danced a quiet happiness, fashioning a room for stars and skimming our palms across cities kept behind mirrors. We drank ambrosia from each other's cupped palms and tended to our garden of glass. And on and on it went.

I remembered . . .

. . . how acrid heartbreak tastes. I remembered the walk to the edge of the reincarnation cycle—the chill of marble, my plumed breath, betrayal prizing apart my heart.

I remembered fury enthralling me body and bone. I remembered light lapping over my eyes and my soul unraveling, fracturing into prisms of amethyst, lapis, topaz. I remembered a needling twinge of regret and the secret, terrible knowledge that somewhere in Naraka my abandonment would leave behind a chasm of obsidian threads—a chronic rift.

I saw . . .

. . . Amar slumped onto his throne, refusing to look at the empty seat on his left. Gupta was at his side, his face pinched, skin sallow.

"Go over every birth record, every horoscope until we find her again. I want—" He stopped, jaw tightening. "I need her back. I made a mistake."

"How will I know it's her?"

"The stars will not lie," said Amar. "A girl partnered with Death, a marriage that puts her on the brink of destruction and peace, horror and happiness, dark and light. Find her."

"But even if you bring her back, how will she know—"

"I have taken care of that," he said sharply.

In his hand was a small branch and a fledgling candle. "I have preserved every memory in the heart of Naraka."

"A fitting place," said Gupta in a small voice, but he frowned. "But then what? Mortals cannot receive such divine information. It destroys them. Not even you can break those sacred boundaries."

"There is a way," said Amar, breathing deeply. "I cannot tell them to a mortal. But if she becomes immortal . . ."

"Ah . . . clever," said Gupta. "The Otherworld may stop you from divulging those secrets, but a mortal that does not pass through the halls of the dead would eventually be deathless."

Amar nodded. "Sixty turns of the moon. A handful of weeks in our halls. And then I can reveal the memories of her past life. Her powers will be restored. She will be a queen once more. But until then, she needs protection. Nritti will no doubt try to find her. She knows she has gone missing. She can feel it, and it fuels her destructiveness. Nritti can never know where she is. Or who she was."

I jolted backward, my breath knocked out in a rush. Spots of light appeared each time I blinked. I shut my eyes tightly, but the images wouldn't relent. All the love and resignation of my former self, each memory of my past life drifted through me, fitting into my mind like lost pieces of a grand puzzle.

But it was short-lived.

The memories fled as quickly as they came, leaving only ghostly imprints. Like plunging into a vat of warmth before being thrown back into the cold. I shivered. My soul was nothing more than a patchwork of half-memory dipped in rime. Incomplete. And made worse by the knowledge of its own fragments.

Around me, there was nothing but the expanse of evening sky. Stars were beginning to shoulder their way for a place in the tapestry of night. Cold that had nothing to do with myself seeped around me. It was frigid. And yet, the air was full of smoke.

Naraka was gone. No marble met my feet, no splintered branches filled with burning memories fell across my ankles. There was no Amar, pulling my face to his—one last kiss before I damned him. There was no Nritti. My hands curled into fists. Now here I was. Exiled. I had no idea what Nritti had planned, but Amar's words—*save me*—clung to me. My head was spinning with questions . . . why had I left Naraka? What *happened*?

A thousand questions gripped me, but no question cut me deeper than one:

What had I done?

PART TWO

THE FORGOTTEN QUEEN

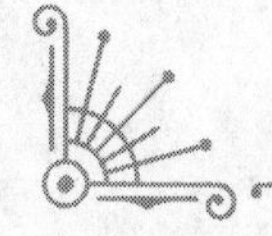

•» 19 «•

THE *SADHVI*

At first, I didn't know where I was. But then the landscape became familiar. I had seen this place, once, from the turrets of Bharata. The stench of smoke and charring bodies filled my lungs. All along the horizon stretched nothing but gray piles of ash, studded with bone. They unrolled toward the horizon, thick as sand dunes. No light penetrated those hillocks of the dead. Small fires wrapped around them, feasting on burning logs and pine. The over-sweet scent of flaming marigolds, *tulsi* and mint stamped the air.

Cremation grounds.

Why was I here?

I choked back my nausea until I saw that I was standing in my own grave. Around me, like the mementoes of the dead, were small objects covered in a fine sieve of dust. I knelt down, my fingers closing around the broken bracelet of my hair that had been around Amar's wrist. Tears burned behind my eyes.

My hand closed around other things too. An onyx stone that was no bigger than my thumb. Its edges had been sawed off into slick rock. The color was the same velvet black of Amar's eyes. I turned it over. Two glittering pinpricks of light shimmered beneath the surface of the onyx. I traced the light, something sharp burgeoning within me. They were memories. *My* memories. Against everything, a half-smile quirked at my lips.

And then there was my mother's necklace . . . still dotted with rusted blood. The sapphire pendant dulled to a near navy-black. I clasped it around my neck, the barest ghost of strength warming me. By now, the sun was beginning to rise and a gray dawn ate away the night.

I knelt on the ground, my knees pressed against my chest. Ripped from Naraka, my soul was left *grasping*. All those memories had flown through me. For one peerless second, I was whole. I knew, only vaguely, who I had been. The Rani of Naraka. But it lacked all the real weight of knowledge. It was just something I had been told. There were other things, though, that I couldn't forget. I knew that what was between me and Amar was real. And I had destroyed him, lulled by what Nritti had shown me. We had been friends. We had been sisters. What happened?

I was no *apsara* like Nritti. That day, what felt like a century ago, she had told me that I was a forest spirit, a *yakshini*. But I had seen me. I had recognized myself . . . sooty dark skin. Coated with stars. And I felt that she was wrong . . . that maybe, she had lied. It wasn't arrogance, just a deep-seated instinct in my chest. But instinct, so far, had betrayed me. I had nothing to go on but what two people had shouted at me before a burning tree. Even now, even after everything Nritti did, I loved them.

I clambered out of the hole, gripping the two tokens I had of Naraka. Beside me, a silver puddle of water caught the light. I had not seen myself since my time in Naraka. My father had said I looked different. Changed. But leaving Naraka had changed me too. When I looked down, the sari of darkest sapphire was gone. No anklets adorned my feet. No bracelets cuffed at my wrist. I was wearing the torn, turmeric-yellow robes of an ascetic *sadhvi* woman.

In Bharata, *sadhus* and *sadhvis* were considered dead. They held no records. No land. No property to claim their own. Some were even known to attend their own funerals, to signify their separation from the mortal world. Somehow, being exiled by both Bharata and Naraka had turned me into one of them. A member of the living dead. My skin was gray, slicked in ash like rough, interlocking scales. I knelt over the pool, my heart hammering. What had I become?

Black hair coiled around my forehead, strung with porcelain beads. My skin was the same sooty, dusky complexion I had always known, but there was something more. My face had changed. I had finally grown into my nose. My forehead was high. Full lips curved downward in a grimace. Thick brows framed my eyes and my gaze was an angry, furious . . . heartbroken thing. But I was not unlovely. And, more than anything, I began to recognize a little of that woman from the memory. The woman who had pruned a crystal rose in a garden of glass. The woman whom Amar had looked at, as though she held the universe in her gaze, as if galaxies lined her smile, as though she were myths and love and song contained in one body.

Tears burned behind my eyes. Cursed impulse. Foolish decisions. I kicked ash and bone into the puddle, scattering my reflection before I turned once more to the bleak landscape. There was no one attending the fires. Family members or loved ones who had lit the pyres had since left.

There had to be communes for *sadhvis*. Places where people would allow them to enter their homes. I remembered from the archives in Bharata that they were at once revered as much as they were repulsed. No one would break bread with a *sadhvi*. But no one would turn her away either. It was best to throw money at her feet, bow and run away before she could ask for more.

Mother Dhina's needling comments flickered in my head. "*Sadhvis* hold communes with ghostly *bhuts*, whisper to snakes and make their beds on funerary ash. Perhaps *you* should join them, Maya."

I grimaced. She had been right.

Still, how would I get to Naraka? How would I find my way back to the Otherworld?

I was still turning over Amar's words, trying to find some sliver of reason when the darkness rustled. Something tall and bestial rose on unsteady legs, unfolding itself from the shadows and pools of flame where a dead body had charred into something nearly unrecognizable. My heart thudded in my chest. What *was* that? I had nothing to defend myself. No weapon on hand except for the blunt end of my mother's necklace and I knew that would do nothing.

A painfully thin horse emerged. It looked like it had one hoof on death's doorstep. Although, given where I stood, maybe it did. Its bones jutted out of translucent skin and a dark bulge that could only be the animal's heart quivered between spindly legs. The horse turned its skeletal face toward me, snorting to remove the gray wisps of hair from its face. A pearly sheen coated its milky eyes.

"What are you?" asked the horse. Her voice was rasping, shadowy, like corrugated steel dragged across marble. "You can see me, can't you, false *sadhvi*? Oh, your fear is a thing so lovely. Like a salt wheel. I could lick it if you gave me the chance. I am all out of sustenance, as you can see."

I'd never heard a voice so cold. My knees buckled. The horse jolted her head to the charring body beside her.

"He dreamed of barley his whole life and yet he worked in rice paddies. Strange are the ways of humans. But I am more interested in you. Not human. You don't smell of sweat and reek of lust. But you are not Otherworldly either."

The horse cocked her head to one side, a quizzical motion. And then she smiled, revealing bloodstained teeth. I suppressed a shudder. "I don't think I've ever eaten anything like you. Such a delectable morsel. May I take a bite? Just one . . . or maybe two . . ."

"No," I said firmly, digging my heels into the ground and crossing my arms.

"Oh, look at that," said the horse. "Feisty too. I bet you taste like spice and cinnamon. I bet you taste like heartbreak. Young things always do."

Something caught in my throat and the horse laughed and it was a terrible thing, like blood sluicing between broken teeth.

"Oh, I am good, I am good. I want to play again. May I guess again? You are heartbroken. You are broken, broken. Which is to say, you are like *me*. Where is your tail, false *sadhvi*? Where is your soul? Do you feed off of them too? Where are your hooves?"

The horse trotted forward, snuffling at me. I could smell rot and blood on her breath, and bit back the urge to gag.

"I'm not like you at all," I said, stepping back. I hesitated, trying to look straight into the dead horse's eyes. "I'm . . . I'm the Rani of Naraka. At least, I was."

The horse stared. Blinked. And then laughed. She laughed so hard she fell to her side, snorting and neighing, casting up clouds of dust and ash so that I had to cover my mouth with my arm.

"I am!"

"And I am a beautiful stallion," said the horse through laughs.

I wasn't a liar. I remembered, like a soft breath against my neck, that real feeling of power. Like the world was something pulpy and easily pushed aside, something I could sift through . . . something I could *change*. And the more I heard the horse's laughter, the more fury growled to life inside me.

"I *am*," I shouted, this time with so much force that thunder clapped in the sky and lightning seamed across the gloaming earth like a broken eggshell veined with light.

The horse stopped laughing, jerking its head to the sky.

"Do it again," she said.

But that flash of power was gone.

"I—I can't," I said lamely.

"What are you doing here then, oh great queen?"

"I don't know."

"Why are you dressed like the living dead?"

"I don't know."

"Why—"

"I don't know anything!" I shouted.

The horse considered me for a moment.

"What do you know?" I asked, sarcasm coloring my voice.

"I know emptiness," said the horse. "I know the taste of blood against my teeth. I know what it is to fill your belly with iron. I know hunger. I know pain. I know memories that won't stay. I know the ghost of life and the perfume of souls."

Memories that won't stay. I almost laughed. Perhaps this horse and I had plenty in common.

"I need to get to the Otherworld. I need to get back to Naraka. He needs me."

"Who?"

"Am—" I stopped and swallowed his name. I wouldn't say it again until I saw The Dharma Raja.

"Handsome, handsome. Even I would die for him," said the horse, smacking her lips. "I've seen him so many times. Times, times, times. Oh, and he is cruel. Oh, and his horns are wicked, piercing things; they like to slice through stars and falling birds. Does he taste like bone and kiss like—"

"Enough," I hissed. "Or I'll kill you where you stand."

"With what? Your soft words? Your young hands?"

But the horse wouldn't laugh and when she spoke, she looked up to the sky, waiting for a thunderclap, some signal that she was wrong.

"You don't believe me, do you?" I asked.

"I believe in nothing," said the horse. A touch of her mania was gone.

"If I knew anything before I became this, I have since forgotten. I have forgotten, even, what it is like to speak to another."

The horse looked once more to the sky, and this time I did the same. Maybe it was the lights from all the palatial buildings of Bharata, but whatever remained of night had left the sky so thick with stars that they looked more like dollops of cream on a black platter.

Once, I would've hurled curses at the stars.

But the longer I looked, the less I hated them. The stars, filled with cold light and secrets, held no emotion in their fixed language of fate. Emotion belonged to life, a thing the stars could never experience. I, not the starlight, shaped my decisions. And it was me, not the evening sky, who shouldered the responsibility for decisions gone wrong. My horoscope had already come to pass, leaving nothing before me but a future ripe with the unknown. The stars had already told me everything they knew. And even though it left me untethered from any cosmic map I had once known . . . I felt freed.

Once, I had shaped the fates of others, even though I couldn't remember how. I didn't even know if I could ever do it again. I didn't know whether the life that I had left behind was something forever out of reach, a relic of a former reincarnation, or something that was mine to claim. But I had no one to tell me otherwise. And I wouldn't cast away the possibility that maybe it could be reclaimed. I wouldn't allow myself to be *lesser.* To fall into the lulls of Nritti's whispers that I was nothing and no one.

"What exactly are you?" I asked the horse.

"I am a shadow. I am a *pishacha*."

I shuddered. I knew that name from the folktales. A flesh-eating demon. A haunt of cremation grounds.

"But you know where the Dharma Raja goes?"

"Oh yes, maybe-queen-maybe-liar. I know. I know. I smell him."

"I need to get to the Otherworld, where the Night Bazaar is," I said, thinking of the bright orchard where he had led me. The nexus between the human world and Naraka. It may be the only place where I could find him and set things right.

The horse laughed. "And you expect me to take you?"

"What can I give you? What do you want?"

The horse's eyes narrowed. "I'd like to take a bite out of you. Maybe two, if you'd let me."

Cold frissons flared along my spine. "But I'm the Rani of Naraka. You wouldn't want to do that."

"You don't sound so convinced," said the horse in a singsong voice. She sounded delighted.

"But if I am, I mean, I *am*," I stressed, scolding myself, "then you would want someone else's blood. Not mine. That might get you in more trouble than it's worth."

"Oh, but you smell so good . . . and what are repercussions and consequences to something not even alive? Not even dead? A half-being . . . like *you*."

I stared at it. "Maybe . . . when I prove myself to you, about *who* I am. Maybe I can get you a new soul."

"To eat?"

"No, to inhabit. A soul that's yours."

The horse whinnied and hissed, red steam billowing from her nose and splattering like blood spray on her muzzle.

"Fine words, fine words. False words, false words."

"If I'm wrong"—I closed my eyes, praying that I wasn't—"then I'll let you take a bite—"

"Or two," interrupted the horse.

"—or two, of me."

The horse stared at me.

"Well?" I prompted.

"What assurance do I have? Give me something."

"What do you want?"

The horse flicked her eyes over me. "Your hair. It is matted, but it is lovely. It looks like coal and soft earth, and I would have it."

I was already in rags. Already caked in someone else's death. Even if it was a small thing, I hesitated a little. This was the same hair that Amar had cut a length of and wrapped a bracelet from its strands, slid it onto his wrist and proclaimed it the finest piece of jewelry he had known. But there was no time for vanity.

I knelt to the ground, knees sinking into the soft ash, and bowed my head forward, never once letting my eyes move from the horse's. She could kill me in a second if she wanted.

"And you?" I asked. "What will you give me in return?"

The horse blinked. "My name."

"What good is that?"

"It is all I have," said the horse, bowing her head. A flicker of pity went through me. "It is all I remember."

"Then it will suffice."

I closed my eyes, tilting my head down. The horse moved softly over the ash, hesitant. I heard her jaws creak open, smelled the rank thickness of rot and sour breath. A soft tear, a strange—but not ungentle—pull, and a single word murmured in the thicket of my scalp:

"Kamala," said the horse over a mouthful of hair.

I pulled away, wincing as some of my hair tore through her clamped teeth. What was left fell wetly against my neck. I shivered. I thought I would be furious, disgusted with myself, but when I stood, I felt nothing but calm. I felt light. I shook my head, nearly smiling at the now-torn strands about me. Kamala had taken more than just hair. She had taken some weight and burden from me.

She regarded me with mild eyes. No longer quite as bloodshot. Perhaps just a deep garnet.

"How do we get to the Otherworld?"

"Climb atop my back, maybe-queen-false-*sadhvi*."

I balked. Kamala barely looked fit to walk on her own, let alone bear the weight of another person. Her bones jutted out, catching the light. Ghostly reins sprang up around her body, fashioning into a saddle the color of marble.

I flashed a weary smile before hoisting myself up.

Kamala reared onto her hind legs and broke into a run. My hair, still damp from Kamala's mouth, whipped about my face. I flattened against her back and tried to glimpse our surroundings, but all I saw was a blur of valleys that looked more dead than alive. A strange smell filled my senses, of sulfur and water.

"Where are we going?" I managed to choke out.

"You want to cross into the land of the Otherworld, but it is a guarded thing, full of anger," responded Kamala. "To do anything, you must receive the permission of its guardian. We must get to the ocean."

Ocean? My eyes widened.

Lashing wind burned my eyes. Eventually, we began to climb over a gray valley before arriving at the rim of a great ocean. My legs ached as I dismounted and my lungs filled with the briny air of the sea. Tall waves rolled toward us like watery giants, white crests like crowns. A split sky stretched over the ocean—half-night, half-day.

Kamala nudged a conch shell toward me. "Make no sound, merely hold it to your lips."

I did as I was told and the crashing waves froze.

•» 20 «•

THE CLOUD BRIDGE

Something dark appeared beneath the surface of the waves. The waves crashed over the spot repeatedly, unearthing two pale mounds in the water.

"What is that?" I asked, trying to keep my voice still.

Hadn't I had enough of monsters? I was already standing next to a flesh-eating demon.

"Airavata," said Kamala. "Tricky elephant. He likes to knit."

"What does he knit?"

"Clouds."

"Oh."

Kamala ignored me and stared with her milky eyes at the white piles in the sea. I followed her gaze, my mouth nearly dropping open. What I had thought were small hillocks of stone were Airavata's gigantic white ears. He rose out of the waves, water trailing through his wrinkled trunk and pooling along the dents of his back. I had never seen an elephant like Airavata. Across his tusks lay a thin cloud and in his trunk he carried an ivory comb. As Airavata combed the cloud, out drifted dark puffs of air that glinted with lightning. His eyes were filled with warmth and he flapped his ears in greeting. Artfully looping his trunk around the cloud, he unhooked it from his tusks and placed the comb and cloud onto his back.

"And what is this?" asked Airavata, leaning forward. His voice was rich and deep, streaked with friendliness and a wizened timber. "A demon near my waters and someone who smells of secrets."

Kamala turned to me, whispering, "Which one am I?"

"The person full of secrets," I muttered.

Kamala whinnied. "Oh, I hope you are a queen. You are funny. Funny, funny. What does funny taste like?" She paused. "Maybe I hope you are not a queen. I would like to taste funny."

"I am certain you do." I smirked before turning to Airavata. "We seek passage to the Otherworld, to the Night Bazaar."

"Strange place. Stranger still, with chaos alive and angry."

I swallowed nervously, my thoughts jumping to Amar. Where was he? Was he safe?

"What do you mean?"

"It means that I am spinning storm clouds of late," said Airavata slowly. He waved his trunk toward a dark cloud that darted around his legs.

"Will you let me pass? I have to get there."

Airavata stared, before bowing his head. "No."

"No?" I repeated dumbly. "You don't understand, I *need* to be there. I need to speak with the Dharma Raja. I need to get back to—"

"It does not matter to me how or why you must get back. I am merely a spinner of clouds. Not a diviner. I cannot augur your heartbreak like entrails any more than I can speak the language of faraway stars."

"Why won't you let me in?"

Kamala turned sightless on me. I thought I saw hunger in her gaze. *Not today,* I murmured in my head. *I will not be demon feed.*

"I demand that you let me in," I repeated.

Airavata only batted his ears. "You see, that is why. You can only enter the Otherworld by invitation, self-worth or sacrifice. Or by standing beneath a double-rainbow with a belly full of cold, cold sapphires. And I have not seen a double-rainbow in five hundred years. And I know you have no invitation, for your name is on no list. The way you seek before me now is the way of self-worth, and that you have not earned."

"There are demons inside the Otherworld. Flesh-eating *bhuts* and wraiths the size of whole countries and you're telling *me* that I have to prove myself to join them?"

"I never said it had to be good self-worth. You could slay a million children. Maybe then you could come. But in your current state, your soul cannot handle the Otherworld."

"But I was let in before!" I protested, thinking back to my wedding day, and the hours spent with my arms around Amar's waist while we walked through jungles, our bodies close. I thought of his promise, his palm welling with blood. His assurances. His kiss. "Why is now any different?"

"It is different because you are different."

"And when I 'prove' myself, I'll somehow find my way back in?"

Airavata nodded.

"Isn't there something I can give you?" I asked, furiously thinking back to the head of hair that Kamala had eaten off. "Something you want?"

Airavata bowed his head. "Poor thing. Poor being of secrets and nighttime. There is nothing you can give me that I would ever take willingly."

"What do I need to do?"

"I do not know. I only know that I cannot let you in. There is something unfinished that you carry with you. Rid yourself of it and you may enter."

The elephant regarded us patiently, not breaking the exchange. I sensed that he was hiding something, but he wouldn't say. And I wasn't going to press him. I could tell, from years spent battling Mother Dhina and Mother Shastri, when an argument or a rationalization was useless.

I opened my mouth to say something, but Kamala spoke first.

"Then give us a cloud bridge. To get back to the other side. There is more than one way into the Otherworld."

"We're just going to turn around?" I asked incredulously.

"If you know the area where the Dharma Raja will be, I can sniff out his location," said Kamala.

"How?" I asked.

"When death is close I become alive . . ."

I stared at Kamala. I had already given her my hair and pledged her a bite of my skin. I knew she was bound to help me. But it never struck me that she might do so voluntarily.

"Why are you helping me?"

"Why do I do anything? Why do I hate beets or lust after the feeling of hair in my mouth instead of blood? Maybe I like the thought of being filled. Of being less empty," said Kamala with another ghoulish grin. "Maybe I am bored and your company is a funny thing. Your energy is a strange one. You are a pillar of salt I want to lick and break, but save and love."

Where would I even go? I couldn't chase false horizons hoping it would somehow land me in front of him. There had to be a specific place, somewhere he'd be drawn despite himself. Amar's words floated back to me:

I love you, jaani. *My soul could never forget you. It would retrace every step until it found you.*

Retrace every step . . .

Death always visited his familiar haunts. Blood-damp stretches of battlefields, sage-sharp mats of midwives' huts, rain-slick rocks of riverbeds. But maybe there was another place he would go. A place that, once, had meant something to *us*.

I fished out the onyx stone filled with two memories. I could use it to find my way back to Amar. Back to the Night Bazaar. Back to Nritti and her ice and honey words. Back . . . to myself.

Airavata batted his ears. "And what do you expect me to do?"

"We need that cloud bridge." I turned to Kamala. "When we get back, there's something I must do, and I hope that will tell us at least where the Dharma Raja will be. And then we can use your . . . talents . . . to get us all the way."

"Delightful," murmured Kamala. "I have not been so excited since a massacre twelve years ago. All those bodies. So delicious."

Airavata bowed his head in assent.

Hooking a cloud between his curved tusks, he began to comb it. A billowy vapor formed a mist over the ocean before flattening into a uniform stretch of white, dotted here and there with iron and purple storm clouds. I reached for Kamala and swung myself onto her back.

Gently, I kicked my heels into her side and we took off onto the cloud bridge. I had thought the cloudy material would be soft, like running on sand or fresh grass, but the cloud bridge was as hard as stone. Airavata walked beside us, sinking ever deeper into the waves until only his head was visible. His eyes twinkled, a knowing glint in his eye. But if he had a secret to tell or a thought to give voice to, he would not share it with me.

And with that, he sunk beneath the water. As Kamala raced over the bridge, I leaned over, reveling in the occasional spray of seawater. Tears burned in my eyes, but I wouldn't let this failure set me back. I had to succeed. I clutched my mother's necklace tight around my throat, praying it would give me strength, and looked around me. On my left, I could see what the ocean looked like at night. Its waves were higher, the crests of its ripples stretching far onto the shore. I caught glimpses of luminescent creatures bobbing just under the surface. Occasionally, a dorsal fin cut the water. On my right, sunshine capped the waves gold. Fish as green as parrots wriggled by the cloud bridge and twice I saw a limpid pink jellyfish.

Where was Amar? I turned back to the shore. Already the

beach seemed like a distant gray line. I drew out the bracelet of my hair. With my memories came the love I had always felt for Amar leaving me heavy and weightless at once. I hated that I didn't tell him that I love him. And I hated how those memories—though fleeting—felt like wounds reopened. But even then, I found hope. My heart had not been false and that knowledge was unshakable and scrawled on the secret joints of my soul, like a spell that kept it whole.

"Are you weeping, young queen?" asked Kamala.

"No," I lied, "the salt is stinging my eyes."

"Pity," grumbled the horse. "I have not tasted tears."

My whole body felt worn out from tension and I closed my eyes, my arms wrapped around Kamala's neck as I fell asleep. In my dreams, I danced with Amar. We spun in circles to the heavenly music of the *gandharvas*. We danced around a wide courtyard filled with colorful birds until I stumbled forward, my arms spread out to brace my fall. I cried out loud and my eyes fluttered open—

"We are here," said Kamala.

The ocean remained, but the sky above was a normal hazy gray-blue. Before us, a great jungle unfurled dark green leaves in invitation. I rolled my neck. Whatever peace I had found in sleep vanished. All I could feel now were my aching muscles. My skin reeked of salt water and my hair was whipped around my face. I glanced at Kamala and bit back a gasp. Her once thin flanks bulged with muscle and her coat gleamed with soft white hairs. Even her eyes were now a dark crimson instead of the rheumy white from earlier. Kamala plodded forward carefully, occasionally warning about low branches.

"Is death nearby? Is that why you look—" I faltered, gesturing at her dramatically different body.

"We are fully in the human world, so death is always nearby. You should see me when we are truly close, false queen. Then, I am a sight to be reckoned with. Sometimes I have lulled away beautiful maids and handsome youths just with my borrowed glory alone."

I didn't ask what happened next.

"Now what?" asked Kamala.

I took the small onyx stone and pressed it to my lips. The memories shifted under my gaze, translucent and wispy.

"Now I find out where he will be."

I sank myself into that memory, into the moment where we first met, bending my whole body into a single event captured within one of those glittering pinpricks.

I had been walking through the Chakara Forest. Fat moths the size of palms wreathed my hair like pearls and moonstones. And then, as I had done since before language burgeoned in the velvet clefts of the mind—I danced.

Not a slow dance, but sharp, punctual movements. My dance organized the shadows of trees, canceled the cloying plumes of wind-fallen fruit, aligned the moonbeams themselves. My back arced gracefully as I moved, neck extended like an oryx, fingers conjuring sharp *kathas* of rhythm, when a sound crunched not far from me.

I spun around. "Who's there?"

From beneath the heart-shaped leaves of a *peepal* tree, something rustled. And a voice, so lush it made ambrosia acrid, answered me.

"Only the lowly painter who tries each night, in vain, to capture evening herself."

"What do you want? Show yourself."

The stranger stepped out of the *peepal* tree. He was broad-shouldered, his features as severely beautiful as a strike of lightning. He wore a crown of blackbuck horns that arced in graceful whorls of onyx, catching the light. But it was his gaze that robbed the clamoring rhythm in my chest.

His stare slipped beneath my skin. And when he saw my eyes widen, he smiled. And in that moment, his smile banished my loneliness and limned the hollows of my anima with starlight, pure and bright. He moved toward me, grasping my hand, and his touch hummed in my bones like an aria. A song to my dance. The beginning of a promise.

I pulled myself out of the memory. My breathing was ragged. I couldn't push out the feeling that the memory left. Something so whole that my body craved and curled around it. I thought my soul was leaning toward the stone, wishing desperately to cling to a truth, a beacon that could guide me back to myself. That raw tenderness. That *kiss* that said *goodbye, come back,* and *I love you* all at once. This memory showed me hope. And that was something I could chase to the ends of the earth.

"We need to get to the Chakara Forest," I said, turning to Kamala.

She had not moved once since I sank into that memory. She had not laughed, nor gnashed her awful teeth, claggy with blood.

"You changed," she said slowly.

"What?"

Kamala whinnied. "You looked different. Shade-play, shadow-play against my eyes. Trust me, false queen"—she paused—"*maybe* queen, I know shadows."

"What did I look like?"

"Like ink-spills and umbra, cloudless nights and winter mornings. Lovely, lovely," said Kamala in her singsong voice. "But you wore no crown of blackbuck horns and something swirled across your skin. I almost tried to taste it, but I did not want to get swatted by a maybe-deity. Maybe-deity! Maybe-deity! Oh, what a song."

I glanced at my arm, ignoring Kamala as she pranced about in a circle, tossing her head and singing *maybe-deity* so loudly it might summon thunder. There was nothing on me but the crust of sea-salt and dried ash. I dusted it off. Kamala's words put flesh on the bones of my hope. Still, that didn't give me as much comfort as I'd like. I was asking a flesh-eating demon for comfort.

"You wish to go to the Chakara Forest?" asked Kamala when she was done dancing. Pearly sweat left a sheen on her coat.

"Yes. But there's something I must do first."

My hand closed around my mother's necklace and I tried to swallow down all those past hurts that had hardened into iron knots.

"I need to bury this in the place where its last owner lived."

Even through my grief of losing Gauri, Airavata's words rang true. To enter the Otherworld and save Amar, I had to release the ghosts of my past. Kamala jutted her nose against my neck and snuffled the necklace before loudly snorting.

"That necklace lived in a kingdom that smelled of stone. It is kinder to *sadhus* and *sadhvis* than its own people and its turrets are fat with mango blossoms. It is on the way to the Chakara Forest."

My heart clenched. Somehow, I felt like Gauri had given me her blessing.

"Bharata?" I guessed.

"I suppose that is the name it goes by now. Cities shed names like maidens their tears. Does its Raja look like a toad in a golden jacket?"

Skanda had never been . . . athletic.

"Perhaps," I said, then thought for a moment. "Probably."

"Then it is so. It is Bharata."

"We have to go through it?"

"It is the only way."

"Then perhaps the stars are on our side." I hauled myself back onto her saddle and we took off through the jungle.

The moon turned motes of pollen into drowsy glimmers. I watched them drift past me, snatching them out of the air. They looked like the wishes from Naraka's glass garden. I closed my eyes, letting myself sink into the quiet of it all. In the silence, I wished for all the things I had lost—love, lives, memories. *Myself.* And I wept for those things as I wept for the dead. And then like the dead, I released them and hoped with all that was left of me that I could give them new life.

I faced the tree-blurred horizon. Somewhere behind that tangle was Bharata. The same Bharata I had abandoned to warfare. Or was it? Guilt slid up my spine.

I would soon find out.

•» 21 «•

THE WARRIOR OF BHARATA

The jungle zoomed past us, a flurry of brown and green branches with slants of scattered sunlight. Within an hour, Kamala slowed to a trot. Up ahead shined the familiar gates of Bharata. It was missing some stones, but remained sturdy nonetheless. I squinted, leaning forward; there were more guards than I remembered. An outdoor pavilion that I had never seen towered above us, strung with pennants and bearing a strange crest.

My father's sigil, a lion and an elephant—for strength and wisdom—had been replaced with a fire bird arcing its way toward the sky, while below it was a small golden city. It was superficially lovely. I imagined Skanda thought it meant something meaningful, perhaps an envisioning of a kingdom soaring into the ranks of legend. But to me, it reeked of arrogance. It said, *Let me abandon this city and leave it forgotten in a quest of borrowed greatness.*

A crowd had formed outside the city gates, people cursing under their breath and exchanging pointed glances. We stopped some distance away from them, and as I jumped off Kamala's back, clouds of dust coated my ankles. I never thought I would be here again. It was strange, like moving through a dream. I held out my hand, closing my eyes to feel the sun beam down on me and wash my skin in bright gold.

Hundreds of people crowded the city, but when they saw me and Kamala, they fell silent. My palms turned sweaty beneath their gaze. What was it that *sadhus* and *sadhvis* did? Did they utter blessings or stay silent?

This thought, however, didn't seem to cross Kamala's mind. She lunged forward, baring her teeth and shaking her mane. Half the crowd scattered.

"Effective," I said, patting her neck.

"You're most certainly *not* a *sadhvi*," huffed Kamala. "You can go up to them, you know. You can ask for anything you want, and they'll probably give it to you. Nobody wants your curses."

"How do I curse them?" Wouldn't be a useless skill to have, all things considered.

"Oh, I don't know. You could set me on them?" Kamala smiled and her eyes flashed red.

I cringed. Horses should not smile.

"Can we get around them to the palace?"

All I wanted was to bury the necklace in peace.

"I can rend flesh," Kamala huffed. "I can't fly."

The crowd had re-formed around the gates, still chanting. Their sweat smelled sour, their eyes were bloodshot. And their clothes . . . tattered things. No better than the ascetic garb I wore around my body. My father would have never let his people dress in such a manner.

"I can smell their hunger," said Kamala softly.

I took in their hollowed stomachs and cheeks, the yellow tinge to their skin.

"I believe you."

"It is the scent of drought and famine. An imbalance, no doubt."

"Of what?"

"Of the worlds," said Kamala.

The memory of the tapestry loomed in my mind. The texture of the tear that rent down the middle. Threads writhing, blackened and burning beneath them. The tapestry stretched out, engulfing and weaving the patterns of an infinite number of stories. It's what kept the worlds in balance. The flicker of memories from my time in Naraka rushed through me. I remembered my feet sliding into the reincarnation pool and the dull warning in the back of my mind . . . that fleeing would leave behind a horrible tear. A chronic rift. And what better evidence than the threads in the tapestry? I looked at the crowd of people in front of the gates. I didn't want to know how far the consequences of my actions had gone, but I was beginning to get an idea.

I couldn't simply bury Gauri's necklace and run. Bharata had once been my home. This earth, now dry and cracked as parched lips, had once hid me from danger. I owed it more than a casual run across its surface. I owed it whatever help I could give. My home may have been broken and shadowed, but it was mine all the same.

"Come on." I pulled on Kamala's reins.

"What about the Otherworld?" Kamala's ears swiveled. "I thought you wished only to cover your cold stone in colder dirt?"

"It won't crumble away in the time it takes us to know why everyone is furious," I said. But my voice trembled. I knew I was gambling against time.

Amar's plea—*save me*—was an urgent thing. But I had to trust my instinct to tell me what was right and wrong. I heard his voice, echoing and filtered through lifetimes. I remembered when I saw the tapestry for the first time, the gut-wrenching nausea of fighting its pull to rearrange the threads. I remembered when Amar had left me alone in its company. Then, his parting words were simple, unfettered: *Trust yourself.* And I would.

"Do you know when the Dharma Raja will come to the mortal world again?"

"Oh, anywhere between an eon and a blink."

"That's not even a remotely useful range," I pointed out.

"It is what it is."

"Well, would you be able to tell when he is here?"

"Yes."

"And we could get to him in time from Bharata?"

"Yes."

"Are you sure?"

"Yes."

"Are you just saying yes?"

". . . Yes."

Kamala snorted and laughed.

"What's the real answer? And tell me the truth this time, don't forget our deal." I placed my arm against her muzzle, sliding it across her nose like it was a piece of salted corn. Drool, at least I hope it was drool, fell with a thick splash on the ground. Kamala stared at my arm hungrily.

"Maybe. It all depends. That is how things are. Perhaps my first answer was the truth. Anytime between an eon and a blink."

I rolled my eyes. "Then I suppose that will have to do. But the moment he's here, you need to tell me and we'll go."

Kamala nodded begrudgingly. I kept my head low as we pushed through the crowd.

"Act like you're chanting a prayer," hissed Kamala in my ear.

"Like what?"

"Mutter something," said Kamala. "Do you know how many *sadhus* I've listened to? Let alone eaten? If you don't start muttering something, they will turn on you. And I don't want to eat them. They look like they'd taste horrible."

"I—"

"A list or something."

"Uh," I stammered, trying to draw out the sound into the beginning of a chant. The people of Bharata were beginning to frown at me. Some had even stopped hurling shouts at the gates to watch me fail.

"Skies . . . fingers . . . teeth . . ."

Kamala nodded approvingly.

"Can they hear you?" I hissed.

"No, not at all. Continue talking to me. That will definitely make you seem crazy. Very convincing for a holy person."

"Are you sure?"

"Quite," said Kamala. "You are like me. Half a thing. Mildly insane. A little of the Otherworld."

"How comforting," I muttered, continuing with my ridiculous list as we shouldered through people. I held my hand open, smiling and grinning when fat coins were dropped into my palms. But it didn't feel right to take them. Especially when the people who were giving the most seemed to have the least to give.

So I gave the coins back.

And that's when things started getting strange.

"The *sadhvi* has returned our offerings!"

"She is a saint!"

"It is a sign that the world has forsaken us!"

Kamala was laughing again.

"The horse is also holy! Make way! Make way!"

"The first holy *sadhu* among us is here!"

"We are not forsaken. Make way!"

"Hear what she prophesies!"

The crowd around us parted. People's hands were outstretched, running their fingers through my hair, across my collarbones, along my arms. They tried to touch Kamala, but she took it less kindly and snapped her teeth.

"You're a holy horse now," I chastised. "None of that."

Kamala growled at me. "Don't forget that I get to take a bite of your arm when all of this is through."

We stopped short of the iron gates of Bharata. My father had never closed them. From what I remembered, they were just symbolic and never meant to keep anyone out. In the distance, I could see Skanda sitting on a pavilion wreathed in lotus blossoms and flanked with serving girls. He was, as I had guessed, fat. And in his golden jacket, he indeed looked like a toad.

"Ah, I remember him," muttered Kamala.

"He's my half-brother."

"Nasty, nasty."

"I know."

"Would you like me to eat him?"

"Definitely not," I said, a little too quickly. I patted Kamala's neck. "But I appreciate your offer. It was almost nice."

"It is nice to be nice," said Kamala with a sage nod. "And it is also nice to eat people," she added as an afterthought.

The crowd of people pushed forward. The iron gates were beginning to open.

"A king would never deny a holy person that has come to his doorstep," said Kamala.

My skin was damp with terror as I allowed the crowd to buffet me to the front. A man pulled me from the swarm, his eyes so bright they looked like gems.

"You must beg the Raja's audience. He has sent so many of our sons into that war. He has claimed so many of our daughters and not returned them. And now he has forsaken our war hero."

Another woman ran forward, pressing my hands to her cheeks. "*Sadhvi*, please. Please help. The Ujijain emperor will not let any of them go. He is calling them all prisoners of war and the Raja Skanda will not ask for their release."

The Ujijain emperor . . . could that mean Vikram? I remembered his mother walking through the Otherworld. She had died the same day, still carrying a bundle of wilted flowers. It meant that

Amar had chosen to pull out the red thread. It meant that many of my people would die, but that the kingdom would be saved. Peace would come.

I couldn't look the villagers in the eye. Another person tugged on my arm. I looked down to see a boy with a gap-toothed grin. "Tell him to send Gauri-Ma. She will win him back."

I stopped walking. "What name did you say?"

"Gauri-Ma," said the boy again, this time staring at me as though I were a fool.

The man who had first approached me nodded fervently. "Everyone knows her. The princess with the dimpled smile and the deadly aim."

"She is there now," said the woman by my elbow, still clutching my hand. "The courtiers are talking about forcing her to break her vow of chastity. The Raja will make her marry. He will make her leave Bharata and her wedding will be her exile."

"He is furious," whispered the boy. He mimicked his hands as if he had a swollen belly. *Skanda.*

Joy and fury warred inside me. Gauri was *alive*. But now they wanted me to send my own sister to the forefront of a war against a kingdom that would claim so many of Bharata's people. The crowd pushed us forward, smiling around mouths full of blessings as they damned my sister.

"Is this what fame is like?" whinnied Kamala into my ear. "How delightful."

"This isn't fame," I whispered back to her. "This is fear."

As we walked forward, I wondered if Skanda had kept our father's sanctum the same. Maybe that's why he held court outside.

Maybe he never wanted to see helmets piled up, their spaces in the iron opened up for smiles and screams or blood-choked cries. Or maybe, it was too full of helmets to make room for people and plans. Maybe it was just a mausoleum now.

The people formed a dense semicircle around me and Kamala. We stood at the end of the Raja's welcoming "hall." It was a makeshift platform. Up close, the lotus blossoms that I thought had strung its sides were nothing more than artfully folded ribbons of silk. Had we run out of flowers too?

Skanda braced his elbows on his knees. The smile he flashed was too narrow.

"You are the first ascetic to pass through the realm of Bharata in quite some time," he said.

A layered greeting. Skanda had at least some shadow of our father's style. But there was also a glint in his eye. He did not believe I was a *sadhvi* and I didn't blame him. I moved awkwardly in my hermetic garb, constantly tugging at the turmeric-yellow robes and pushing the crusted ash and salt off my skin. Maybe a real *sadhvi* wouldn't do such a thing.

"To what do we owe this honor?"

Every pair of eyes turned to me. I pushed my body a little closer to Kamala, fumbling for the right words.

"I—" I paused, racking my brains and thinking of the boy's words. "I'm here to see . . . Gauri."

Skanda's eyes narrowed.

"The Princess Gauri."

Oh God, I hope I am right. I hope that's who the boy meant. I hope he didn't take me for a fool.

"Why?"

"I have traveled across . . . places . . . places of great woe. Of great"—I turned, looking at the crowd of people pressing up one against the other, and thought about everything they'd said and everything they wanted—"of great sorrow. I am here to warn you that no place is safe. And that an army is necessary to protect its people."

"We have enough of our army remaining."

Before I could say another word, a furious growl ripped across the platform. I jerked my head up just in time to see Gauri storming across the stage and pushing aside the weak efforts of Skanda's guards to block her.

"*Remaining*," she repeated in a furious voice.

I could hardly speak. Joy blossomed in my heart. Here she was. Gauri was safe. More than that, I realized, as I followed the expressions on the citizens of Bharata's faces: She was *adored*. Gauri was strongly built, and she wore her hair like I once had, scraped back in a tight braid.

Even as she glowered, dimples flashed in her cheeks. But the most striking thing of all was what she wore. She had forsaken the garb of the harem women and wore the armor of a soldier. But her outfit was different; it was inlaid with emerald, so that when she moved, the light skittered across the metal like light dancing on a pond. She looked like a beautiful *naga* woman, a snake goddess wreathed in light, moving serpentine and sly.

"You cannot be serious, brother, even the *sadhvi* has pointed out the error of your ways. Our city could come under attack at any point. We should be ready. You should send me to reclaim the lost troops from the Ujijain Empire."

"*My* city," corrected Skanda, this time standing up so fast, he toppled a platter of sweets that was waiting beside him. "*My* empire. I have indulged you for too long. I allowed you to train beside the other soldiers. I allowed you to show your feats of archery to the citizens of Bharata. I allowed you to leave the harem and walk through the cities, acting as my ambassador. And now you dare to spar with me in front of an audience?"

One man beside me clenched his jaw, and I sensed that a fight would break out in her defense if Skanda made one wrong move. Skanda must have noticed because he suddenly sat down, his face assuming a blanket of calm.

"Now that the *sadhvi* woman is here, perhaps we could let her decide."

No one would argue with that. Even Gauri bowed her head deferentially. I shifted my feet and attempted some measure of mysticism and authority.

"Does your stomach ail you?" whispered Kamala.

My attempt clearly failed.

"I would be honored to settle the dispute," I said loudly.

Gauri was looking at me quizzically, her eyes roving over my face and hands . . . settling at my neck. Did she recognize the necklace that was once hers? If she did, she gave no sign. I bowed at the hip, deftly spinning the sapphire pendant away from my throat and onto the back of my neck. I loved Gauri, but if she didn't trust me, she might out me as a thief by accident.

"Then it is settled. You will be my guest," said Skanda.

"What about me?" muttered Kamala in my ear.

"And my horse?"

"And the horse," said Skanda, with such false graciousness, I almost considered letting Kamala eat him.

•» 22 «•

EONS AND BLINKS

There's nothing quite as strange as having an old and familiar haunt explained back to you in an alien language, with unfamiliar words and false skins stretched over each place like a new blanket. Skanda and his retinue of yes-men escorted Kamala and me through the grounds, asking us to bless things. I tried to act spiritual, but I wouldn't consider it a rousing success. When Skanda asked me to make an offering that would bring him happiness, I threw an offering on Varuni. The goddess of wine. And when Skanda asked me to prophesy about the future of his reign and his legacy, Kamala urinated on his foot.

Skanda led us through the gardens, his gaze fixed on a pretty attendant who was constantly—although reluctantly—handing him a goblet brimming with some liquid dark as blood.

The gardens were a ghost of their former glory. My father had spent years tending these orchards, walking through them with his hands clasped behind his back. Years ago, there had been mirror-lined fountains to catch the sun. The orchard had been so illuminated that each new blossom wore a golden nimbus. There had been fish in inky ponds, shimmering iridescent beneath the water's surface, lively moons in miniature. There had been thousands of trees heavy with jewel-bright fruit. I knew. I had climbed those trees, plucking fragrant guavas and devouring their rose and saltwater flesh right there.

All of that had changed. Bharata had changed. The air was leeched of all warmth, but that didn't make it any less dry and dusty in my throat. The trees had been reduced to mere spindles. Someone had strung pennants in them, but they hung limply in the windless air. My throat tightened as I stared at the place that had once been so familiar. If Bharata hadn't believed in ghosts when I lived beneath its walls, then it certainly believed in them now. This place, this city looked carven and gaunt. When we stood in the garden, Skanda dismissed everyone. Even Gauri, despite how stubborn she was about never letting us out of her sight, caught his mood and left.

"This is where my father once instructed me," said Skanda, pointing to a familiar row of now desiccated *neem*, sweet-almond and fig trees.

Scolded, more like. I resisted the urge to laugh. "It is rare that a ruler would spend time in the company of his offspring. No doubt you are quite blessed, Your Majesty. What lessons did he impart?"

"He once told me to remember that the illusion of power is just as great as actual power," he said slowly.

I stiffened. He knew I was no *sadhvi*.

"You understand my predicament," said Skanda in a wheedling voice.

Kamala cast me a sidelong gaze and whinnied, pawing at the ground. She didn't need to say any words of warning. The moment Skanda spoke, my eyes sharpened.

"Tell me what I should understand," I said.

Skanda let out a long breath. "Times are very different for the realm than what they might have been once upon a time. My father died valiantly in battle. After that, people lost faith. There has been a war raging on the outskirts of Bharata long before I became the ruler of this realm. At one point, we had the upper hand. My father invited the war leaders here for a wedding."

My hands clenched. "What happened?"

Skanda shrugged. "We don't know. One minute the girl was there, the next minute she wasn't. It made the leaders furious."

"What happened to her?"

Skanda snorted. "Who knows? Who cares? She escaped all this."

"No one remembered her?"

"I believe she had some horrible horoscope, one way or the other. I cannot remember. But horoscopes have gone out of fashion. No one cares about those things anymore. The stars have lied so much to us."

I didn't know whether his words were more comforting or dismal. The Bharata I knew had fixated on the abstract language of comets and star patterns. Listening to Skanda felt like examining an old scar. I saw the wound Bharata had left in me, but it was a relic of something time and magic had sewn together. If Bharata could have changed over so many years into some entirely different beast, then maybe I had too.

"The people have not seen a *sadhu* come through our palace walls in years," said Skanda. "And I know for a fact that you are no *sadhvi*."

My head jerked toward him. "Sire, I—"

"No need," said Skanda. "Didn't you hear me? I don't care if you're a fraud or not. The illusion is enough. I haven't seen my people this excited in years. I'll pay you whatever you want, just make sure you put on a good show. In particular, silence my sister. You already met her."

"What exactly has she done wrong?" I tried to keep the protective edge out of my voice, but Skanda's gaze turned flinty.

"She wants to volunteer herself on a useless reconnaissance mission to find out what happened to a handful of our soldiers."

"Were they important?"

"They were elite members of the service. But new ones can be trained. Anything, and anyone, can be replaced," he said, falling silent. "Even me."

I regarded Skanda. He wasn't as dumb as he seemed. He was, even though I hated to admit it, a little perceptive. If only he wasn't so lazy. Perhaps he really would have made our father's legacy something noteworthy. But I could sense his weakness. He was scared. He was selfish. And that was a dangerous combination.

"Why don't you want the Princess of Bharata to go?"

"Illusion," he said, gesturing with sweaty hands toward the failing orchard around us. "I need to hold on to the illusion of power.

If that slips the moment Gauri leaves, then I am finished. They'll probably throw me out."

"What exactly do you want me to do?"

"I do not know. You're the charlatan. Fake something. Some ceremony where you can counsel her otherwise, and then announce it to the realm. It has to be something that all the people can understand and empathize with."

Kamala snorted, pushing her muzzle into my hand and leaving dark tracts of mud—and something else, which I didn't want to discover—on my palms. Her anger was a palpable thing.

"You have my word, sire," I said.

Kamala whinnied, nibbling on my arm, and I swatted her.

"Excellent," said Skanda. "You can settle up with the royal treasurer at the end. What do you have in mind?"

Behind him, a slight shadow dipped in and out behind a banyan tree. I held back another smile. Gauri. No doubt she'd heard everything. There was no way I would follow Skanda's plan, admirable though it might have been. His heart wasn't in the right place. At least when my father made sneaky decisions, they were always for the good of the country. Never just to save face.

"With your permission, sire, I'd like to hold vigil outside the palace temples and allow those members of the royal court to speak with me at will. If you can convince the Princess Gauri to join in one of the sessions, perhaps have another member of the court... a harem wife whom Gauri is close with... to join and stand as witness to our session, I can craft the correct words to announce to the court."

"Excellent."

He tugged his hand through his hair and my heart clenched, a brief memory of Amar flashing in my mind. There were so many times in Naraka that I had watched him do something similar. So many times that he had twirled one dark curl around his long fingers. I needed to get back to him. I couldn't let go of too much time.

"By your leave, Your Majesty, I would like to hold that session today."

"Today?" repeated Skanda, stunned.

"I believe it would look more natural to your citizens. An immediate announcement revealing the change in the princess's mind would show some transparency. That perhaps you had not bullied or bribed me into saying such words by holding me within the palace walls for more than a day."

Skanda nodded approvingly. "You're quite bright for a charlatan *sadhvi*. How long have you been in this business of deception?"

Oh, if only he knew.

"Years," I said through a thin smile.

"Consider it done."

Skanda pointed me to the palace temple, cast a nervous glance at Kamala and stalked off in the direction of one of his yes-man advisers.

"What is it?" I hissed at Kamala. "I thought you were going to talk right then and there and then we would've been thrown out."

Kamala wouldn't look at me. "It's the Dharma Raja."

I froze. "What about him?"

"I can sense him." The blue veins that once stood out so prominently on her skin had begun to sink beneath pearlescent hair.

Even the garnet gaze of her eyes had receded into something bright and black. Thoroughly animal.

"And?"

"He was here, but only for a moment."

"Where did he go?"

"I couldn't tell you that, not for all the salt-skin in the world." Kamala sighed.

"Do you know where he was?"

"That's the thing I was trying to tell you, maybe-queen!" exclaimed Kamala, pawing at the ground. "He was at the Chakara Forest. You were right."

I was right. There was a soft glow of warmth in that knowledge, even if knowing that I had just missed him rent through me like a new wound. I had trusted my instinct and it had been right. I could have reveled in her words if they didn't make me furious.

Kamala sighed. "But there is something else."

"What?"

"He left something in his stead."

"In the same place?"

"Yes."

"What did he leave behind?"

"I don't know. My own senses do not tell me such things. Though that would be a great help. I wouldn't have to lie in wait, hiding behind bushes and hoping some unsuspecting stupid person would wander past me. They might even wear such signs on their heads proclaiming, 'Eat me!' and such a thing would be—"

"Is the thing moving?"

"Yes, yes, but only in the area. I think it is dormant. It is waiting, I suspect, for something."

"How do you know?"

"Oh silly Rani, silly *sadhvi*, I have had so much experience with death. I know that it is waiting. It is waiting for the soft thud of freshly culled souls. It is waiting to paint its lips red with blood. It is waiting to crunch bones and wear them like clattering raiment and robes."

"Does that mean the Dharma Raja will return to the spot?"

"Yes."

"How long does death usually wait?"

"Eons and blinks."

I couldn't abandon Gauri. Not now. Not when I had come so close to seeing her for the first time in weeks. I had to move quickly.

"Tell me the moment the Dharma Raja's representatives seem to move. Or do anything. Can you do that?"

"I can, I have, I shall, I will," sang Kamala.

"Good."

I tugged her reins, about to lead her to the palace temple when I heard a soft jumping sound behind me and felt the pointed edge of a dagger at my neck.

"Stop where you are, imposter."

I stopped.

Kamala bent her head to me. "Surely I can eat that one."

"No," I hissed.

"No? You won't stop?" said the voice, laughing. Gauri.

"I wasn't talking to you. I was talking to the horse."

Kamala snorted indignantly.

"I heard you talking to my brother."

"So what?"

"I know exactly what you plan to do and I won't allow it."

This time, I turned around and faced her. Gauri was a full head taller than me. Strange that she used to run to me, wrapping her arms around my waist in a hug. I fought the urge to throw my arms around her. There was murder in her eyes, a calculating gaze no doubt caused by a quick and sudden immersion in court politics. And she had a military background to add to that. Smart girl. The moment I held her gaze, she paused, lips parted for just a moment before she looked away.

Had she recognized me? I wanted her to. I wanted her to see who I really was beneath the saffron robes, torn hair and ash-covered skin. But she shook her head, as if ridding herself of a momentary lapse, and refocused her dagger at my throat.

"You heard what I *said* to your brother. That means nothing in Bharata."

A smile quirked on Gauri's face.

"You don't strike me as a charlatan," she said.

Her tone, a questioning lilt, slammed me back through memory. In a blink, we were back in the Bharata I remembered, the capitol carpeted with lush trees and heavy with the perfume of wind-fallen fruit. And Gauri was once again the hesitant, soft-voiced eight-year-old who asked what we would be in her next life. Twin stars? *Makaras* with tails long enough to wrap around the world? I swallowed the lump in my throat, tamping down the memory like a dead fire.

"And you don't strike me as a murderer," I said, flicking aside the point of her dagger. "I want to help you."

Gauri looked taken aback. A familiar rosiness spread across her cheeks.

"Why would you do that? What did you really come here for?"

I hadn't known until now, but I saw it, felt it. I came here for her. Because it didn't matter whether I had lived in another realm for years that I thought were mere days. It didn't matter that I had tasted fairy fruit, fallen in love and broken a heart. Some bonds were impervious to all manner of experience. And the truth was that, no matter what happened, we were sisters.

"I came here because I've known about the villagers' concerns for some time. I once lived in Bharata," I said. "It is my home, and like anyone else I want to see that it will be safe. Loved. Cared for. The citizens prefer you far more than they do the current raja—"

"Careful, *sadhvi*, what you're saying reeks of treason—"

"People always have their favorites," I said calmly. I hated myself for even encouraging her to leave this place, to risk her life when I knew that I couldn't protect her. But there were worse things that could happen to her if she stayed. She would be a prisoner. She would never get the chance to make her own choice. And if there was anything I could give her, some parting present for never being there when she grew up . . . it was that. A choice.

"What I'm suggesting would help you as much as it would help him. You could go and reclaim those lost soldiers. Boost morale. Do you really think you can do it?"

Gauri nodded, her eyes shining. "I know I can."

Tears burned behind my eyes. *Come back safe.*

"And will you go alone?"

Gauri nodded again. "It is safer that way, not to risk anyone's lives. And I know where they're being kept. I've received word."

She fell silent, her gaze distant and eyes fixed on a shaded area sequestered in a copse of once-bright lime trees. I knew that place . . . it was a rendezvous for lovers.

"The person you received word from," I said after a while. "You love one of them, don't you?"

Gauri started, a protest on the tip of her lips.

"I . . . ," she began before weakly trailing off. She quickly regained composure and her eyes narrowed. "That's none of your concern."

You are my concern, I wanted to say. *You are my sister.* But I said nothing. I just let her words hang in the air.

"The best motivation is love," I offered.

Beside me, Kamala nodded vigorously. "And food!"

Gauri's eyes widened. Like a ghost of sound laid atop the other, I heard what Gauri did—a sort of mangled neighing.

"Your horse is rather strange."

Kamala nodded again.

"So what's your plan, *sadhvi*? I heard what you said to my brother. If your grand design is announcing that I should go, he'll never let you leave alive. He'll call you crazy and denounce you. Trust me. I've been around long enough to witness how he handles dissent."

"Then we won't give him the chance. You will leave as soon as our meeting concludes. Right under his nose. And when you return, you will praise him."

Gauri balked. "*Praise him?* He did nothing!"

"You would do well to learn how to play the games of court," I said. "Sometimes an illusion is just as good as the actual thing. The difference lies in the telling. Make this one concession. Find out what happens next. If you bring back these soldiers and word gets out that it was your idea and your escape, he may punish them on your behalf."

Gauri considered me. "What are you?"

"A maybe-false-queen!" butted in Kamala.

It must have come out as another deranged horse whinny because Gauri nearly jumped.

"I told you," I said, not meeting her gaze. "I'm a person who lived here once upon a time."

"You know far too much about the political schemes of Bharata."

"My father was a diplomat."

"No, he wasn't! No, he wasn't!" sang Kamala. "Lies are fun. Lies are nice. They taste like rice soaked in milk and sliced and diced with cardamom and—"

"Is your horse ill?" asked Gauri.

"No, not at all," I said and smacked Kamala on her flank. "She's eager."

"For blood," said Kamala.

I forced a grin on my face. "Send the harem wife that you trust the most. We're going to need her to cause a distraction."

Gauri nodded approvingly. "If you're starting anything at the harem, that will get his attention. It's where he spends most of his time anyway. Give me some time before you send the wife to start a distraction. I need to gather my belongings and say some goodbyes."

"You have my word," I said, before adding, "and my admiration."

Gauri leaned close. "So far, I like you, whether or not you're a real *sadhvi,* although I have no doubt that you aren't. But make one wrong move, hurt a single hair on the head of the harem wife I send to you, and you can be sure that I will have you kicked out of these gates or worse. And my brother will be none the wiser."

In my head, I heard the Gauri from what felt like only four days ago. She had thrown her arms around my waist and told me she would protect me. At least I knew the protective instinct wasn't something she'd lost.

Gauri jogged off in the direction of the harem and I pulled Kamala along to the palace temple. "Well? Any word? Any news about the Chakara Forest?"

"None-none-none," sang Kamala. "But they are still there."

"How can you recognize their presence against all the others?" I asked. "Surely death isn't just waiting inside the Chakara Forest."

"Death is just a little pulse, like a splinter in my veins. But *this* is different. He rarely leaves so many representatives at once. Certain people, the Dharma Raja culls individually, and then there is a surge in my heart like fire and a thousand carmine flowers blooming all at once."

"Representatives?" I repeated.

But then I realized. The hounds in the halls, their mouths thick and writhing with human spirits, their coats brindled like emerald and diamond. Living jewels turned monstrous. They were Amar's messengers, his representatives gone to fetch troublesome souls and bring them back to Naraka. But why have all of them in one place at the same time?

"Beasts," whispered Kamala, affirming my suspicions. "Four-eyes. Tongues like lashes. Fun to kick. Prone to chasing and nervous flop sweat. They chew on bones, but only the tibias and femurs of virgins with mixed eyes. Preferably when one eye is black as a cygnet and the other is green as a grass shoot."

Not a very pleasing image. Now, all I could see were giant hounds chasing down the souls of those who wanted to cling to life a little longer. It also meant that they were waiting to gather something and bring it back to Naraka, but why? And why would he need so many? At least I knew where all of the beasts and the people would end up: Naraka.

Perhaps there'd be a way to figure out how to follow them. To get back to Amar. But how could I save him if he wouldn't know me? How would going to Naraka even make a difference?

"Do you think clouds prefer to drop rain all at once or to test the ground occasionally?" asked Kamala. She was staring at me with a strange intensity. It was either hunger or thoughtfulness.

"Why does that matter?"

"Because you are splitting yourself, maybe-queen-but-certainly-liar."

Splitting myself.

"You are a fraying, fragmented bone. And no one, not even *I*, would deign to eat such a thing."

"What do you expect me to do?"

"I don't expect anything," said Kamala archly. "I expect sunshine and moonshine. But I am telling you to stop being a broken bone. You are in one place, so be in one place. Or I'll bite you."

Be in one place. I was here. I wouldn't leave Gauri. It wasn't like last time, when I had no choice but to flee or die. Right now, she was the one who needed me. And truthfully, I needed her too.

By now, we had nearly reached the palace temple. Beautiful sandstone walls arced around us. I stayed outside, near the pillared *mandapa* halls where deities with half-lidded gazes considered us stonily. There was a figure moving toward us, an emerald veil pulled low over her face. She must be Gauri's friend from the harem. I wondered who she was. The figure didn't look familiar. The woman moved slowly. She was older. Stockier. She had none of the lissome watery-grace of the harem wives I remembered. She moved like someone who had no one left to impress.

Sweet incense wafted from the temples. The afternoon sun of Bharata looked like thick yolk as it dribbled slowly into evening. The parched air had lifted. Insects practiced their enigmatic songs in stark bushes and wilted flowers.

The harem wife approached. I practiced how I would greet her. Should I bow? Should I do nothing?

"What's your plan?" asked Kamala.

"I'm going to ask her to start a fire."

Kamala's eyes gleamed. "Oooh . . . I do love when they're served up hot and piping and charred."

"You and I will be gone by the time the fire starts. It's just a distraction for Gauri."

The harem wife was finally here.

"It is a great honor to meet you," I began. "I am so pleased that the Princess Gauri has placed you in her confidence. It will make this next task much easier."

The harem wife stopped, her fingers still tightly clasping the edge of her green sari. She removed it, slowly, from her face, peeling back the silk until it showed a chin that I knew wobbled when she screamed, thin lips now parched dry from repeated inhales at a water pipe, a smirk scalded into the sagging flesh of her left cheek, and eyes made for watching you burn and never once—not even to wipe away particles of dust and ash—blinking.

Mother Dhina.

·» 23 «·

A SHARED CONSTELLATION

All my words, whatever they wanted to be, fell out of me in a long whoosh.

"You," I breathed.

I forgot that I was wearing the garb of a *sadhvi*. Mother Dhina glared and took a step back.

"How dare you speak to me in such a manner, beggar? I don't know why Gauri placed our trust in you."

Our trust? I had to be mishearing her. The Mother Dhina I knew had never helped a single person. I didn't even know whether she cared about anyone beyond her daughters and they were probably married and long gone from the mirror-paneled foyers of Bharata's harem.

I dug my heels into the ground, preparing for a slap that never came. And why should it? I wasn't Maya anymore. That girl really had become a ghost. I was clinging only to the emotions she stirred in me—hate and anger. But also . . . regret. There were so many times I had waited outside the gossamer curtain of the court's inner sanctum, waiting for them to notice that I was more than my horoscope. More than some girl they could tack all their half-remembered suspicions to.

I gathered my breath, and said something I didn't expect:

"I apologize for insulting you and your—"

"My daughters died of the sweating sickness," cut in Mother Dhina. "I am not Princess Gauri's mother. In case that is what you thought."

Parvati and Jaya *dead?*

I had no fondness for them. Yet I wouldn't wish such an end to their lives either. Where had I been when the world was pulling up its roots and razing the places and people I knew? I wondered if they walked past my chambers while I slept, dreaming up nightmares and gardens that splintered underfoot.

"I am not anyone's mother," said Mother Dhina softly.

Her face was unguarded. Grief transformed her and for a moment, the Mother Dhina I knew sank away. I saw a woman with ruined beauty, kohl-dark eyes ringed with dryness. I saw a woman who had placed her faith in an era that had not treated her any differently, that had taken her children and left her with the double-edged sword of a long life.

"Broken-bone, broken-bone, smash her with a silver stone," trilled Kamala in my ear. "Maybe-queen-maybe-liar, you share something with this crone. Is it blood? Is it sinew? Let me rend and taste her tissue."

I shoved Kamala. "Why don't you go graze?"

"Graze?" she retorted. "I do not *graze*."

"Go stalk a peacock."

"You are not very nice," said Kamala, huffing and trotting away.

"Now you want to take away my last consolation in old age," said Mother Dhina, her voice heavy with accusation. "You want to send Gauri into some no-man's-land and you expect me to help."

"*She* expects you to help, and if you didn't agree with her yourself, I doubt you would have accepted," I said. "Besides, I can assure you that it is not what either of us want."

That much was true.

"What would you have me do?" asked Mother Dhina.

"The Raja Skanda is fond of his wives, yes?"

A cruel smile turned up the corners of Mother Dhina's lips. "Oh *yes*. He adorns them with jewels and spends each night in their company. He gives them the largest rooms and drives out the old. He lets the wives stomp on those of us who had been there first, who had served the realm longest, who had yielded the palace children that didn't live long enough to deserve names."

Her voice had lost none of its smoke-rasp, but where it was once husky and sultry, it was now like dragged-over stones. The darkest sense of triumph snuck into my heart. Now she knew what I had known all those years.

But I felt something else too. Pity. The thought that it would even find its way to me was its own irony. Still, I felt it, a humming in my throat. A desire—though I tamped it down—to forgive her. I knew the future that had been before me, and I had escaped. Even if it felt like days since I had left Bharata, I always knew that my future there had been a lonely cage. Mother Dhina had only recently come to that conclusion.

"Start a fire in the harem," I said.

Her eyes sparkled. She smiled.

"Don't harm anyone," I added quickly. It was best not to stoke Mother Dhina's particular brand of cruelty. "The last thing we want is for Gauri to be blamed for any deaths."

Mother Dhina considered this and nodded reluctantly.

"Send them all to me. All the wives, all the women of the harem. The Raja Skanda will be able to take care of the fire, but by the time that happens, Gauri will already be gone."

"You speak her given name," warned Mother Dhina. "That is far too familiar for my liking." She took a step closer to me, her eyes scrutinizing my face. Whatever ash and paint streaked my features, her gaze seemed to chisel everything away. "Do you know the Princess Gauri from before?"

I swallowed. "No."

Mother Dhina stared at me for a long while. "You remind me of someone."

I could guess who.

"She died in childbirth," said Mother Dhina. "She left behind a daughter who needed a mother—" She broke off and her face, even through the veil, was stony. I knew who she was talking about. *Advithi*. My mother.

"She was not afraid to trust and hold someone's trust in return," said Mother Dhina, in a tone of begrudging respect. "Though that didn't earn her any admirers. Or my friendship, for that matter."

"And her daughter?" I prompted, trying to hold back the tremble in my voice.

"She had an affliction, one could say," said Mother Dhina. "This was during a time when the realm gave credence to horoscopes." She sighed. "That time is gone. But the girl had a poor one. A dangerous one. And we were living in strange times, not nearly as strange as now. But it was a start, you understand. We were not used to it. We wanted answers and had none. We wanted an explanation for our grief but could find none. So many of us had lost children, brothers, families in war . . . and so the girl became, well, she—"

"Became someone to blame?" I finished.

"You have to understand that it was easy for us." Her voice was choked on tears.

A familiar acidic feeling gripped my chest and I turned from Mother Dhina and spared a glance at Kamala. She was watching a peacock drag a bejeweled train across a tangle of brambles.

"Why are you telling me all of this?" I asked.

Mother Dhina blinked at me. "Gauri asked me to stay away for a while before I did as you asked. But I believe I would have come to you anyway. The Raja Skanda told us that you are here to offer spiritual consultations. Counsel me, then."

Had she asked me this years ago, I would've had a more colorful response. But that was in a different time that no longer belonged to either of us.

"You haven't asked a single question."

"Weren't you listening?" said Mother Dhina. "I have told you my story, my shame. There is no one left alive that I may beg of for forgiveness. So what would you counsel me?"

I kept waiting for the desire to see her cry, to let my mouth fill up with so much anger for another person that I could feel it claggy between my teeth. I waited and waited until it felt like a century had pried its fingers off my hate one by one. At the end of it all was nothing but pity.

Mother Dhina stood before me, her lips slightly parted to reveal a row of decaying teeth behind her lips. Nothing I could say would serve as absolution. Mother Dhina was past the point where she might believe in words. She had even given up on horoscopes.

My gaze fell on a statue that no one had moved for years. The stone was fashioned in the lithe shape of an *apsara,* her torso jutting dramatically to one side, hair frozen in tendrils of polished diorite and granite. It looked surprisingly heavy, but I remembered that the one time I had moved it aside, it had been light. It was hollow, after all, and the space inside was large enough to hide small things within—things like books you didn't want to part with or candies wrapped in linen or even . . . a pair of slippers that didn't belong to you.

I pointed to the statue. "Look inside."

"You must be daft," she said with a huff. "That statue is far too heavy to be moved."

"Just because it hasn't been moved doesn't mean that it can't be," I said, conjuring the most sage voice that I could.

Mother Dhina went to the statue and, with a pointed glare in my direction, moved to pick it up. It gave way with ease, as I knew it would. The only sound was the soft *whumph* of upturned earth.

"It's hollow," she said.

She reached in, drawing out a pair of dirty but altogether unscathed slippers. The tassels were still intact, as were the annoying pair of bells that used to jangle each time she stomped through the harem. Mother Dhina held them in the air for a full minute before clutching them to her chest, as though doing so could seal some terrible void within her.

"The daughter," she said through soft gasps, "she had hid these from me. I could never find them."

I considered scrubbing my face and telling her who I was and that I had forgiven her, but that wouldn't be true. I did not forgive her. I pitied her. I preferred our screen. She had her veil. I had my costume of a *sadhvi*. That would serve us both.

"I should go to the harem now," said Mother Dhina, her gaze not moving from the slippers, an awed smile on her face. "Enough time has passed. Is that all I should do? Start the fire?"

"That is all. If you see Gauri, you can tell her I will be at the palace gates. She can let me and my horse out that way, facing . . . north?"

I checked with Kamala that this was the right direction and she grunted. Mother Dhina was still staring at the shoes, her fingers tracing the seams of silk that shone like light upon water.

"You're not a *sadhvi*, not a thief and not entirely a charlatan," said Mother Dhina. "Who are you?"

If I could tell her, I would. But that answer was beyond me, so I gave the only one that felt right.

"I'm a dead girl walking."

Kamala kept pawing at the ground.

"Let me, let me, let me," she pleaded.

"No."

"I'll be so very nice. If you let me, I'll only nibble at your skin. You won't even bleed too much. I swear on my soul."

"You have no soul."

Kamala considered this. "Just let me, let me—"

"There are *no* bodies to be found there. Trust me. She gave me her word no one would be injured."

"Then let me make sure," wheedled Kamala. "Let me make sure that the nasty crone kept her word—"

"No. We are waiting for Gauri and then we are leaving."

"You are not very kind."

"You are not very patient."

Kamala harrumphed and snuffled my hair, sending showers of something wet and stinking down my neck. I suppressed a groan. I wanted to sink into a frothing hot bath and collapse into pillows bursting with feathery down. Instead, I had Kamala's increasingly bony spine to look forward to.

"Are the Dharma Raja's representatives still there?"

"Yes, yes, but they are restless as trees in a storm."

"What do you think it means?"

"They are waiting. They are salivating. Their spittle drops into the ground, fat as newborn babies, heavy as the sighs of lovelorn boys . . . oh, how it mocks me."

The smoke rose and formed inky coronets atop the parapets

of the harem. Shouting voices converged, thick as the smoke itself, until it became a collective fug of surprise. Night had draped herself languorously over the courtyards I had once roamed. No stars gleamed above. No moon watched my treason. I waited for Gauri, my breath held for the moment to see her once more . . . and then I did.

She was riding toward me on a horse the color of rain-drenched tree trunks. All the guards had fled their watch for the palace gates and had rushed to fetch pails of water to extinguish the fire. There was no one guarding the iron gates, but still I had waited. I wanted to see her go. Besides, I had something that belonged to her.

Gauri's face was shining by the time she pulled up to the gates. I clambered onto Kamala's back and together we dashed into the bramble of forests. As we ran, the moon striped us silver. Damp leaves kissed our skin and we wore crowns of starry dust motes. Beside Gauri, magic thrummed in my veins and I believed, after so long, that perhaps we really could be the things we dreamed of—dancing bears or twin sea dragons with tails made for ensnaring oceans. But now I knew that it wasn't the magic of past stories that made me feel this way. It was the same thing I recognized in Naraka but could not name. *Love*. Impossible love.

When we stopped running, Gauri heaved, eyes squinting on the fire that was beginning to die down, leaving nothing but smoke. She turned to me and her lips were pursed.

"The fire has been smothered. Why did you bother waiting? You have done your duty."

I jerked my head toward the smoke unfurling into the skies. "Any casualties?"

"Nothing but a couple silks, I imagine," said Gauri. "Mother Dhina constructed her fire quite cleverly. And painlessly. But while I am indebted to her, I imagine that it is you that I have to thank."

I smiled. "No need."

"I need to know why you did it."

"I already told you."

"No, you didn't," she said, this time her voice soft. "I recognized your necklace the moment you came into the city walls. My sister had given it to me before she disappeared, no doubt taken by some foolish king."

Her eyes were hard and glassy with unrestrained tears. "Do you know what happened to her? Did she send you here to look after me?"

I couldn't hide my hurt when I looked Gauri in the face.

She hadn't recognized me.

My own sister had no idea who I was, even after she saw the necklace around my neck. My words to Mother Dhina rang true. I was a dead girl walking. I was a ghost making peace with the places I once haunted.

I took the necklace off, letting my fingers graze its small seed pearls just once before I handed it to Gauri.

"I saw her once, in a faraway land that no horse or boat can reach, but that all will find," I said, my voice thick.

"How was she?" asked Gauri.

This time, tears were sliding down her face, shining against the helmet she wore.

A part of me wanted to grab Gauri by her shoulders and shake her into remembering me. But that would've done nothing. And so, as I had done so many years ago, I told her a story. I glossed over the grotesque and emphasized the beautiful. I created details where there were none, things pulled out from my imagination, things as I may have imagined them myself at some point or another.

In the end, I did whatever I could to stave off her nightmares.

"She is happy. She fell in love and ran away, but she misses you very much. Her husband is a kind man with a large smile, who treats her as an equal and never shares his bed with anyone but her."

Gauri laughed, more tears falling from her eyes.

"I passed through her land not too long ago, and she asked me to bring this to you and tell you this: in the Night Bazaar, trees bear fruit of edible gems and the *naga* women enviously stare at one another's scales. She told me to tell that she loves you, thinks of you often and will always be proud of you. She asks that you stay safe. Always."

Gauri pressed the necklace to her lips before tying it securely around her neck. She checked the straps of her horse before smiling at me.

"Thank you, *sadhvi*. I wish you well on your journey. If you see her again, please tell her that I love her and that I think of her often. Tell her that I will come back alive. For her."

Tears blistered in my eyes, but I would not cry. I had done what I came here to do and for that I was happy. Kamala pawed the ground. There was no time to share my stories with Gauri or explain all that had happened since the last time we met. "And thank you for everything you have done for us today," said Gauri. "I have every intention to return alive, and when I do, I will make sure people will remember you and sing your praises. Tell me how I can reward you. Where can I find you?"

I smiled. "Don't you remember? We can always find each other in our same constellation. The Solitary Star."

Gauri's gaze widened, glittering with the promise of tears. I dug my heels into Kamala's side and as we leapt into the forest, I looked back only once, to see Gauri grinning and waving, just as a veil of trees stole her from view.

•» 24 «•

THE LADY OF THE FOREST

Arrow-sharp tree limbs cut the path ahead of us. Darkness draped across polished jet trees and shadows shivered into existence—slow as a turning head. Only daubs of moonlight marked where the trees stopped and the sky began.

We moved quickly over the hills and scrubland. I kept my face close to Kamala's back, taking comfort in her heavy breaths and the muscles of her flanks gaining thickness and life with each passing step. Now that Bharata was behind us, my thoughts lurked once more like monsters. I kept thinking of Amar, and a pain more real than all the scrapes along my body clawed into my skin, sinking nails deep as years.

Every time I closed my eyes, I saw him next to me, his hands in my hair, his lips against mine. But each time they opened, all I saw was dark. I had no idea where he was, what he was doing. My last glimpse of him remained seared into me, until my thoughts were clouded with his eyes dulling in pain and unlocking all those memories buried deep within me.

The world I had known now loomed sunless and lurid. Trees were dying. People were wilting. Cities were crumbling. And I knew that this downward spiral had something to do with the ruined balance of the Otherworld. I had to get there. Even if it turned out that everything I did would be as useful as pitting a broken leaf against a buffet of wind, I had to try.

Kamala slowed to a trot before a copse of trees that crouched over foul-smelling warrens. A hundred mushrooms pale as bodies bloomed out, teeming over the roots of trees so that at first everything seemed blanketed in flesh.

"This is where the Dharma Raja's representatives are?"

Kamala pawed the ground, "Yes, oh yes. Can you not feel them, maybe-queen?"

"No."

"That is because you are not trying!" scolded Kamala. "You must let yourself go. You must let yourself be dead. Imagine you are their succor and absolution, imagine their bloodlust, their eyes . . ."

I closed my eyes, forcing myself into stillness, into quiet. I tried to find a hole in the silence around me, some place where noise was a tangible thing, something I could cut through and cloak around me . . . I imagined myself as the pale mushrooms, flung out and life-leeched . . . I imagined myself *wanted*, like a thread untamed, something that needed to be resolved and tucked back in, something that needed to be *hunted* . . .

. . . and then I heard them, saw them, smelled them. Their paw prints, meaty stamps of blood dampening the forest floor lit up like puddles of light, and I leaned close to Kamala.

"Follow it."

Kamala cackled and laughed, her body swelling beneath me, veins like rivulets of sapphire bulging with life, her mane a dense tangle of opaque frost that I wrapped around my wrist, holding tight as we sped through another mass of trees.

There. Waiting just outside the shadows, three massive hounds napped, heavy as boulders. In the distance, a sound lit up the dark, soft as a dream. It was a glorious and syrupy sound, something I wanted to drench myself in forever. I swung my leg around Kamala, intent on following it, when she growled in warning.

"Don't," she hissed, jerking her head to the dogs.

They were beginning to stir awake. Their paws twitched beneath them, muzzles trembling with some invisible scent.

I pulled Kamala behind another tree, safely at a distance from whatever was making its way toward us. I wasn't sure what I had expected the moment we got here. I thought the hounds would be circling something or on the verge of leaving, but someone had commanded them to stay and sleep, to lie in wait.

The voice became louder and louder and then I saw her. Nritti. She was singing, summoning. She walked slowly through the moonlight and I saw her, for an instant, as if through prisms.

I saw her on a sunny day, her arm linked in mine, laughing about something incoherent and fuzzy with memory. I saw her by the banks of a river, crooning to a sea of fish that swam silver and gold to drop pearls at her feet. Though they lasted no more than a blink, I clutched at my chest, feeling for some invisible slash inside me, some strange wound where all those memories had escaped. When I looked at her, my heart thrummed to a bruised and mournful beat, but I didn't know why. In my head, she was a shining *apsara*, beloved and dear as Gauri, if not more. How could she be evil?

Nritti was still singing. Her hair was pinned back with butterflies whose wings shimmered like stained glass. She wore a *salwar kameez* of green silk, ringed round and round with opal gems so that the light caught and stayed with her. Her arms were outstretched, beckoning something unseen toward the napping hounds. Golden beetles darted in and out of her hair and her smile was soft, generous. Her expression so heart-stoppingly sweet that my legs twitched to run to her, to tell her my secrets.

"Stop that," grunted Kamala, unmoved.

"Why? She's . . . perfect."

"Hmpf. She smells like blood."

I grinned, and my head was dizzy and cottony, drunk on her singing.

"Are you jealous?"

Kamala bared her teeth at me.

The beings following Nritti soon came into view and all of my drunken thoughts stopped abruptly.

Children.

There were at least ten in the clearing, and the chatter of voices and laughter hinted at more. The hounds stood up, shaking their brindled coats, watching the crowd of children carefully. Their haunches twitched and drool puddled around them. They were *hungry*. Every now and then, their eyes darted back to Nritti and a sickening realization went through me: they were waiting for a signal. Waiting, I realized, to take the children.

But that couldn't be possible. That was not how the balance worked. That was not how the threads operated. They were overlaid and knitted in their own patterns. They could never be lulled into a situation and *deliberately* broken. It violated the careful balance of the tapestry.

A young girl with braids that hung to her wrists stepped forward, wrapping her arms around Nritti in an embrace that tugged at my heart. Gauri had once hugged me like that. The girl was lulled by Nritti's voice and who could blame her? It was a voice heavy with loveliness. Nritti's song was unlike anything I had ever heard. It had no words. Instead, the sounds conjured clear images in my head. She sang of warm warrens in the ground, slick caves behind waterfalls and the stillness of water. But it was more than a melody; it was an offer of friendship, it was a . . . request. Nritti's song grew faster, the tone shifting. Now she sang of the acceptance of changes, and her melody summoned images of ripe pomegranates bursting with ruby seeds and lightning slicing through the sky.

Kamala hissed and tendrils of steam rose from her flared nostrils.

I watched as the girl nodded, smiling. Her expression was clear: *Take what you want.*

Nritti stopped singing. Around her, the children froze, smiles slicked onto their faces, their cheeks coated with sweat. They were so entranced they probably didn't even notice their feet torn, brambles and burrs and thorns piercing their ankles.

The butterflies in Nritti's hair dipped in and out of sight. They were nothing more than illusions.

The golden beetles stopped moving, shimmery chitin flashing black and matte as coals. Beady eyes wriggling themselves free of magic until they took on the hunched, feathered shape of cormorants. Even Nritti's dress began to change color . . . from emerald to nothing more than ash and a translucent black cowl. Her skin and face, so lovely and bright, faded. She was color-sapped, bleached white as a bone. Her hair turned stringy. The voice that had lulled all the children to this one spot lengthened into a croak. Nritti's lips pulled back into a smile of spite. Jagged teeth peered out from the ruin of her lips and she screamed her song. But this was no song of *asking*, it was a song of *taking*, and the louder her words became, the more I saw what it was she wanted.

The moment the girl with the shining plaits nodded, Nritti leaned forward, bending as though to kiss the girl on the brow . . . slowly, breath teased out of the girl. Nritti laughed and that's when I heard it. The voice of the woman from my room. It *had* been her. Maybe my mind couldn't believe it before, convinced that my instincts were a broken thing. But I was right. The proof of it filled my ears, fury snaking through me.

I jumped off Kamala, about to run forward and get the girl out of harm's way, when I felt the drag of teeth at the nape of my neck pulling me back.

"Can't you see what she's doing to that girl? If she won't hesitate to do it to a child, she certainly won't blink twice to do the same thing to you!"

"Let me go!" I said, fighting against her, but her teeth had latched on to me and I had no choice but to watch, dangling from the incisors of a demon as the little girl's eyes widened.

I thought Nritti meant to kill her. But life wasn't what she was taking. It was *youth*. The more she inhaled, the less of the girl's ethereal sparkle was left. Her skin paled. Hair grayed. Honey voice sharpened.

Nritti pulled away, dragging her arm across her mouth like she had just finished a meal.

"Thank you," she said, and her voice was all sweetness.

Next, she approached a boy with nut-brown and golden skin who had stood transfixed the whole time, his eyes glassy with magic. She trailed her fingers against his jaw, first softly, then—her lips curled up in a weird smile—harder, until she was scrubbing away at the color of him. The boy winced, his skin flushing crimson with the promise of blood, when Nritti finally pulled away from him. Gone was the paleness of her skin. She was shining and auric, the image of the sun as seen through cut topaz. Glorious.

Nritti flexed her arms, examining the length of her tawny skin and polished hair. She hummed a trill and the things that had once flitted like innocent living haloes around her head took their real form—shrieking cormorants and blood-slicked beetles. Things meant to harm, to scissor, to pinch.

"Much better," she said. She turned to the hounds. "Drag the rest down to the Otherworld. I want to look my best for my wedding."

Wedding? My hands went cold.

Nritti snapped her fingers. "Summon him."

The hounds nodded. They bayed as one, heads thrown back and throats bared to the night, howls cleaving the sky with thunderclaps and a violent wind.

The forest shadows crept forward like spilled ink and my pulse quickened. And then, in the clearing . . . there he was. Amar. His crown of blackbuck horns was gleaming, his arms clasped behind his back. In his hands swung a noose.

I dropped wordlessly from Kamala's mouth, scuffed knees thudding softly in the dirt. I sat there, my legs curled beneath me, heedless of the bugs tracking their way across my thighs or the incessant nudging of Kamala's nose against my back, trying to shove me into standing. I couldn't move. Half-remembered memories transfixed me to the spot. I saw him through fractals, veil after veil of memory that was once mine.

The woman I was then and the person I was now may have shared a soul, but everything else between us was a mystery. I knew she had spent her life in the Otherworld. I knew she had ruled Naraka. I didn't know whether she was a good ruler or a foolish one, but I knew that everything she saw of Amar fitted neatly in my heart, warm as a fire kernel and fierce with belonging, with *rightness.*

The only thing I didn't know was why she—*I*—had left. I remembered the betrayal, but not the reason. I remembered the fury, but not the fire.

The longer I stared at Amar, the more images flashed behind my eyes—him gathering me in his arms, our eyes drunk on the sight of each other. The silk of skin against skin, the hum of a connection tethered at our marrow, hinging on breath patterns, voice inflection, intangibles of love. I tasted his lips against mine—fervent, firm—smoke and cinnamon and the panic of not catching yourself right before you fall.

Nritti strolled toward him, flashing her glamour of stolen beauty. Lightning splintered across the sky, throwing his face in relief, highlighting the sharp line of his lips and his narrowed eyes. Nritti tilted her head up expectantly, lips pursed and tugged into a shadow of a smile. She stared at him like he was a toy possessed, something that did her bidding.

And it seemed, for an instant, that she was right. My heart stopped.

Amar leaned over mechanically, lips pressing against hers in a kiss that was cold, unfeeling, but . . . a kiss all the same. Nritti smiled smugly and patted his cheek. I hardly heard what words she uttered. I had drawn my knees to my chest. Kamala had stopped nudging me.

"Come, come," said Nritti to Amar, as if she were speaking to a child. She threw one last lovely glance at the children standing immovable and paralyzed behind her. "I thought they would be good witnesses."

Amar's brow quirked into a frown. "But why?" He surveyed them indifferently, his gaze occasionally flitting to the hellhounds at his side who looked at him with unconditional love. "Their time has not come. They have no place in my halls—"

"*Our* halls," said Nritti. Around her there was only a haze of glamour and lust. "Don't you remember when I found you? You were broken. And wasn't I the one to save you? I pledged myself to you, so we could change the Otherworld forever . . . isn't that what you want? Aren't *I* what you want?"

Watching them was like slamming my arm repeatedly through a door of thorns, trying to get to the other side. Amar's hand flew to his temple, his face crumpling with a sudden headache. Nritti watched impassively, a small wisp of light forming in her palm that she raised to her lips and blew . . . like a kiss.

The light sank into Amar's skin and he drew his hand away, a dazed and remote expression slipping over his face.

"The pain doesn't stop, does it?" asked Nritti. "It's because you can't rule over the dead by yourself. You need me. And what better way than to pair us together? What better way to relieve you of this tension than to will your power to me?"

Nritti stroked the noose in her hand as if it were a pet. Amar nodded, but the movement was wrong. Limp. His face was ashen. I wanted to rush to him, but I saw now that everything he had said in those last moments in Naraka were true. He was lost, and in need of saving. But I couldn't subdue Nritti the way I was. Whatever latent power had once curled at my fingertips was gone.

"Come, come, my pet," said Nritti, patting her leg like she was calling a dog to her.

Amar didn't even notice; his gaze was far off, his arms like phantom limbs at his sides. The children clambered to her, gathering hold of anything they could—the ends of her hair, her dress, her fingers. She smiled thinly at all of them, shaking off their hands like they burned her and calling the hounds to howl once more at the sky.

"Take us back," she commanded.

Lightning flashed once more through the sky. The noose glimmered in Nritti's clenched hand, shining like an eel. Beside her, Amar was a specter of himself. Neither of them was looking at the other. Amar's gaze was downcast, fixed on the sky. Nritti's gaze was on the children. She was looking at them with a rapt desire.

In a flash they were gone. Nothing remained of where they stood except for a burnt ring in the ground. Within seconds, oily black mushrooms sprouted through the ground, unpeeling into blackened rings. Where the children stood, poisonous plants pushed themselves from the soil—violet petals of monkshood, horse-chestnut branches with pale blossoming heads, purple columbine and sorrowful betel palms.

My throat was thick with pain and I blinked wildly, trying to restrain the tears prickling behind my eyes. Anger had gouged a pit inside me. I tamped down my doubt. Whatever the reason behind why I left Naraka, Nritti and Amar together wasn't it. I wouldn't let my insecurities drape a noose around my mind. I was done with that.

Wordlessly, Kamala stepped forward, and she was thin, thin as false hope. But still, she swung her neck, bringing me to her until my tear-stained cheeks were dampening her bony neck.

"There, there," she crooned, "would that I could eat anyone that made you unhappy."

I laughed despite myself.

"Perhaps not so much a maybe-false-queen after all," said Kamala.

I looked down at my skin, still sooty and tracked with brambles. I could feel my shorn hair move against the nape of my neck and my robes were as tattered as before.

"What makes you say that?"

"It is in your eyes," said Kamala. "You do not look for yourself. You look for *them*. A true queen knows that doubt is as unwieldy and powerful as a forest fire. It is good, good, good. Good as mangoes during summer. Better than the flesh of new brides." She smacked her lips. "If you do not doubt, you do not see."

"I doubted too much," I said, walking to the scorched earth where Nritti and Amar had disappeared. "I need to get to the Otherworld. You saw her, she was taking children from the *human* world, who had no business going to that blasted realm, let alone *dying* before their time."

Kamala nodded. "Her hunger is worse than mine."

At this, I looked sharply at her. "What is she hungry for?"

"Oh, I don't know. Maybe bones, like me. But I doubt it. It's only those that deserve nothing that want everything."

"It's not right."

"What is right? What is wrong? Too complicated," said Kamala with a huff. "Better to do as I do and not think about those things. Live eternal damnation with the utmost simplicity: Stay on your own cremation grounds and eat only the bones that you find yourself."

"As ever, brilliant advice."

"I try."

"Is our questing done now?" asked Kamala, trotting up beside me. "Will you nurse your broken heart and moan over it forever? May I now take a bite of that lush-lush arm?"

I snapped my arm back. "No."

"Good," said Kamala. "Because I hate the taste of cowardice."

"There's no way we can get back to the Otherworld."

Kamala cocked her head. "Yes, we can."

"What, do you have a bellyful of sapphires and a double-rainbow?"

"No. But you have something that will make the world open," said Kamala. "A sacrifice."

That other way.

"I have nothing to give."

"Everyone always has something to give. Always. It does not matter whether it's worth something to anyone but you; all that matters is that it is cherished."

Her gaze leapt to my pocket, where the last memory lay buried in the cold onyx stone. The last full memory I had. I held it close to me. Aside from the bracelet of my own hair, this was all I had left of Naraka. It had guided me to the Chakara Forest, left me with a single burning hope that I wasn't foolish for coming here, that I had some place in all of this. This was the last claim I had to a life I could only remember in wisps. A life that, while I acknowledged, I couldn't reconcile.

"Why couldn't we do this earlier?"

Kamala looked at me shrewdly, one eye dark as dried blood.

"Could you have done this earlier?"

I knew what she meant. Before seeing Bharata and Gauri, I had been lugging along the ghosts of my past. But not anymore. Still, something stung me, like tiny insect bites of regret.

"What is the matter?" asked Kamala.

I pulled the stone from the makeshift pocket in my robes. "I feel like I'm losing a piece of myself."

"Oh, nonsense."

I glared at her. "You don't know what happened back there. You don't know what it's like to feel like for a moment you were entirely whole. Like you finally knew yourself and then to have that ripped from you."

Kamala regarded me for a moment. "Yes, actually, I do. That is the whole purpose of a curse. To remind you that you are lacking, but never know what that hollow is."

I stepped away from her, chastened. "I'm sorry."

"Do not be. Do not be anything. Do not mourn a life you do not know. It is done, it has happened. It is a riven bone, without meat or memory."

"But it was *me*, Kamala."

"You have more than one self."

"But—"

"But nothing. It is foolish to cling to ghosts or spent bones. It is better to forge ahead. It is better to leave what you do not know and make yourself anew. I have slung the ghosts of memories across my back for years and it has done me no good and earned me no victuals."

I nodded. She was right. Souls had no shackles. They knew no nationality and swore no allegiances. Whoever I was, whoever I could be . . . that was a choice. And I had made mine.

"How do I give it away?"

"Consign it to the earth with blood," said Kamala, before tossing her head at the scorched earth. "Bury it in the ground."

Despite the curiosity burning inside me to know that last memory, I forced it away. It was part of me, but separate, and I wouldn't let it define me. I used the sharp edge of the stone to prick the pad of my finger.

"Oooh," crooned Kamala. "How about a lick, then?"

Ignoring her, I smeared blood across the stone and dropped it to the ground. It landed with a silent thud against the dirt. I knelt toward the stone, bringing the memory close to my eye. I let myself sink into it just barely, teasing only the slightest detail of the memory before I forced myself to drop it.

I blinked back the barest of images—a samite curtain, an upturned hand. I held the emotion coiled inside me, the knowledge that the memory was potent. Beloved. My voice trembled:

"This is what sacrifice I offer you for passage to the Otherworld. Take a memory that I lay claim to only in name, but not in spirit. I will be less whole without it. But let the weight of it, its promise of love and tears, of something lost and beautiful, serve as fair barter."

I kicked a small hole into the ground and buried the memory there. Earth ate the offering, flashing pale threads of tubers like gnashing teeth until the stone had disappeared. Above, thunder groaned in the bellies of the sky. Kamala and I both started, shocked by the sound. Thunder never used to bother me, but this was a horrible, wrenching sound—like the sky screaming.

Kamala inhaled sharply. "Look!"

I turned.

The memory was gone. The hole I had made for it had fallen in on itself; moon-bright roots clung to the sides, forming a tunnel veined with quartz.

"Is that how—" Kamala began.

"Yes," I said, pushing her back, "get in, get in!"

"I don't like being underground."

"Not the time!" I said. I squatted to the ground, kicking my legs into the hole, and suppressed a shiver. It was cold and damp. But not like dirt. Like sweat-covered skin cooling in the wind. "Ready?"

"Absolutely not—"

I grabbed hold of her reins. "Not looking for an answer."

And then we slid forth.

•» 25 «•

IMPOSSIBLE HUNGER

Roots tore through my hair. Lodes of quartz banded around the tunnel, but the light was stingy and pale, and refused to illuminate what lay ahead. I threw my hands out against the dark. My insides slammed together and left me weightless. Dark fell in such cold, thick veils that for a moment, I didn't know whether my eyes were open.

I blinked, squeezing my eyes shut before opening them just in time to see the earth leaping out to meet us. My shoulder knifed into the ground. Light spiraled across my vision and pain needled into my joints.

Kamala tumbled beside me. The moment she found her bearings, she cast a withering glance my way.

"I do not like you."

I winked at her.

She bared her teeth at me.

Around us, the Night Bazaar was more than just unrecognizable—it was gone. Where the sky had once been divided by perpetual day and night, it now appeared uniformly black. Haphazardly strewn gems poked out of the ground, casting a cold light that joined the glow of bone-white corpses hanging from trees in a shadowy orchard. The vendor stalls were gone. Snapped wheels, chipped signs and shattered jars littered the outskirts of a large clearing in the middle of the bazaar. Except for some shriveled trees, it was deserted. Everything had a haunted look. Scorch marks covered the dais where the *gandharva* musicians had once played beautiful music.

And in the orchard where Amar had handed me a fey fruit, nothing remained but charred stumps. Beside me, Kamala suppressed a shiver before glancing around. Sounds fluttered from a haze-riddled section of the Night Bazaar. The noise was at once soft and deafening, like a frenzied heartbeat or a scream unleashed underwater.

"He is here."

I didn't need to ask who.

I pulled my robes tightly across me. Heat slapped the air, but the atmosphere held not warmth, but fury. The ground changed beneath us. Where it had been coarse and ashy, now it was smooth and cool. I glanced down and my stomach flipped. We were walking on sanded bones. Their slender, asymmetrical shapes were fitted together like slats of wood. Strange crenulations like teeth marks dented the bone floor and I looked away sharply. By now, my sandals were hardly more than thread and I could feel each bone's smooth ridges curl beneath my feet.

The sounds around the corner were deafening and chaotic, not at all like the alluring music the *gandharvas* played. Even the air felt foreign. Where the Night Bazaar once smelled of secrets and the promise of adventure, the smell of the Netherworld had a cloying unpleasantness ripe with the stench of fermenting fruit and sulfur.

"What happened to everyone else?" I asked.

Kamala shuddered, her withers rippling with goose bumps. "They have fled."

"Where did they go?"

"In the trees, in the rivers, in the glens," murmured Kamala, swaying her head from side to side. "In all the hidey-holes left in the world."

I remembered the first time I came to the Night Bazaar, how the crowds parted like water before Amar and me, how their gaze was frantic, but always *reverent*. He had kept them safe. Whatever had happened, they must not have thought he could keep them safe anymore. I couldn't blame them. The Night Bazaar was in disarray. Lightning hung from the torn seams of the sky, flickering weakly in the air. The shadowy dome above held no signs of the sun, moon or stars. Here, there were chalky square outlines in the floor where towering *rakshas* wrestled and sparred. In a darkened corner, a horde of footless *bhuts* swayed in a terrifying dance to the rhythm of their own screams. On the outskirts stretched an expanse of black water. Something skimmed the waves; great fins and a jaw jutted outward—poised for biting and crowded with teeth. A *timingala*. Its eyes never blinked and I couldn't shake the feeling that they were fixed on me, shining with hunger.

"I miss my cremation ground," said Kamala, sniffing disdainfully at the scene before us.

I ignored her, my throat suddenly tight.

I saw Amar. Perched on a towering throne of thorns. There was no compassion in his eyes. Only steel. But there was also a blank look to his expression, as though he couldn't quite remember how he'd gotten there or what he was supposed to do next. Images rustled beneath my skin, lighting up behind my eyes. I saw us along the ocean at the edge of the world, his hands twisting the black curls of my hair. I saw him standing near the shore, smiling as he placed a wreath of rosemary and honey myrtle around my head like a crown. I saw our fingers interlace, felt the roughness of his hands against my own and heard him speak my name like a prayer.

Beside him, Nritti leaned out on a throne of bleached bones. Her full lips curled in a smile as she lifted one perfectly groomed eyebrow and surveyed the destruction.

A hum gurgled through the air, like a thousand stomachs rumbling. A wrenching pain twisted through my gut and I doubled over. Beside me, Kamala keened. A *dakini* sank to her knees in front of us, her necklace of animal skulls scraping against the ground and flinging dirt onto my legs. Five *peys* wailed and clawed at their faces so deeply that blood welled to the surface. They sucked on their fingers greedily.

I fought against the fug of magic—it was an enchantment of *hunger*. I'd never known an appetite this furious. It was in my skin, under my nails, like grit between my teeth. My throat was parched. The air tasted stale on my tongue, but I lapped at it anyway. I wanted to fill up my emptiness with anything. Everything.

"Do you feel it?" hissed Kamala. Her hoof stamped the ground, like the hunger was just an itch she could get rid of. Even if I could speak, I didn't have the chance. A sound bellowed at the front of the chamber.

"Too long we have been confined to the rules of the Otherworld . . . too long we have starved for more than the scraps the universe throws our way," said a voice. *Nritti.* "But I ask that you stay hungry just a little longer before we glut ourselves on the world. For our victory, I want you *hungry*."

My head snapped up. I clamped down on my lower lip so hard that the rust and salt taste of blood surged in my mouth. I licked it away, focusing all my attention on her. I stepped forward unsteadily, my feet slipping, legs bowing under the weight of unnatural starvation.

"We are! We are!" chanted a thousand voices.

"I want you *aching*," she crooned.

One more step. Another. Another. I was dragging my feet through the dirt, fighting my way to the front.

"We do! We do!" rose up the voices.

"Good," she said. "Tonight, in honor of my pending nuptials"—she stopped to stroke a finger against Amar's cheek; he shuddered and my heart flipped—"I will let you go *anywhere* you please."

Horror surpassed hunger. I pictured all these horrible bodies slinking across the lands I loved, living nightmares with empty stomachs and lips pulled back to reveal teeth made for rending. Gauri's determined face flashed in my mind. *No.*

Nritti stood, reaching behind her for the boy I recognized from the glen. He stared up at her and his face was incandescent with joy. He was so distracted that he did not see the blade glinting or notice how Nritti's smile stretched thin and predatory.

"Let this soul pave our way," screamed Nritti to the crowd.

They roared with happiness, surging together. Bodies pressed against my back and I reached out blindly for Kamala. Her muzzle pushed against my neck and her jaws snapped when a *churel* moved too close to me. The *churel*'s feet were twisted, her toes wrenched in the opposite direction of her face, and when she met my gaze, I saw her longing—hands twitching to feel something more than dust against palms, lolling mouth aching to be slaked with shuddering hearts and slick organs, anything to feel alive.

Amar never once raised his head. Beside Nritti, he was a shadow. I leapt onto Kamala's back and leaned close to her ear:

"Run."

And she did.

Nritti raised the knife, her head tilting, voice crooning. Her voice broke my heart, but still we kept moving. Never stopping. Lightning flickered above us. A *pey* lay trampled in the rush. I never once looked away from Nritti. I didn't know what had happened to the girl who had been my best friend. Whatever reasons once existed had gathered moss and dust in their edges. All that mattered now was the scene before me—laughter seeping into my ears, the floors thick with spilled blood, hunger that hollowed your innards and coated your tongue with dust.

Kamala reared to a halt, her forelegs clinging for purchase. I leaned across her back, my hand outstretched—"Stop!"

There was a moment where I didn't know if anyone had heard. My word felt like little more than a croak. Silence fell around us. Nritti's blade clattered to the ground and the boy stumbled back, unscathed.

Amar's head snapped up and for the first time since leaving Naraka, we stared at one another. His expression hadn't changed since the glen. It was flat, but not unkind, just . . . out of reach.

He looked as though someone had summoned him from stone. The more I looked at him, the more images prickled behind my eyes—him walking toward me, in one hand carrying a glass rose while his fingers reached for me, eager to close the space between us; his hand slung over my waist while we slept, two bodies curled into the shadow of each other.

But those images were mine alone. Amar blinked, his brows furrowing before he looked away. My heart slammed against my ribs. If I had any doubt about his last words—that he wouldn't remember me, that I would be lost to him—this moment cured them.

I was a stranger.

•» 26 «•

A DUEL OF RIDDLES

Nritti was staring at us and her face was blank and controlled.

I leapt from Kamala's back. The gaze of a thousand eyes slapped against my skin. *Think, Maya.* Anger flared inside me. Anger that she had ousted those who belonged here and ushered in those who did not. Anger that Amar was by her side. Anger that she had lied. But I tamped it down, swallowing my fury like a bitter draught. And then I did what anyone would do before a false sovereign—

I bowed.

Kamala glanced at me sidelong, a ghoulish grin across her face, "I know what she is hungry for and she is starved as the earth. Her teeth are grinding, grinding, churning stars. Do you hear it, false *sadhvi?*"

"What are you talking about?" I muttered back, my head still bent to the ground. "What is she hungry for?"

Kamala leaned closer. "*You.*"

A whip cracked through the air and I jerked my head up, only to see Nritti standing right in front of me. She tilted her head to one side and the movement was so slight, so emotionless that I thought she would slide a blade through me just to see what would happen.

"I do not believe I asked your opinion, *sadhvi*," she said.

I dropped my gaze, my neck burning. She didn't seem to know me. Then again, I was unrecognizable as the girl who had eaten up her lies in Naraka. But just to be sure I pulled one end of my robes over my head.

The point of a knife pricked my throat, tilting my head up. "Perhaps I should just use *you* instead . . ."

I froze, twisting down the fear that had stolen my breath. I wouldn't give her the satisfaction of letting my heartbeat pulse against the metal. My hands curled into fists, ready to grab her blade, when someone's voice echoed in the ruined Night Bazaar.

Amar.

He was standing, his hands outstretched. Fury shadowed his face, but in a blink, it was gone. His expression warred between lost and enraged.

"I want her to speak," said Amar. "Speak your mind, *sadhvi*. You are under my protection."

Nritti dropped the blade by a fraction, but her gaze wasn't on me. It was on Amar. Hope fluttered in my ribs. Nritti looked at Amar like he was a tame tiger who had unexpectedly torn out the throat of an animal. She looked at Amar with a flash of fear in her eyes, and hope poured through my veins.

No amount of captivity could strip the wild from the tiger. Amar was no different. He was feral. He was *mine*.

Nritti, recovering from her lapse of silence, delivered a low bow.

"As you wish, my lord. But if we are to follow through with our plans, we need a soul. What better than one that offers itself so freely?" She pointed to the little boy at the edge of the dais, knees drawn up to his chin, staring at Nritti like she was his salvation. "Look at him, he longs to be cut. I should do as he asks."

"Your enchantment has robbed his will," I shot back, the words tumbling out before I had a chance to stop them.

Wrong move. Kamala moved closer, her nose nudging into my shoulder, nostrils flaring protectively. I wanted to hug her. Beside me, a *churel* sucked in her breath and a *rakshasi* stumbled backward, as if my words would put all of their lives at risk.

The crowd around us laughed but it was thin and forced. Nritti leaned closer to me.

"When we have hollowed the world above, wouldn't death be a kinder fate to the boy? Do you want him to return to find his home destroyed? Because that is what they will do."

In the ruins of the Night Bazaar, I was all too aware of my own mortality. My heartbeat enthralled them. I was food. If they could not have the boy's blood, they would take mine.

"You are bound to be a great ruler, my lady. But on the eve of your victory, perhaps you can spare a favor to a lowly *sadhvi*?"

Nritti glared, her jaw tight, but she nodded.

"How about a game?" I asked. "Give me a riddle. If I answer correctly, you will grant me the boy."

Nritti grinned. "I will play your game, *sadhvi*. But if you answer wrong, you will take his place."

Kamala hissed into my ear, "Are you so eager to die, young queen?"

"But on one condition," I said.

Her eyes narrowed. "What?"

I looked from her to Amar. This whole time, his eyes had never left my face.

"I request a private audience with the Dharma Raja."

His face was impassive, but he nodded in my direction and the smallest of victories lodged between my ribs, light as a heartbeat and just as hopeful. Around us, the crowd of darker beings sank into the shadows. Some licked their lips. Others just stared.

"You will receive no help," said Nritti.

She reached down, tugging at the air like it was a handful of chains. Gupta was yanked out from behind the throne of thorns. His face was haggard, dirt creasing his skin. I lunged toward him, but Nritti slammed her heel into the ground and a wall of wind threw me back.

"None of that," she chided. "Take the *pishacha*."

Gupta nodded. I tried to make eye contact with him, but he refused to meet my gaze. Kamala whinnied, rearing onto her legs, fighting to stay close to me.

"We have a deal," Kamala whispered into my ear. Her voice trembled. "You may not die. Not until I have a bite, or two, of that lush-lush arm, like you promised. If you die, I will kill you."

I searched myself for a smile. "Have you grown fond of me, then?"

"As one who has grown fond of a particular dish. Nothing more."

She huffed but she wouldn't look at me. Gupta dragged her away. My hope felt bruised and cold. Winds teased the ends of my shorn hair and the *sadhvi* robes did nothing to keep out the chill.

"Which animal is the most cunning?" asked Nritti, stroking the blade between her fingers.

I frowned. That wasn't a riddle. It was a matter of opinion.

"Flustered so soon by our game?" asked Nritti. She raised the blade, tracing small, sharp circles on the exposed tops of my feet.

Bear? Too lumbering. Tiger? Too noticeable. Sweat broke out between my shoulder blades. I didn't know the answer. I paused. *I didn't know the answer.*

I cleared my throat. "The one we have yet to discover."

Nritti's smile curled into the barest of snarls. Behind her, one corner of Amar's lips quirked into a grin. Kamala laughed, stamping her hooves and tossing her head. But our game hadn't ended yet.

Nritti stepped forward. "I am clothed but cannot grow; what am I?"

I swallowed my fear. "You're either referring to one of two things. It's either me or moss over stone."

Behind Nritti, Amar let out an exhale that might—if I strained that weak hope in my ribs—have been a laugh.

"I am pleased with her answers. Give over the boy," said Amar, with a lazy wave of his hand.

Nritti smiled like her throat was full of broken glass but she did as he said. She walked the boy to me and lifted her hand off his shoulder. The room was silent and still. I reached for him immediately, but no sooner had I done so did she snatch him back.

She laughed and tilted her head. "I said I would give you the boy. I didn't say for how long."

She swiveled toward Amar, and as she moved, I saw that there was something more than just a blade clasped to her *salwar kameez*. It was Amar's noose, coiled tight against her hip. She gripped it tightly. "We need a soul, my lord. You said so yourself. If I do as you ask, the *sadhvi* must take his place. A soul for a soul."

Amar wasn't laughing anymore. The muscles in his neck tightened. His jaw clenched. But he didn't say anything. Nritti's grip on the noose turned her knuckles white. She was controlling him. I bit back a snarl.

Nritti turned back to me and her face was triumphant. "No soul, no bargain."

Kamala whinnied, pulling against Gupta. I dropped my gaze to the ground, my heart frantic when I saw my sandals—mud crusted, tearing at the seams. I grinned. *Don't worry, Kamala,* I thought, *I'm not dying.*

"I have one."

When I spoke, my gaze was for Amar alone.

"Here," I said, tearing off the sandal and throwing it at Nritti's feet, "a sole for a soul."

Kamala began to laugh and the deranged sound pitched off the walls, scattering between the bodies of the dark Otherworld beings. They stood slack-jawed and still. Only their eyes moved—

bounding between me and Nritti and back. Before Nritti could speak, a creaking sound clattered through the room.

Amar scooped the dirtied sandal in one hand before pulling me away from Nritti. His grip crushed into my arm, strong as iron. But there was something else . . . he was trembling. I could feel it through my skin.

"I accept her barter. Release the boy," he said tonelessly. "But have her locked into the chamber to Naraka." He turned to Nritti. "Her demand insulted your honor. That cannot be allowed."

The blood drained from my face. Scaled and roughened hands tugged at my arms, and I was dragged from the dais. I kicked, trying to throw off my assailant's arms, but they were like shackles. From his throne, Amar stared and beside him, Nritti's face glowed smugly.

The beasts of the Otherworld threw me behind a metal door sunken into the knotted trunk of a banyan tree. Inside, the sounds of the Otherworldly beings outside stuttered into silence. In this shadowed room, softly glowing moths lit up the walls. Fear left me trembling. They were going to kill me.

I turned around, looking for escape. Behind me was a great obsidian mirror, like the one I had once found in the room with the tree full of memories. In its reflection, the stone halls of Naraka glittered.

"You are not a *sadhvi*," said a voice.

I looked up, stunned to see Amar standing before me. He helped me to my feet, but I couldn't look at him. Every time I glanced into his face, that flat look of no recognition slashed through me.

He jerked my chin up. "Do not lie to me. Who are you?"

Tears prickled hot behind my eyes and the answer I gave him was so true, I could feel it echoing through all my hollow spaces: "I don't know."

He released his hold on my chin but he didn't step away. "You asked to see me alone. Why?"

Because I love you. But that didn't matter. Any moment now, Nritti could rush inside. All she would have to do was hold tightly to that noose and Amar would be powerless against her. Maybe I couldn't save us or what we once had. But I could save him. I could save Gauri.

"You need your noose back," I said, my voice low and urgent. I looked to the door, my heart thudding. "Nritti is *controlling* you. I know you. You would never drag a thousand children to these depths or unleash monsters into the world. Power is about *balance,* remember?"

He stepped back, his face paling, black eyes narrowing to slits. "I did not ask for your wisdom, false *sadhvi*. You do not know me."

My heart was breaking. I thought I knew, finally, what it meant to be a ghost. It meant speaking your words around a mouth full of loss. It meant grasping onto echoes and hoping, praying that the words still meant something.

"I know your soul," I said, my voice cracking. "Everything else is an ornament."

"You have a strange effect on me . . . why is that?" he asked softly. "Beside you, I am reminded of something I have forgotten."

My hands fell to my sides. There, beneath the rags of my robes, the fabric was raised and bumpy and I knew what lay beneath it—a broken circlet of hair. I fished it out of the pocket. My whole body was trembling, shaking against its restraints of bone.

Amar reached out to cup the back of my neck. I shuddered. I had forgotten how cold his hands were, like the soul of winter had tangled itself in his fingers. He stared at me and his gaze had all the finality of death—it was ferocious and terrible, a ravel of locked horns. He was *searching* me. I knew exactly what he was looking for—

Himself.

I twined the bracelet together, letting it hover mere inches from his skin. I had no expectation, no method, no strategy. I was blind and clinging to a bruised piece of hope. But it was all I had.

"You once said your soul could never forget mine," I said, sliding the mended bracelet around his wrist. "Do you remember now?"

He inhaled sharply, like something had rent through him. Around his wrist, the bracelet glowed like a caught star.

"Jaani," he breathed, staring at me.

He clutched his chest, an amazed smile turning his face incandescent. I grinned so widely that I thought the air would bend around us, pushing us together. His fingers entwined in my hair and he tilted my face up. I was leaning toward him hungrily, but in the next instant, his smile faltered. Amar's brow crumpled with pain. He stumbled, his knees buckling.

"What's wrong—" I started, moving to help him.

The door swung open. Nritti stepped in and our eyes met. I

knew, then, why she had avoided looking at me. She had known who I was the whole time.

"Let me kill you," she said soothingly, drawing out the blade. "I've already told all the beings outside that you have corrupted the Dharma Raja. They will descend on you like dawn upon the vestiges of night, and I will do nothing to honor your memory." She paused and spared me a smile that sent icicles blooming across my chest. "I will not wipe up your blood. I will not mourn you. I will not *care*.

"Trust me," she said, stroking the edge of the blade. "It is better this way."

Nritti spared a glance at Amar. He had sunk to his knees, his hands clutching his heart.

"Stop this," I said through gritted teeth. "Give him back the noose. You're killing him."

She tilted her head to one side, staring at the blade.

"I'm not killing him," she said calmly. "Not yet. The Dharma Raja is weak." She stretched the noose tight and Amar seized up, his breath coming out in staggering gasps. His face paled.

"Stop!" I cried, lunging toward Nritti, but with a flick of her wrist, I was thrown back against the wall.

My head slammed against the metal with a resounding thud. Nritti laughed and twisted the cord between pale fingers.

"I take no pleasure in squashing an ant. But you are a very peculiar insect. And all because the all-powerful Dharma Raja made a foolish mistake."

"What mistake?" I asked, my voice barely above a whisper.

"You once knew me so well. You know how I am. Why would

I give up the secret before the game is done?" Nritti took a step toward Amar.

I fought to get to him first, but each step took me farther and farther away from him until my body was pressed against the rickety frames of the room.

"You said I was killing him," said Nritti, kneeling beside him. She glanced at the dagger then at Amar. "Who am I to make you a liar?"

My body contorted into a scream. But all the sound I might have scraped up from every recess of myself was useless against a sharp blade. I watched, paralyzed, as Nritti sank the blade into his heart. Amar shuddered, his body tense. The muscles of his neck stood out in sharp relief. His eyes rolled back, the whites of his sockets glistening before they focused on me.

"Jaani," he said, a shaky smile curling his lips.

Amar tapped his lips twice, one hand fluttering to his heart. And then he went still. I blinked back tears, and a scream wrenched from my throat. Grief cut me, separating me like a soul from its body. I was nothing more than a being of fury and heartbreak.

"Don't worry, my friend," said Nritti.

She yanked the dagger from Amar's chest. It came away with a sickening, unclasping sound. Nausea roiled in my gut. Whatever magic Nritti used kept me pinned to the wall, but that didn't stop my limbs from trembling.

"I won't let you languish alone. Let me put you out of your mortal misery and finish my efforts," said Nritti. "It's an honor, truly. You will be the last person to die. After that, death is nothing."

•» 27 «•

A TANGLE OF THREAD

Nritti flicked her wrist and this time I fell to the ground, my knees slamming into the packed earth. Blood thrummed in my ears. Pain radiated through my body. I looked at Amar, sprawled across the floor, his wrist flung out. The bracelet gleamed pale as moonstone against his skin. His eyes were fixed on the fathomless ceiling above us. He may have been immortal, but Nritti's control had rendered him into a mere echo of himself. He was worse than dead.

Nritti's shadow fell across the floor. She was coming for me. I began to crawl toward Amar, ready to fold him to me in my last moments, but I stopped. That was what she wanted. What she *expected*. But that was where she was wrong. She had mistaken my strength for weakness. I loved Amar. I loved him enough that it catapulted my fear into frenzy, my hurt into hope.

I didn't run to him because I had loved and lost.

I ran from him because I loved him. And I would not lose him.

Nritti sent a sickening wave of magic my way. For a moment, I faltered. My legs nearly crumpled beneath me. Tongues of flame lit up the floor, turning everything around me ghastly and shadowed. But I didn't stop. I didn't turn. My gaze was fixed on the obsidian mirror glittering at one end of the room. In the portal's reflection, Naraka's stone halls twinkled.

My feet stamped into the ground, closer and closer. Heat seared my lungs. The moments between escaping Nritti and entering Naraka sprang out like thorns, each one pricking at me, each one sharper than the next, each one a knot of pain. Until—finally—my hands touched the mirror's cool surface. My singed fingers skimmed something smooth as glass . . . and I *pushed*.

The stolen moment from entering one world to the next raised the hairs on the back of my neck and twisted my insides, but then, I was through. Behind me, the portal shivered, the surface curdling black.

I stood in one of Naraka's pale halls. Lanterns sprang along the stones. Beside me, a carven niche in the wall held a small statue of a mynah bird. I grabbed it and, with all the strength I had left, pitched it straight into the mirror. The surface crackled, light seaming along the edges.

I didn't know whether it would keep Nritti away long enough for me to do what needed to be done. But I had to try. Against her,

I was powerless. I was *mortal*. She thought that was a weakness, but I knew better.

Being mortal meant that I had a thread hidden somewhere in that tapestry. Being mortal meant that I could free myself from the tapestry. It meant that I still had a chance to claim the powers that were once mine, to fight back against Nritti.

I blinked back tears, trying to forget how still Amar's body looked on the floor. He wasn't gone. He couldn't be. I flew down the halls when I saw it—the throne room. A sieve of dust coated the floor. The air settled heavy and neglected around my shoulders. Outside, the sky of Naraka was a lurid yellow and ice spidered and crackled against the ledges.

The moment my feet hit the floor, a familiar tug in my gut wrenched my gaze away from the window. The tapestry. Its pull had not diminished; if anything its strange lull from before had turned into a pulsing, writhing frenzy. It twisted in and out of sight, shapes sinking and remolding the longer I looked at them. In one second, the threads became bleached as bone, bulging out from the surface until it turned into the beveled form of a white elephant who shook his head with sorrow and bent his trunk to collect a thunderstorm. *Airavata*.

Color burst prismatic into the threads, each piece of silk or worsted crewel sliding into the burnt landscape of a realm I knew so well—*Bharata*. Again and again, the tapestry changed: a horse with its ribs poking out of its sides, garnet eyes rolling back into its head; a young man clambering onto a throne; Gauri riding in the dark; the sea of cells beneath my feet in Naraka . . . each individual in its confines shivering, waiting, wondering. I even saw my father in those threads. His brow was creased, his fingers skimming over the mirrored walls of his prison, wondering when he would be released into the next life. And I saw myself. Not as a former queen who had once commanded the tapestry, but as a woman with her back bent in sorrow and age, still wearing the same saffron *sadhvi* robes, peddling tales to anyone who would listen.

Tears ran freely down my face. The tapestry was taunting me. Every single one of those images was an invitation to fall to my knees and admit that I couldn't save them. That I couldn't save *myself*. I steeled my heart's frantic, veering beat.

The tapestry was testing me. It wasn't prophetic. It could augur nothing from entrails of thread. It was a design. And designs could be altered.

Somewhere in that swirling thicket was my thread.

And I had to untangle it from the black, widening hole of the tapestry. I marched forward, letting the tapestry call to me, sing to me, serenade its secrets and entwine about my ankles. I let it fill me and guide me to myself. I flung out my hands, breathing slowly and deeply, pushing out all the sounds I imagined in the background—of mirrors crackling, and an entrance tearing. My fingers skittered over the tapestry, hovering over threads that I knew weren't mine . . . and then I felt it. A pinch in my soul, and something startling me, like a word caught in my throat.

I reached forward, my eyes burning at the sight of the tapestry. Sweat beaded on my skin and my breath fell out in damp heaves. My thread was slick, shining as indigo and oil. But it was caught in something, another thread that was white-hot and iridescent. *Nritti.*

I braced myself, knowing what would happen the moment my skin touched the threads. I remembered my insides wrenching around Vikram's thread all those days ago. I remembered the tapestry weighing me and finding me wanting. I remembered his past flickering like a beating heart in my hands. It had been hard then, and that was just one soul. Now, I was plunging myself into two lifetimes.

The two threads seared against my palm. Pain flared behind my eyes and I was falling, my feet slipping against the dusted marble, my whole body tilting around the inferno of the tapestry. I clutched the two threads and my hands burned. I screamed, but never heard myself. The room had lapped up my shrieks.

The skin on my hands peeled back. I was being pried open, each bone lifted from my body to make room for memories—memories stout as trunks, thin as lightning, furred and fanged, solid and slippery. Memories that were mine and Nritti's. Memories that were starving for recognition. Memories so hungry, they *consumed.*

The threads called, and I answered—

It was too late to turn back now.

•» 28 «•

LOST NAMES

I remembered my lost names. I unfurled them, smoothing their worn creases, inhaling their scent of star-swollen evenings and monsoon dusks. Nritti had lied. I was no *yakshini* by the edges of forest glens. I was *more,* so much more. I clasped my lost names to me—

Yamuna. The name barreled around my ankles, brackish and forceful. A river striped with tortoises and water that glowered and snapped. A force that could drown.

Yamini. The name pressed a cool hand against my heart, warm as freshly wrought stars flung into the winter-black of night.

The names gave me strength. They gave me history. They gave me one more secret to myself, and I would know them all. I opened my eyes, squinting against the brightness as two images spun around before converging into a single scene.

Nritti was dancing in Patala, a part of the sprawling Otherworld that held neither sun nor moon, but remained bright with sparkling, unearthly jewels. She danced in a hundred courts, content. Happy. The pride of all the *devas* and *asuras*. And then she met Vanaj, the youngest son of a mortal king, brought to the Otherworldly court for his role in vanquishing five *rakshas* who had plagued sacred grounds.

He loved her.

And she loved him.

And in such bliss does devastation grow.

They spent years in each other's arms. Wandering groves, living as hermits in an ashram of marble where nothing grew around them but lush fruit trees. No one murmured their discontent but the silver fish in the nearby rivers. Nothing interrupted their lovemaking but the cusp of dawn and the famished growl of their own bodies.

Then came the war of the two sundered families.

And Vanaj was called away.

Nritti stood before me, her lovely face wasted, gaunt. She stood in Naraka's palace, facing the thrones where Amar and I sat.

"You must help me, sister. He is dying. I know it. I have done everything I can." Her voice cracked. "I have performed the severest of penances. I have begged each sage. I can do no more."

Amar looked at me and my heart clenched. I knew that gaze. Resignation. Already I knew where Vanaj's thread hovered, flickering, unraveling from the grand tapestry. But there was nothing that could be done. Some threads left no ambiguity for life or death.

And Nritti saw it in my face.

"Traitor," she hissed.

"What can I do, sister?" I beseeched her. "Even we are powerless. But I can follow his soul, remake him anew. You need only wait and he will be your Vanaj again."

"I. Want. Him. Back."

"You cannot," said Amar softly. "We know your pain, but—"

Nritti laughed, her eyes wide. "*You*? You don't know my pain. Neither of you do. You sit there, commanding life or death as though it was nothing but a foolish child's game."

Amar stood up, his face stony. "There is nothing we can do."

"Yes, there is!" she screamed, tearing at her hair. "He doesn't have to die! Who let you decide? Why are either of you fit to take away life? Death is unnecessary."

She hissed, hurtling her curses at both of us. She would not listen. Even when I tried to find her, day after day, year after year. I spent hours poring over the tapestry, seeking out her thread, but it was as though she had vanished.

I saw Nritti stalking burial grounds and defiling ancient temples. She walked through crowded villages, murmuring under her breath. The moment she touched something—tree bark, cow skin, a boy's forehead—they burned and burned. She entered in silence and left in chaos. She trailed it, dropping fury like candies.

The golden-skinned *apsara* with the quick smile and eyes like crystal was gone, replaced with an equally beautiful but terrifying and bloodless version of herself. I saw her watching me through the obsidian mirror that we used to summon one another.

I saw her pressing herself against it and snarling:

"One day, your inadequacy will sneak up on you, like shadows upon bodies. One day, your pride will fall like glass. And when it does, I'll be there to take back what is mine."

I remembered the terrible decision that fell to me. A *deva* had been cursed to rebirth as a mortal man. I weighed his crime of theft and measured his life thread, spinning out his doom and death, inscribing those truths on his forehead. For his terrible crime, a terrible end—death on the battlefield, a bed of arrows for his funeral pyre. He would take no wife. He would bounce no child upon his knee or know the joy of love. But he would be illustrious and wise. And when his time on earth expired, the heavens would embrace him once more.

And as I spun it, sang it and wrote it, so it became.

Fury and rumors flitted to the Otherworld, that the Rani of Naraka had befouled her title with her decisions. I paid no attention to the rumors.

But Amar did.

"If this continues, they will storm our palace. I cannot let that happen. We have the sanctity of the balance to maintain."

I flinched; something in his words felt strangely distant. "Do you believe them?"

"Of course not," he said, waving a dismissive hand. But I caught a tremor in his fingers. "Still, we need to control the peace. We must care what they think."

"Why? It won't change anything."

"It's your"—he caught his words—"*our* reputation."

The realms held council in illustrious courts above the clouds, where thunder stalked in the corners and lightning crowned each throne. The air was uncommonly bright, livid with sunshine and splendor. Many-limbed *devas* reclined on carved clouds, clutching ambrosial *soma* in golden goblets as they questioned me.

Throughout my questioning, the Dharma Raja stood by my side, a silken shadow against all this light. I believed in myself, and with Amar supporting me, my decision was invincible.

"How could you be so cruel?" exclaimed one. "No wife in his mortal life?"

"His wife would not be reincarnated with him. I will not give him another."

A woman with a white veil, whose skin glowed like dawn, shot me a trembling smile.

"And what about his brothers? Did they not also partake in his crime of theft?" retorted another.

"They did," I said.

"Then why must he endure a whole life as a human when his brothers live less than a year in that realm?"

"Because they were accomplices. Not the instigators of the crime. It was he who committed the most wrong. It is he who must live the longest."

The *deva* beside me stomped his feet and lightning flared behind him.

"And what say you, Dharma Raja? How will you defend your queen's decision?"

I remembered holding my chin high, surveying the crowd with the tasteful indifference of one who knew she was impervious. And I remembered when that moment fell with his next words:

"If you doubt her, then I propose an *agni pariksha*. Fire will always tell."

The *devas* and *devis* nodded approvingly to themselves. A trial by fire. Humiliation burned through me. I dropped my hand from his and the world broke between us.

Betrayal felt bitter and acrid in my throat, and the ghost of it was everywhere, taunting my reflection. How could he do this to me? How could he doubt me so much to expose me to the ridicule and glances of the celestial world? All this time, Amar said nothing. Our bed became a cold thing and my heart froze with it.

I remembered the night I awoke all alone, my eyes still puffed and swollen from weeping. Our bed was empty, the room echoing. I heard my name called through a mirror portal that Nritti had once used. Silently, I walked through the halls, my hair unbound and catching along the newfound icicles hanging across marble eaves.

Nritti was there. Waiting. I ran to embrace her, not once seeing that her fingers were stained red, that the smell of rot clung to her. I was blind.

"I forgive you," she said tonelessly. "And I come in warning."

"Of what?"

"Your Dharma Raja has turned on you, sister."

Her words became my poison and I let it fill me, blind me, until all I saw was betrayal.

Nritti fed me images through an obsidian portal—Amar tearing out the tapestry threads like throats, of him gloating in the fallen lives, of him ignoring my words, waiting for the moment where he could use the *agni pariksha* to exile me forever.

"You were nothing but his dark plaything," Nritti said.

And I let myself believe her.

On the day of the *agni pariksha,* light transfixed Amar's face.

"I have every faith in you, my love," he said, trailing fingers along my jaw. "This will put an end to every rumor. This will keep you safe from them. I know our days have been cold, but after this, we will be as we once were."

Inside, my heart snarled, but I kept my face blank. "I will not disappoint."

All the members of the Otherworld assembled for my trial. I wore white, the dress of mourning. In the Night Bazaar, a dim glow lit up the faces of the attendees, clinging to well-oiled horns and scaled skin. Leonine *rakshas* waited patiently, weapons quivering in their grip. If I failed, they were free to depose me. If I succeeded, they would end their bloodshed in the human realms.

Sacred flames lapped up from the ground. Ribbons of fire snaked out like tongues and grasping hands. I looked to Amar. His face was stern. Hopeful. For what outcome, I thought I knew. But I was wrong.

The *agni pariksha* scraped through me, burning talons that combed through my being. Survive unscathed and it was proof of my worthiness as queen. I did not doubt that I would pass. The question was what to do after. Nritti's words floated through my mind as I burned and burned and burned. *He wants you to fail, sister. He does not know how strong you are. When you succeed, leave. Leave his horrible kingdom. Let him fend for himself. Let him weep. Let him fail. Start anew. With me.*

Nritti had fed me so many images—Amar dancing with a

beautiful *nagini* in a sea palace carved of glass. Amar flinching from my touch. My tongue was full of smoke and heartbreak. My mind was full of lies.

I don't remember when the *agni pariksha* ended. I only remembered emerging, my ankles encircled with ash. A deafening roar—applause or resentment, fury or joy—as I left. And I remember Amar's face, one dark eyebrow arched as he surveyed the crowd, a proud smirk on his face as though he expected this all along.

All that time, I thought he was merely pretending.

In Naraka, a feast awaited me. Every room dripped silver, glass blooms and petals carpeted the floor. The walls of our kingdom shimmered as if underwater and moonlight glimmered through the lattice windows. Sweet *kafir* cream and *pista* cakes in golden bowls lay piled high among the tables. But I would touch none of it.

"Are you disappointed?" I asked coldly.

Amar slipped his arms around my waist. "I always believed in you. It is the world outside who needed convincing."

"Liar," I hissed, stepping out of the ring of his arms.

"What is the meaning of this?"

"You humiliated me. You left me to them like carrion before vultures. And like vultures, they devoured me."

My voice was hoarse and brittle. I hated him. I hated him for abandoning me. I hated him for needing him.

Amar stepped back, his jaw clenched. "I did it to quell dissent. To keep you safe. I was ashamed that I had to ask you to undergo the *agni pariksha*."

"So ashamed you distanced yourself from me the moment *you* demanded that trial?"

Amar looked stunned. "I am the Dharma Raja for a reason. I would not have my own impartiality questioned by favoring you. Surely, you knew this."

"What would you have done if I failed?"

"You couldn't fail," said Amar. "That's why I did not worry. You were meant to be the queen of these lands. We were meant to rule together. For all of eternity."

"I would rather die than rule by the side of a coward."

Shadows curled away from Amar's body.

"Coward?" he hissed. "Cowardice is running from the difficult choices made by the ones that love you most. If I have been a coward, so have you, *jaani*. But we may start anew. Let us not speak of this time any longer."

He tried, once more, to tilt my face into a kiss, but I moved away.

"I saw you spread the rumors yourself in the Otherworld. I watched you take solace in another's arms. And if surviving the *agni pariksha* means spending eternity with you, then I would rather live life as a mortal."

The room became damp and sticky with darkness.

"What *lies* you hurl at me," he murmured.

"I don't trust you."

He stepped back, wounded. "Has your judgment become so compromised? If you truly do not believe the truth in my words, then you have no place here."

We stared at one another, fury swelling between us. The silence expanded, solidifying our words like manacles.

"Once, I thought you loved me," I said in a broken voice. "I refuse to live in your shadow for the rest of eternity."

His eyes widened, obsidian eyes searching and disbelieving.

"Then leave!" he said, gesturing to the door angrily.

So I did.

I stepped into the reincarnation pool, letting the waters tease my life apart, inflicting upon myself the same curse that had forced me to undergo the *agni pariksha*. In the distance, Amar's voice roared for me. Pleading. But it was too little. And far too late.

I blinked furiously and the images spun away. The two threads lay against my palm, scalding and writhing like twin serpents. My head was full of what I had seen and what I now knew. I had allowed myself to hear lies and never questioned their truth. I had let suspicion rule me at a terrible price.

My grip on the threads tightened. I had to release myself from her hold.

Outside, the sky pulsed yellow and the marble floors of Naraka sweltered with heat. In the distance, I heard the faintest shattering sound and my heart lurched. Nritti had gotten through. Any minute now and she would run into the throne room. She would wield her powers and I—still powerless, still mortal—would fall.

I tugged at the threads. But they wouldn't budge. My lungs filled with fire. *No. No, please . . . not now.* The tapestry was leering and weighing, waiting and wondering. The weight of its magic was a crushing thing and my mind was splintering beneath it. Images skittered across my skin, pushing up beneath my fingernails, prickling against my feet. I heard Nritti's voice filtered through the threads—"unworthy." I heard my own thoughts echoing, tilting around my hurt.

And then I stopped. Those moments were mine, but they didn't define me anymore. I wouldn't let my doubts cripple me. I had to accept who I was, what I had done and, more important, who I could *be*. Amar's voice wrapped around me. *Trust yourself. Trust who you are.* I hadn't listened to him then, but I would now. I stared down the tapestry. I knew, now, why it had refused my touch. It didn't know me because I didn't know myself. And so I spoke as if in greeting:

"I am Maya and Yamuna and Yamini. I am a frightened girl, a roaring river and night incarnate," I said. My voice was strong and clear. Around me, the tapestry shrank back, like a scolded animal. "I have been a forgotten princess, a stubborn queen and a false *sadhvi*. And I will not be tethered."

Calm spiraled around me. I no longer saw Naraka's livid sky, nor heard the scrape of glass along the halls. I had slipped into a moment of lost time, a moment for me alone, something sacred and inviolate—as precious as self. I grasped hold of my thread, untwisting it slowly from Nritti's.

"My life belongs to me," I said.

And then I pulled.

•» 29 «•

AN END. A BEGINNING.

Light seeped through my skin like water. Light pressed its fingers against the cracks in my being, patched the rifts and ravines with memory until I was drenched in color, in sound, in *life*. When I stepped away from the tapestry, I felt . . . heavier. As if all this time, my existence was an ethereal thing spent searching for myself.

It was time. Time to leave this limbo. Time to embrace the light that was neither banished nor tainted, but buried deep within me, waiting until I could claim it once more. The tapestry shivered. I thought I heard a sigh of relief echo in the halls. Before me, the threads convulsed, weaving an entirely different image—*Amar*. His eyes were still open and unseeing, but I knew he wasn't lost. The tapestry was trying to tell me something. I thought about his last moments, his last actions . . . he had called me *jaani* and tapped his lips twice before his hands fluttered to his heart.

And then I understood. I knew why Nritti couldn't destroy him.

I was his *jaan*. His life. Kill me, and he would be rendered useless, an echo of himself.

"I will save you," I whispered to his image.

The tapestry sank away, shimmering into a mirror-portal where I could see the Otherworld's reflection glittering in the distance. I could see Amar's body sprawled out, waiting for me. I was about to push through the portal when the sound of a blade dragging through dust stopped me.

"Found you," sneered Nritti.

I didn't turn immediately. Her voice rippled in my head. Despite everything, I mourned her. I mourned *us*. I mourned for the girls that had crouched beside a riverbank and fished out tortoises and pearls. I gathered all that sorrow . . . and then I let it go.

"I was not hiding," I said, turning to face her.

Her face blanched. "You've . . . you've changed."

I looked down. I had changed. But not in looks. I was not splendidly clothed like Nritti and neither bangles adorned my wrists nor did tiaras sparkle at my temples. Instead, inky clouds scooted across my skin before fading softly into rose-gold and plum-velvet. Warm stars dusted my palms and storm clouds danced about my ankles. I was wreathed in light.

"So did you," I said softly. "Is this what Vanaj wanted? He loved you."

Nritti stepped back, flinching. "He did. And you wouldn't save him. You were too weak to do anything for me."

"No, my friend. It was you who was weak."

I looked past her, to the ruined Night Bazaar in the portal. The sky should have shown the sun and moon dancing above. Instead, there was only clammy dark. And I was tired of the dark. I closed my eyes. In my mind, I pictured the mango grove outside my room in the harem. I pictured the sweetness of Amar's kiss, the fierce look in Gauri's eyes, Kamala's blood-curdling laugh. Those moments were parsed pieces of myself and they held a power more potent than chaos—it was life, strong and pulsating.

I stretched out my fingertips, letting their strength leak onto the ground, pooling into golden puddles that sent a force of light between me and Nritti. She screamed, throwing her hands to shield herself. And as she did, Amar's noose was thrown out of her hands and soared into the air. I reached out—

—and caught it.

I grinned. This time, I didn't look back to see what I had lost. I felt the mirror-portal against my hands, let hope swell between my ribs, and then I *pushed.*

I stumbled through the portal. The sounds were deafening. Outside the small room where Amar lay, voices hollered for war, for blood. Nritti's enchantment of hunger hadn't ceased. If anything, it had only grown. Within seconds, they could storm through the barriers of the Otherworld and sink their teeth into the human realms. I couldn't let that happen. But I couldn't stop them alone.

I gathered Amar in my arms. For the first time, there was no nagging absence in the seams of my soul. I was whole. All the frayed patches of my spirit mended. The tapestry's glittering threads had climbed through the fissures of memory and half-dreams and filled them with color. I looked at him and *love* filled me. I loved him with the force of a thousand lifetimes, made greater by the fact that my love was returned.

I clasped his hands around the noose. A touch of color returned to his cheeks.

"You are my life too," I said and then I pressed my lips to his.

A burst of heat met my hands before it tempered to something cool and distant. Amar stirred on my lap, solid hands reaching to clasp my fingers. He blinked, shaking his head. Slowly, as if he was approaching something fragile and hallowed, he traced the length of our tangled fingers before his gaze trailed past my arm, my neck, before fixing on my eyes. We were truly, *finally* visible to one another.

Neither the secret whirring song of the stars nor the sonorous canticles of the earth knew the language that sprang up in the space between us. It was a dialect of heartbeats, strung together with the lilt of long suffering and the incandescent hope of an infinite future. Amar searched my face, his fingers hovering over my jaw-line, lips and collarbones. But he didn't touch me. Instead, he took in a shuddering breath.

"Are you real?" he managed, his voice a shadow. "Or are you an illusion? Some final punishment for losing my way?"

"I'm no illusion," I said, staring into his eyes.

The ferocity of his stare laid my soul bare for him to judge.

"I thought I would be lost forever," he said hoarsely, pulling me to him.

His hands tangled in my hair, the kiss resonating at my core. He pressed his lips to mine with the intensity of lifetimes and when we finally broke apart, his lips curved into a fragile smile.

"You've saved me."

"Did you have any doubts that I could?"

He hesitated. "Your abilities are something I could never doubt. Your *will,* however, I was unsure of. When I could finally bring you back, I thought you would leave again. I'd never have a chance to explain. Forgive me—"

I stopped him. "I will not let us be beings of regret. I know my past. What I want is my future."

He smiled and moved to kiss me again, when the entire room quivered. The flimsy walls of the room split and tore. The obsidian mirror before us snapped in half and Nritti tumbled out. She stared at us and her mouth curled into a snarl.

"Not again," she hissed.

Amar tried to protect me, but I slipped out of his arms and rose to my feet. I wasn't the one in need of protecting. It was Nritti. Amar smiled and joined me. He stamped his foot against the earth and the walls around us fell. The din of the Otherworld rose riotous around us. Nritti's enchantment nearly claimed my balance, but I held strong.

All that *hunger.* It was plain in the faces of the Otherworldly beings. *Rakshas* the size of elephants had sunk to their knees, filling their mouths with dirt. Even the great *timingala* had begun to keen, slapping its tail into the water and drenching the Otherworld. I watched as a bull-aspect demon slammed his horns into the ground, upheaving dirt. My stomach flipped. If Nritti wouldn't lead them to the human realm to sate their bloodlust, then they would *dig* their way to the human realm.

In the fray of people, my gaze flew to the only two beings not moving: Gupta and Kamala. The moment he saw me, Gupta dropped his hold on Kamala. He stared at me, a huge smile tugging at his lips. Kamala snorted and stamped the ground before galloping to me. I caught her around the neck, burying my face in her mane.

"Certainly a false *sadhvi*, but not a false queen . . . ," she said, nuzzling me.

Eyes like lamplight turned to us, glances cutting away from the dirt to witness me and Amar. When the Otherworld beings saw us, they paused, brows furrowing as if they had forgotten something important and had only just remembered. I flexed my fingers. Some of the darkness lifted, blotted away like ink on a page. The space around me was a pelt in need of mending. Even now, I could feel through its rifts, sensing all the pieces that had been knocked askew in chaos like broken bones. Somewhere under the muddled air of sweat and dried blood was the bright scent of fairy fruit. Somewhere between those ragged strips of night lay moonbeams tangled with lightning, stars ripped and furious. I could mend it all.

The whole of the Otherworld fell silent. Some of the Otherworldly beings shook their heads and stumbled backward. Others dropped their weapons and prostrated themselves on the ground. But most of them didn't fall as easily. Instead, they turned their attention toward Nritti, waiting for directions.

"You have gone too far," said Amar.

Nritti grinned. "You have not even begun to witness the destruction I can wreak."

"We won't give you that chance," I said.

Amar moved to my side. He didn't crouch behind or run in front. He stood by my side as an equal. He laced his fingers in mine, his expression handsomely severe.

"What should we do, *jaani?*"

"Restore the light," I said.

Amar grinned. He wrung his hands like he was balancing an invisible sphere, his face drawn in focus. In the space between his fingers, a small pinprick of light began to whirl faster and faster. Nritti roared, flashing her palms up. But I was faster. *Stronger.*

She screeched at the nearby *rakshas* and *bhuts,* pointing wildly at me, but the monsters refused to budge. "What's wrong with you fools?" she yelled. "Forget it! I'll do it myself! You're weak," she seethed at the shrinking fey, "and when I'm the Rani of these realms, I will find each and every one of you pathetic excuses of monsters and show you the meaning of hell."

"For that," I said, "you'll need some experience."

Nritti turned her glinting eyes on me, her lips stretching into a sneer. "And you're going to do that for me, are you? You don't know the first thing about power."

"Then let me demonstrate."

Magic crackled at my palms, twisting serpentine around my

legs and arms until my limbs bowed under the weight of it all. I breathed deeply, sensing the movement of life around me as though it were light through prisms. From one angle, Gupta charged toward the crowd, walloping *rakshas* and *asuras* with his scrolls of bone. Kamala pulled her lips back to reveal sharp teeth, laughing to herself as she ripped out the throat of the bull-aspect *raksha*. I felt Amar's power beside mine, a shadow to my light, a rhythm to match our music. And in that unknown space before me, I sensed Nritti. Her power was a wrenching thing, starless black and sorrow, but my magic was something more . . . it was *hope*.

A rupturing sound echoed and the Night Bazaar transformed into an unlikely arena. *Rakshas* the size of boulders flung themselves at Gupta and Amar. Gupta danced around their bludgeoning movements. From the palms of his hands, inky tendrils of smoke fell over the *rakshas* and *peys* and they fell backward, their eyes glassy. He jumped forward, spinning in tight circles, drenching enemies in sticky, blinding black.

Gusts of wind knocked back *rakshas,* sending them tumbling like avalanches down the ranks of the uprising beings. Nritti screamed, throwing up pillars of black. She darted through them, her reflection scattering. Shadow arrows sprayed across the ruined Night Bazaar.

Nritti didn't seem to care who she hit. My eyes widened in horror as the feathers found less likely targets—*peys* who fought at her side, their last expression choked and bewildered; writhing *nagas* with their cobra-hoods flared open, baring fangs the size of scimitars.

Chaos lit up the riot of Otherworldly beings. They flew at each other, all sense of a common enemy gone. Blood sank into the ground of the Night Bazaar and the earth gathered the offering greedily, leaving nothing in return save for damp plots of dirt and ash. The cacophony of grinding hooves and entangled horns joined the din of lightning and thunder above. Steam rose languidly from the ground, burning where demon blood had evanesced.

I summoned magic to my fingertips until it gathered like a cloud around us. And then . . . I released it, letting it ribbon around the ruined Night Bazaar, bolstering shattered beams, siphoning away its cloak of broken gloom. Beside me, Amar dropped the diamond of light between his hands. It hit the ground and then the air stood still. Pinpoints of light burst in the air. Explosions erupting with heat, with screams . . .

Through the din, Amar's gaze sought mine. Around us, the walls converged, shattering to the ground in thunderous claps. Light sang as it spread across the floor. Above, a great ripping sound echoed through the Night Bazaar. Nritti's sneer faded, pale skin draining to an absolute white. She froze in mid-scream, wild eyes flashing between vacant and livid.

The magic at my fingertips shuddered with ferocity. I spun it in my hands, and then opened my palms, letting my own enchantment of binding wrap around Nritti, folding to encase her and preserve her in a translucent shell of ash and silt.

Not gone, not defeated . . . but contained.

She would never hurt anyone again.

With Nritti's spell broken, the Otherworldly beings collapsed. The dark ones screamed, but the glittering light roared back, engulfing their sounds and bodies. Light washed over us and I felt a tug at my core even as my feet remained on the ground. Above, the sky of the Night Bazaar returned, one side gleaming with the sun and the other shining with the moon. Gupta flew to us, holding up his writing board as though it were a sword. I pulled him into a hug and when I drew away, tears shined in his eyes.

"I missed you, my friend," he said, dabbing his eyes with one dirtied end of his torn coat.

I squeezed his shoulder. "And I missed you."

Kamala trotted beside me, her lips a ghastly shade of red.

I bowed to her. "You can have a bite of my arm now if you'd like."

She tossed her head, gesturing at the fallen demons around us. "I am quite sated. I would, however, ask another thing . . ."

"What is that?"

Kamala bent her head to the ground, her voice low and shy. ". . . I could stay with you. If you'll have me. And I wouldn't eat anyone. That is a promise. Unless you asked me to eat someone. In which case, I would be easily persuaded."

I drew her to a hug. "You may stay."

When we had shaken enough hands and embraced enough people, Amar pulled me away from the sounds, back through the room with flimsy walls where the torn obsidian mirror-portal glowed blearily. There was only a handful of air between us, but it was all illusion. We were closer than that, two souls sewn together with light.

His palm slid to my cheek and my skin sang. I loved him with two loves. One, a relic of another era. Another, unformed and hot, a freshly wrought star. All enigma and song. I think he felt the same way because his next words were almost resentful:

"You are quite deceptive, my queen. Like a handful of light one moment and then winged night the next." He smiled. "I would know all your mysteries if you would let me."

"You can try, but you'll never know them," I said. "I have a thousand smiles, a hundred forms. Not to mention all my names."

He closed the space between us, lips skimming hungrily across mine.

"Then I am pleased we have eternity," he said, pulling me into a kiss.

When we broke apart, I leaned against Amar's chest and I listened. I listened to his heart, to the world outside folding away the shadows. I listened to the absence of my mother's necklace from my throat, wondering whether the sapphire was now cool against Gauri's neck. I listened as the seams of the earth absorbed its wounds, to the light falling thickly over the ruined Night Bazaar. I knew there were a thousand tasks left to complete. Markets to rebuild, a tapestry in need of tending . . . but for a moment, I concentrated on the sound of Amar's heart and the feel of our fingers entwined.

I was free.

I was whole.

I was Queen of Naraka.

GLOSSARY

APSARA: A celestial nymph known for dancing and associated with the water and clouds.

BHUTS: A restless ghost sometimes created from improperly performing a deceased's funerary rites.

GANDHARVAS: Male nature spirits, often depicted as celestial musicians in the court of the gods.

PISHACHA: A flesh-eating demon known to haunt cremation grounds.

RAJA: A title for an Indian monarch.

RAKSHA: A demonic being, though not always malevolent.

SOMA: A golden nectar which first gave the gods their immortality.

SWAYAMVARA: An ancient Indian practice where women chose their husbands from among a list or lineup of suitors.

YAKSHINI: Female mythological creatures who guarded earth's treasures and are often considered the equivalent of "fairies."

Keep reading for a sneak peek of
the next Star-Touched novel

A Crown of Wishes

•⟫ **PROLOGUE** ⟪•

THE INVITATION

Vikram had spent enough time with bitterness that he knew how to twist and numb the feeling. Tonight, he didn't draw on his years of experience. Instead he let the acidic, snapping teeth of it chew at his heart. As he walked to the network of wooden huts that formed the ashram, the echo of laughter hung in the air. He stood in the dark, an outsider to a joke everyone knew.

Since he was eight years old, he had spent part of every year at the ashram, learning alongside other nobility. Everyone else resented the part of the year where they returned to their kingdoms and endured having to put their lessons to use. Not Vikram. Every time he returned to Ujijain, he was reminded that his education was a formality. Not a foundation. He preferred that. No expectations meant learning without fear of being limited and growing opinions without fear of voicing them. His thoughts preferred the fertile ground of silence. Silence sharpened shrewdness, which only made him embrace the title his father's empire had, albeit grudgingly, given him: Fox Prince.

But shrewd or not, the moment he entered the ashram, he wouldn't be able to ignore the celebrations of another prince called home to rule. Soon, Ujijain would summon him home. And then what? The days would bleed together. The hope would shrivel. It would be harder to outwit the council. Harder to speak. He tightened his fists. That bitterness turned taunting. How many years had he spent believing that he was meant for more? Sometimes he thought his head was a snarl of myth and folktales, where magic coaxed ignored princes out of the shadows and gave them a crown and a legend to live in. He used to wait for the moment when magic would drape a new world over his eyes. But time turned his hopes dull and lightless. The Council of Ujijain had seen to that.

Near the entrance of the ashram, a sage sat beside the dying flames of a ceremonial fire. What was a sage doing here at this hour? Around his neck, the sage wore the pelt of a golden mongoose. *Not a pelt.* A real mongoose. The creature was napping.

"There you are," said the sage, opening his eyes. "I've been waiting for you for quite some time, Fox Prince."

Vikram stilled, suspicion prickling in his spine. No one waited for him. No one looked for him. The mongoose around the sage's neck yawned. Something tumbled out of the creature's mouth. Vikram reached for it, his heart racing as his hand closed around something cold and hard: a ruby. The ruby shone with unnatural light.

The mongoose yawned . . . jewels?

"Show-off," said the sage, bopping the mongoose on its nose.

The creature's ears flattened in reproach. Its fur shimmered in the dark. Bright as true gold. Bright as . . . magic. When he was a child, Vikram thought enchantment would save him. He even tried to trap it. Once he laid out a net to catch a wish-bestowing *yaksha* and ended up with a very outraged peacock. When he got older, he stopped trying. But he couldn't give up hoping. Hope was the only thing that lay between him and a throne that would only be his in name. He clutched the ruby tighter. It pulsed, shuddering as an image danced in its face—an image of *him*. Sitting on the throne. Powerful. Freed.

Vikram nearly dropped the ruby. Magic clung to his body. Starlight raced through his veins, and the sage grinned.

"Can't speak? There, there, little Fox Prince. Perhaps all the words are knocking against your head and you simply can't reach out and snatch the right one. But I am kind. Well, perhaps not. Kindness is a rather squishy thing. But I do love to lend assistance. Here is what you should say: 'Why are you here?' "

Shocked, all Vikram could do was nod.

The sage smiled. Sometimes a smile was little more than a sliver of teeth. And sometimes a smile was a knife cutting the world in two: before and after. The sage's smile belonged to the latter. And Vikram, who had never been anxious, felt as if his whole world was about to be rearranged by that grin.

"I am here because you summoned me, princeling. I am here to extend an invitation for a game that takes place when the century has grown old. I am here to tell you that the Lord of Wealth and Treasures caught a whiff of your dreams and followed it until he found your hungry heart and cunning smile."

The ruby in Vikram's palm quivered and shook. Crimson light broke in front of his eyes and he saw that the ruby was not a ruby, but an invitation in the shape of a jewel. It shook itself out . . . unfurling into gold parchment that read:

THE LORD OF WEALTH AND TREASURES CORDIALLY INVITES YOU TO *THE TOURNAMENT OF WISHES.*

Please present the ruby and a secret truth to the gate guardians by the new moon.

This ruby is good for two living entries.

The winner will be granted their heart's wish.
But know now that desire is a poisonous thing.

Vikram stared up from the parchment. Distantly, he knew he should be frightened. But fright paled compared to the hope knifing through him. That shadowed part of him that had craved for something *more* was no childhood fantasy gone twisted with age. Perhaps it had always been a premonition. Like knowledge buried in the soul and not the sight. True but hidden things.

The sage nodded to the ruby. "Look and see what awaits you."

He looked, but saw nothing.

"Try singing! The ruby wants to feel loved. Seduced."

"I wouldn't call my singing voice seduction," said Vikram, finding his voice. "More like sacrilege, honestly."

"It's not the sound of your song that coaxes out truth. It's the sincerity. Like this—"

The sage sung no song, but a story. Vikram's story. An image burned in the ruby. Vikram clutching the Emperor with one hand and tightly holding a bundle of blue flowers in the other. Voices slipped out of the gem: muffled displeasure, the title "heir of Ujijain" spoken around a laugh. He saw the future Ujijain promised him—a useless life of luxury wearing the face of power. He saw the nightmare of a long life, day upon day of stillness. His chest tightened. He'd rather die. The sage's voice had no tone. But it had texture, like a scattering of gold coins.

"If you want a throne, you'll have to play
The Lord of Treasures loves his games and tales
A wanting heart will make his day
Or you can waste your life recounting fails
But say it, little prince, say you'll play this game
If you and a partner play, never will you be the same."

The ashram huts loomed closer and the fires crackled like topaz. The idea took root in Vikram's mind. He'd built his life on wanting the impossible—true power, recognition, a future—and now magic had found him the moment he stopped looking. It breathed life into all those old dreams, filling him with that most terrible of questions: *What if . . .*

But even as his heart leapt to believe it, the sage's words made him pause.

"Why did you say partner?"

"It is required of your invitation."

Vikram frowned. The princes in the ashram had never inspired his faith in teams.

"Find the one who glows, with blood on the lips and fangs in the heart."

"Sounds as though they would be hard to miss."

"For you, doubly so," said the sage. His voice expanded. Not quite human. The sound rose from everywhere, dripping from the sky, growing out of the dirt. "Say you will play. Play the game and you may yet win your empire, not just the husk of its name. You only get one chance to accept."

The sage sliced his hand across the flames. Images spilled out like jewels:

A palace of ivory and gold, riven with black streams where caught stars wriggled and gave up their light. There were prophecies etched on doorframes, and the sky above was nothing but undulating ocean where discarded legends knifed through the water. A thousand *yakshas* and *yakshinis* trailed frost, forest brambles, pond swill and cloudy coronets. They were preparing for something. Vikram felt as if he'd tasted his dreams and starved for more.

Magic plucked at his bones, begging him to leave this version of himself behind. He leaned forward, his heart racing to keep up with the present.

"Yes," he breathed.

As if he could say anything else.

The moment split. Silently, the world fell back on itself.

"Excellent!" said the sage. "We will see you in Alaka at the new moon."

"Alaka? But that's, I mean, I *thought* it was myth."

"Oh dear boy, getting there is half the game." The sage winked. "Good for two living entries!"

"What about two living exits?"

"I like you," laughed the sage.

In a blink, he disappeared.

PART ONE

THE GIRL

•» 1 «•

TO BE A MONSTER

GAURI

Death stood on the other side of the chamber doors. Today I would meet it not in my usual armor of leather and chain mail, but in the armor of silk and cosmetics. One might think one armor was stronger than the other, but a red lip was its own scimitar and a kohl-darkened eye could aim true as a steel-tipped arrow.

Death might be waiting, but I was going to be a queen. I would have my throne if I had to carve a path of blood and bone to get it back.

Death could wait.

The bath was scalding, but after six months in a dungeon, it felt luxurious. Gauzy columns of fragrance spun slowly through the bath chambers, filling my lungs with an attar of roses. For a moment, thoughts of home choked me. Home, with the pockets of wildflowers and sandstone temples cut into the hills, with the people whose names I had come to murmur in my prayers before sleep. Home, where Nalini would have been waiting with a wry and inappropriate joke, her heart full of trust that I hadn't deserved. But that home was gone. Skanda, my brother, would have made sure by now that no hearth in Bharata would welcome me.

The Ujijain attendant who was supposed to prepare me for my first—and probably last—meeting with the Prince of Ujijain didn't speak. Then again, what do you say to those who are about to be sentenced to death? I knew what was coming. I'd gathered that much from the guards outside my dungeon. I wanted intelligence, so I faked whimpering nightmares. I'd practiced a limp. I'd let them think that my reputation was nothing more than rumor. I'd even let one of them touch my hair and tell me that perhaps he could be convinced to get me better food. I'm still proud that I sobbed instead of ripping out his throat with my teeth. It was worth it. People have a tendency to want to comfort small, broken-looking things. They told me they'd keep my death quick if I'd only smile for them one more time. I hated being told to smile. But now I knew the rotation of the guards' schedule. I knew which ones nursed battle wounds and how they entered the palace. I knew that no sentinels guarded the eastern gate. I knew which soldiers grinned despite their bad knee. I knew how to escape.

My hair hung in wet ropes against my back as I slid into the silken robes. No coarse linens for the Princess of Bharata. Royalty has the strangest advantages. Silently, the attendant led me to an adjoining chamber where the silver walls formed gigantic polished mirrors.

Slender glass alembics filled with fragrant oils, tiny cruets of kohl and silk purses of pearl and carmine powder crowded a low table. Brushes of reeds and hewn ivory shaped like writing implements caught the light. Homesickness slashed through me. I had to clasp my hands together to stop from reaching out over the familiar cosmetics. The harem mothers had taught me how to use these. Under my mothers' tutelage, I learned that beauty could be conjured. And under my and Nalini's instruction, my mothers learned that death could hide in beauty.

In Bharata, Nalini had commissioned slim daggers that could be folded into jeweled hairpins. Together, we'd taught the mothers how to defend themselves. Before Nalini, I used to steal shears and sneak into the forge so the blacksmith could teach me about the balance of a sword. My father allowed me to learn alongside the soldiers, telling me that if I was bent on maiming something, then it might as well be the enemies of Bharata. When he died, Bharata's training grounds became a refuge from Skanda. There, I was safe from him. And not just safe, but not *hurting* anyone. Being a soldier was the only way that I could keep safe the people I loved.

It was my way of making amends for what Skanda made me do.

The attendant yanked my chin. She took a tool—the wrong one, I noticed—and scraped the red pigment onto my lips.

"Allow me—" I started, but she shut me up.

"If you speak, I will make sure that my hand slips when I use that sharp tool around your eyes."

Princess or not, I was still the enemy. I respected her fury. Her loyalty. But if she messed up my cosmetics, that was a different story. I closed my eyes, trying not to flinch under the attendant's ministrations. I tried to picture myself anywhere but here, and memory mercifully plucked me from my own thoughts and took me back to when I was ten years old, sobbing because my sister, Maya, had left Bharata.

Mother Dhina had dried my tears, scooped me onto her lap and let me watch as she applied her cosmetics for the day.

This is how we protect ourselves, beti. *Whatever insults or hurts are thrown at our face, these are our barriers. No matter how broken we feel, it is only the paint that aches.*

We can always wash it away.

A soft brush swept across my cheek, scattering a fine dust of pulverized pearls across my skin. I knew, from the harem mothers, that the powder could make skin look as incandescent as a thousand mornings. I also knew that if the powder got in your eyes, the grit would make you weep and temporarily rob you of sight.

The scent of the powder fell over me like a worn and familiar cloak. I inhaled deeply, and I was sixteen again, preparing for the palace's monsoon celebration. Arjun said I looked like a lantern and I'd stuck my tongue out at him. Nalini was there too, defiantly wearing the garb of her own people: a red patterned sash around a silk-spun *salwar kameez* sewn with thousands of moon-shaped mirrors.

A year later, when Arjun became the general, I told him I meant to take the throne from Skanda. I had protected my people as much as I could from his reign. But I couldn't stand by the edges. Not anymore. Without questioning, Arjun pledged his life and his soldiers to my cause. Six months after that, I made my move to take the throne from my brother. My brother was cunning, but he would protect his life before his reign. I thought that with Arjun and his forces supporting my bid for the throne, I could ensure a bloodless transfer of power.

I was wrong.

The night I tried to take the throne, I wore my best armor: blood red lips for the blood I wouldn't shed and night-dark kohl for the secrecy I had gathered. I remembered the fear, how I had cursed under my breath, waiting with a handful of my best soldiers beneath a damp stone archway. I remembered the pale bloom of mushrooms tucked into the creases of stone, white as pearls and corpse skin. They were the only things I could see in the dark. I remembered emerging into the throne room. I had practiced my speech so many times that when I realized what had happened, I could summon no other words. But I remembered the bodies on the ground, the lightning breaking the night sky like an egg. I remembered Arjun's face beside my brother: calm. He had known.

"Done," said the attendant, holding a mirror to my face.

My eyes fluttered open. I grimaced at my reflection. The red pigment had crossed the boundaries of my lips, making them look thick and bloodstained. The kohl had been unevenly smudged. I looked bruised.

"It suits you, Princess," said the attendant in a mockingly pandering voice. "Now smile and show me the famous dimpled smile of the Jewel of Bharata."

Few knew that my "famous dimpled smile" was a scar. When I was nine, I had cut myself with a blunt pair of shears after pretending that the wooden sculpture of a *raksha* was real and that he meant to eat me. *Fate smiles upon you, child. Even your scars are lovely,* said Mother Dhina. As I got older, the scar reminded me of what people would choose to see if you let them. So I smiled at the attendant, and hoped that she saw a dimpled grin, and not the scar from a girl who started training with very sharp things from a very young age.

The attendant's eyes traveled from my face to the sapphire necklace at the hollow of my throat. Instinctively, I clutched it.

She held out her palm. "The Prince will not like that you are wearing something he has not personally bestowed."

"I'll take my chances."

It was the only thing I had from my sister, Maya. I would not part with it.

My sister's necklace was more than a jewel. The day Maya returned to Bharata, I hadn't recognized her. My sister had changed. As if she had torn off the filmy reality of one world and glimpsed something greater beneath it. And then she had disappeared, darting between the space of a moonbeam and a shadow. The necklace was a reminder to live for myself the way Maya had. But it was also a reminder of loss. Vast and unwieldy magic had stolen away my sister, and every time I looked at the pendant, I remembered not to place faith in things I couldn't control. The necklace told me to place my faith in myself. Nothing and no one else. I didn't just want to believe in everything the necklace meant. I needed those reminders. And I would die before I parted with it.

"I rather like the look of it myself. Maybe I'll keep it," said the attendant. "Give it. Now."

The attendant grabbed at the necklace. Even though her arms were thin, her fingers were strong. She pinched my skin, scrabbling at the clasp.

"Give. It. To. Me," she hissed. She aimed a bony elbow at my neck, but I blocked the jab.

"I don't want to hurt you."

"You can't hurt me. The guards told me how weak you truly are. Besides, you are no one here," said the attendant. Her eyes were bright, as if touched with fever. "Give me the necklace. What does it matter to you? After all you took? Isn't that the least I can take away from you, one damned necklace?"

Her words stung. I took no pleasure in killing. But I had never hesitated to choose my life over another's.

"My apologies," I said hoarsely, knocking her hand away from my neck. I had been gentle before, careful not to harm the skinny and heartbroken thing standing in front of me. This time she lurched back, shock and fury lighting up her face.

Maybe the girl had lost her lover, or her betrothed, or her father or brother. I couldn't *let* myself care. I'd learned that lesson young. Once,

I had freed the birds in the harem menagerie. When Skanda found out, he covered my floor with ripped wings and told me the cage was the safest place for foolish birds. Another time, Skanda had punished Mother Dhina and forbade the palace cooks from sending her any dinner. I gave her half of mine. He starved me for a week. Those were just the instances where I was the only person hurt. My brother had taught me many things, but nothing more important than one: Selfishness meant survival.

Caring had cost my future. Caring had trapped me under Skanda's thumb and forced my hand. Caring had robbed my throne and damned all I had held dear. That was all that mattered.

The attendant lunged forward, and I reacted. Hooking my foot behind her calf, I tugged. I swung out with my right fist—harder than I should have, harder than I needed to—until my hand connected with her face. She fell back with a hurt yelp, knocking over a slim golden table. A cloud of perfume burst in the air. In that moment, the world tasted like sugar and roses and blood. I stepped back, my chest heaving. I waited for her to stand and fight, but she didn't. She sat there with her legs crossed beneath her, arms wrapped around her thin rib cage. She was sobbing.

"You took my brother. He was not yours to take. He was mine," said the girl. Her voice sounded muddled. *Young*. Tears streaked her cheeks.

"You're a monster," she said.

I secured the necklace.

"We all have to be something."

A
CROWN
OF
WISHES
NEW YORK TIMES BESTSELLING AUTHOR
ROSHANI CHOKSHI